**London Borough
of Hounslow**

0	1	2	3	4	5	6	7	8	9
590			796	9614		3406			
			3193						

P10-L2061

The Poplar
Penny Whistlers

The Poplar
Penny Whistlers

Sheila Newberry

ROBERT HALE · LONDON

ISBN 978-0-7090-9206-3

Robert Hale Limited
Clerkenwell House
Clerkenwell Green
London EC1R 0HT

www.halebooks.com

2 4 6 8 10 9 7 5 3 1

For Glenys, a special cousin
and wise nurse tutor

Typeset in 11/15 Sabon
Printed in Great Britain by the MPG Books Group,
Bodmin and King's Lynn

Acknowledgements

Glenys, for nursing history, who also found an intriguing character who was linked with my family for many years around the turn of the twentieth century. Like Van der Linde in my novel he was 'born at sea on a dark and stormy night. . . .' (As stated on an early census.)

John, for his knowledge of the area, the docks and shipping.

Betty Lee, Nursing Archivist, affectionately known as 'The Oracle'.

Dick Playle, from earlier correspondence re music halls and street musicians.

The late **Mrs Emma Stainsby,** court dressmaker and true Londoner who lived to be 104, and inspired the name of 'my family'.

The original **'Puglet'** who belonged to my intrepid great-grandmother, **Emma Meehan,** midwife, of Wymondham, long-time widow of an officer in the London Fire Brigade.

Bibliography

The Streets of Poplar compiled by Rev. Arthur Royall © 1999
General Nursing, 9th Edition Luckes, Eva C.E., Kegan Paul,
Trench, Trubner & Co. Ltd., 1914.

Acknowledgement as requested re *Oh! Mr Porter* lyrics, to
www.musicsmiles.com

Foreword

The Poplar hospital was not far from the East India docks. Originally a tavern, by 1850 the building was a hostel for migrants. Later, it became a dispensary for the dock company. As the need grew for a charity hospital in the area, various extensions were added, although the Georgian facade was retained. In 1880 an outpatients section was established. Ten years on, although the hospital now owned the freehold, and there were plans to extend the facilities for the benefit of the wider local population, the medical staff still mainly treated workers involved in accidents in the docks. This is where my story begins.

Footnote
Sadly, the hospital was demolished in the Blitz on London in WW2.

One

November, 1890. The Docklands, Poplar.

Hester Stainsby began working as a laundry maid in the Poplar hospital when she was fourteen years old in 1887. She'd had no choice, after her mother's sudden death from pneumonia. Bess had worked in the laundry for sixteen years before her, with respite only when Hester, and later, the twins, Polly and Harry were born. This was when Granny Garter came to live with them, ostensibly to look after the children. It hadn't quite worked out like that: Fred Stainsby and his mother-in-law were incompatible. Hester took on her mother's role as peace maker.

Hester was well aware that her wage was essential to keep the family afloat. Fred, her father, a dock labourer, was poorly paid at that time: competition was fierce among the men each day, for the opportunity to load and unload steamships like *Robin* which carried grain, iron ore and china clay, and the older Clipper sailing ships with their cargo of tea. It was Hester's mother who'd earlier kept the family clothed and fed.

However, following the Port of London Dock Strike the previous year, when peaceful demonstrations organized by the dock workers' leaders were sympathetically noted by influential public figures like Cardinal Manning, most of the workforce joined the union and a rate of 6d. an hour was agreed. Things had improved for the Stainsby family since then, and Hester was proud that her sister and brother were still in school at twelve years old, when many local children were already working. Their pa might be a manual worker, but he was an avid reader – had been ever since he was a lad and discovered the free public library – and he encouraged this in his children. They survived Granny's reluctant care and were a close-knit family.

When she heard the sonorous boom of the foghorn Hester gave an involuntary shudder. In the cavernous laundry where she toiled from dawn to dusk there was fog, too: damp, hot and swirling. Steam billowed from the great cauldrons as the women poked the washing with long poles into the boiling water. Heavily soiled sheets and gowns had already been soaked for some hours before the women struggled to lift and transfer the water-logged linen. Even then, there was the need for diligent scrubbing of stubborn stains with soap and brush on the ridged drubbing boards. Hester's knuckles were often rubbed raw as well. After the boiling, then mangling, there were the cold rinses, one with a blue bag to enhance the whiteness, more mangling, then starching if required, and finally pressing all that damp cloth with sizzling flat irons. More steam, more fog, but time for cheerful chatter. Not today though; there was a general feeling of apprehension.

The mournful boom continued. Then they heard an even more ominous sound: the hooter signalling an accident. The women glanced fearfully at one another, but didn't express their thoughts aloud. There was still too much to do: floors to swab, sinks to scour, ash-pans to empty beneath the boilers. It was like being in a Turkish bath, they sighed, although none of them had enjoyed that particular experience, and the inevitable sweating meant that most of the workers were thin and gaunt looking. They carried on despite winter coughs and colds, as Bess had done before she succumbed to her final illness.

Doors banged, trolleys trundled in the corridors above, voices were raised. The heavy door to the laundry room swung open and a porter stood there, peering through the steam. Hester had her back to him. She jerked around, when she felt his touch on her shoulder. 'Hester, come with me,' he said urgently.

'What for?' she demanded sharply.

'Matron wants to see you. In her office. Now.' The young porter was clearly upset. Alf Hodge was a friend and neighbour of Hester and her family. 'I was told, not to say why . . . I'm sorry,' he floundered.

She wiped her damp brow on her overall sleeve, plucked at her cap. Strands of dark hair came loose from the knot she had fastened first thing that morning. Sweat dripped down her neck soaking her collar. She was a small, slim girl, pale faced, due to lack of fresh air, but strong and determined.

The kindly supervisor, replaced Hester's cap, tucked stray locks neatly inside. 'Go as you are, dearie, Matron'll expect that.'

'Good luck!' Big Peg, as she was known to her friends, who had biceps to rival any docker, called impulsively as she turned the mangle. Water gushed into the tub set to catch it, Peg looked out for Hester, for Bess had been her best friend. Hester was the kind of daughter Peg had hoped to have, herself, but her husband had died of consumption a year after their marriage, when she was only twenty. She was twice that age now. She didn't even have a wedding ring on her finger – it had been sold to help pay for the funeral.

'Yes, good luck,' the rest echoed. They were a tight-knit community, all connected with the docks.

Hester clattered up the stone steps in her wooden soled shoes. Alf knocked on a door, then moved aside. 'I'll be round later,' he whispered. He had a freckled face, ginger hair and rather bulbous blue eyes. As a lad, he'd been the butt of jokes from his peers at school because of his looks, but Hester had soon sorted them out. She'd told the bullies where to get off, with blazing dark eyes and small clenched fists. He'd been devoted to her ever since. He'd been over the moon when Hester's family moved in next door to his. Now he had an excuse to see her every day.

'Come in.' Hester heard the command as if from a distance. She turned the knob slowly, then entered Matron's sanctum. Matron was by the window, adjusting the blind. She was not a forbidding figure as some were, although she wore her impressive cap with pride. Matron was comfortably plump with a maternal manner towards her staff, although she was neither married nor a mother. Daylight flooded the room. Hester blinked, after the gloom of the laundry.

'The fog is lifting, thank goodness.' Matron observed. 'Sit down Hester, please.' She indicated a chair, but remained standing, regarding the girl for a few moments. Then she continued: 'There is no easy way to say this. Your father has been badly injured while unloading cargo on the docks. A barrel broke loose from the hoist, fell on him below . . . his legs were crushed. He was brought here fifteen minutes ago, and the surgeon has been called. He will be in the operating theatre shortly.'

'Can . . . can I see him?' Hester managed, despite the shock.

'My dear, I don't advise it. Go home now, to be with your grandmother. Return here this afternoon and I will be able to tell you how things are.'

'Will he—'

'He's a robust man, Hester. If it is God's will, he will survive. He is in good hands here. You must be brave, accept further responsibility at home. You should take a few days leave, I think. You will receive your wages as usual on Friday.'

'Thank you, Matron.' Hester said, realizing she could go. She still had to face the questions from her workmates, but she would fight back the tears and explain briefly what had happened. Then she must hurry home, to Granny Garter and together they would break the news to Polly and Harry when they came home from school.

Two

May, 1891

After six months in hospital, Fred returned home to his family. He was able to hobble around now on crutches, despite having lost his left leg above the knee. The surgeon had managed to save the other leg, but Fred said ruefully: 'I ain't got one good leg to stand on, nowadays.' He was aware that he would be unable to return to work at the docks.

The new Dock, Wharf, Riverside and General Labourers' Union secured for him a weekly sum of £1 which would pay the rent and upkeep of the company house on the Rise. This was the best place they'd lived in. True, the lavatories and the wash-houses were still outside, but fortunately across level ground at the rear of the terrace. The houses were well-built with two good-sized rooms downstairs, two up plus a box room, and a basement kitchen. The back room would now be a bedroom for Fred.

Fred's workmates rallied round his family. They usually left their gifts on the doorstep; pigs' trotters wrapped in newspaper, a cabbage, bantam eggs, a loaf of bread. Hester had cooked the trotters up for supper, when she arrived home from the laundry. Granny shrieked at the sight of them, 'How vulgar!'

'We stick together,' Fred said, when Hester and the twins visited him in hospital, and he heard about Granny's outburst. 'Us Poplar lads. . . .' He'd been born in Stainsby Road, as he now reminded them: 'Like most of the roads round here, it was named after somebody famous. It was what his widow wanted, in his memory. I was lent a book to read while I was in hospital, by that writer fellow, funny name, same, back and front – what was it? Jerome K. Jerome. He lived in Stainsby Road as a lad. It was a good story about three men in a boat travellin' down the old Thames. But don't go thinkin' *you've* got blue blood – the Stainsby what they called the road after, weren't no relation as far as I know. Mind you, it's a good name to live up to, I always think.'

'Well, we was all called after Royalty,' Polly said. 'Hester got Elizabeth as her second name—'

'That was after your dear ma!'

Polly carried on: 'And I'm Mary Victoria, after the *Queen*, and Harry, he's Henry after old Henry the Eighth and all the other Henrys—'

'Don't I know it,' Harry butted in. 'And *Albert,* into the bargain!'

'If you want the truth,' Fred said, 'You can swaller your pride. When Granny saw you'd inherited her h'aristocratic nose, Polly, she decided you'd be called Victoria, after *her*!'

'That's why Poll's her favourite!' Harry dodged a cuff from his irate sister.

It was Granny Garter who took to her bed, at the thought of caring for Fred all day. She was a fine figure of a woman, as her late husband, the roguish bookie, often said, and he spoiled her to the extent she thought of herself as quite a lady. A woman came in to do the washing and housework in those days. Unfortunately, her husband died, deeply in debt, and she'd descended on her only daughter who'd married a man her mother regarded as lower class.

Hester and Alf accompanied Fred home in the ambulance, one of the new, box-shaped vehicles drawn by a pair of horses. When it drew up outside the terrace, it caused quite a stir among the neighbours, who emerged to wave their encouragement, and to direct their small boys to lurk near the horses with bucket and shovel. They'd known Fred as a jolly fellow before he lost his wife, who on Friday nights in the pub, after a single tankard of beer, entertained his friends by playing the penny whistle. He'd passed his musical expertise on to his younger children, and now they stood, jostling each other in the doorway, waiting to 'pipe' him indoors. They were not identical twins of course, being boy and girl, and Polly was definitely the more dominant, although Harry had a wry sense of humour which endeared him to his elder sister.

Alf brought out the wheelchair provided by the hospital, and settled Fred in this, with crutches in his lap. He and Hester eased the wheels carefully up the flight of steps to the front door. The steps were an important defence against the possibility of flooding in the winter from the nearby culvert, in which children paddled in the summer when their mother's backs were turned. The water was tainted by mud and rubbish including sewage, and reeked like its parent, the great River Thames.

'All right, Pa?' Hester asked at the top. The whistling began, and Fred managed a smile. He nodded.

'Where's Granny?' he asked.

'Resting up,' Hester told him, knowing he would be relieved. 'Thanks Alf, for all your help – we couldn't have managed without you.'

The ambulance was driven off, as Hester pushed Fred's chair into the living room. The table was laid ready for supper.

'You'll stay and eat with us, Alf, won't you?' she asked.

'Thought you'd never ask,' Alf joked. His stepmother was too fond of the bottle to bother much with food for her men folk.

'I made a red jelly,' Polly said proudly. 'I coloured it with cochineal.' She jiggled the plate so her pa could see it quiver. She was already taller than her sister, with ash-blonde braids, hazel eyes and apple-red cheeks. Her looks were deceptive, she was far from angelic. Harry, still whistling, was shorter with a mop of black hair like Hester. They took after Fred.

'So long as it ain't calves foot jelly – can't abide it,' Fred remarked. 'That's for invalids.' He made a wry grimace.

'It won't taste of much,' Harry reminded his sister, after removing the whistle from his mouth at last. 'You watered it down, that's why it hasn't set proper.'

A tussle between the two followed. Alf prised them apart. 'Say sorry to your pa, or he'll turn round and go back to the hospital!'

This did the trick, even though the twins realized this was unlikely.

'All that fuss about jelly,' Hester rebuked them. 'When there's that big fish pie I slaved over earlier, ready to come out of the oven. It smells good, eh, Pa? Polly, Harry, sit down and shut up!'

Polly had to have the last word. 'Hester's friendly with the fresh fish chap down the market. She got two big cod cheap. He even gutted them for her. Fish *stinks*! So does he. . . .'

The kerfuffle had been heard by Granny in the room above. She thumped her stick vigorously on the floor to express her displeasure.

'Now I *know* I'm home,' Fred said. 'And it ain't a dream.'

Alf manoeuvred the wheelchair behind the table. 'All right, mate? I'll help Hester bring the grub up from the kitchen.'

Hester lifted the corners of her apron to protect her hands as she carried the steaming dish from the gas stove to the kitchen table to serve up. Having gas laid on was a great improvement on the old coal range they'd previously battled with, she thought, with all the hard work it entailed, including blacking the stove. The gas lamps too were much better than the old oil lamps, with wicks to trim and that pervasive odour.

The pie had browned nicely on top, she saw, to her satisfaction. She'd cooked and mashed some old potatoes which Alf's step-mum had thrown out. Hester had painstakingly removed any shoots from the wrinkled skins, and planted these in the border of earth round the yard. Later, they would have the pleasure of new spuds, she thought. She'd used a knob of precious butter in the mashing, as this was a special occasion. The flaked, cooked white fish had been coated with white sauce, too, another treat. 'Stick that sprig of parsley on top,' she told Alf, as he counted the plates out. 'I grew it on the windowsill in that box you made me.'

'Like that fishy fellow do you?' Alf asked her.

'Alf Hodge, what's it to you?' she teased.

'He's as slippery as them eels he sells on his stall. You should see him chatting up the barmaid in *The Ship*—'

'Not likely, seeing as I don't drink,' Hester retorted. 'You take Pa's and your own plate, I'll carry the twins' dishes up, then come back for Granny's.'

'What about your own supper?'

'I'll keep it warming, with the teapot, while I see to Granny. The rest of you must tuck in. You slice the bread – Polly's too wasteful. I'll be as quick as I can.'

Fred looked at the pie appreciatively. He wouldn't say that he'd had enough steamed fish in hospital to last him a lifetime. 'Good cook like your ma,' he said to Hester. 'She'd be proud of you.'

Granny was sitting up in bed in the big bedroom, which she had taken over when Fred was away. She'd turfed out young Harry, who'd shared the room with his pa, into the box room, which smelled musty, being a repository for Granny's old finery. This was much to the girls' relief, as they no longer had her in their room.

With a sheet of newspaper protecting the fancy bedspread from her former home, Granny Garter offered no praise for the meal. She said instead, 'Fish again. I fancied a nice bit of steak.' Her small mouth was pursed and she looked disagreeable.

'Who don't?' Hester responded with spirit. 'Wouldn't you care to hear how pa's doing?'

Granny feigned deafness, as she poked at the potato crust with her fork. 'Send Polly up with my cuppa. *She's* always got time for me.'

So have I, Hester thought, but Ma had taught her to respect her elders, so she couldn't say it. Granny wasn't yet sixty, and was still a handsome woman, surely she wasn't past stirring herself and making the most of life, even if it was not the one she'd chosen.

'Good to be home,' Fred said later. He looked tired. It had

been a long day. Being so dark, he always had a stubbly chin by nightfall. Granny often said he ought to shave twice a day, but his smart reply was always, 'You want to try it, Missus! Bess never objected . . .' Now, he passed a hand over his face and felt the roughness of it. If he left it a day or two, he could be old Bluebeard! It had all been rather too much, coming home, and wondering how they would cope.

'I'll take you out back,' Alf said tactfully, 'Then help you into bed. I can come in again before I leave for work, and get you dressed, and young Harry'll see to your needs when he gets in from school at midday, eh.'

'Alf's a wonder,' Hester said to Pa. 'He shifted the bed and that, downstairs for you, and Granny agreed to let you have the commode.'

'*She's* got to make do with the chamber pot,' Polly put in, grinning. 'That's a balancing act, I reckon.'

'Maybe it'll decide her to get up and come downstairs,' Alf said.

'I ain't always going to be helpless,' Fred said suddenly. He sounded fierce, and they knew he meant it. 'I don't intend to be a burden on me family. Don't look so solemn. I might get practising the old penny whistle again meself – go down the market and play a tune or two for my supper. I'll be one of them street musicians, eh?'

'Oh, Pa,' Hester wiped her eyes. 'Surely it won't have to come to that?' She was glad Granny Garter hadn't heard him say it; she would have thrown another fit of hysterics, she thought.

Fred held out his arms. 'I ain't give none of you a hug yet! No more tears. . . . I'm here, ain't I? That's all that matters.'

Three

It was Hester's Saturday morning off from the laundry, if not from the household washing. She rose early as usual and lugged the rush linen basket out to the wash-house, which they shared with next door. Kind Alf had filled the copper with water and lit it before she arrived. The whites would go in there, as they did at the laundry, but there was plenty of washing to do by hand in one of the big sinks. They didn't use lye any more, but a big bar of yellow soap. She was sorting the clothes when Alf turned up with a couple of kettles of boiling water – there was a cold tap, as there was in the kitchen, which had eliminated the arduous task of pumping water into buckets every day.

'Want a hand?' Alf asked diffidently. He had a bundle of his own clothes to wash in the sink in the hot, soapy water when Hester had finished with it. He'd looked after himself since he was Harry's age.

'Women's work, Alf!' Hester grinned. 'But I won't say no!'

'Where's that lazy sister of yours? She ought to wash her own drawers and petticoats.'

'Don't you be so cheeky, Alf Hodge! You shouldn't know about such things. She'll need to grow up soon enough after she leaves school when she turns fourteen. Anyway, she takes after Granny, thinks she's above all this drudgery. She and Harry are going to wheel Pa down to the market later on and get the shopping. Polly enjoys that.'

'What about you? Don't you fancy being out and about?'

'Purkiss the fishman did ask me if I fancied a stroll down by the river,' she teased him.

'What did you say?' Alf demanded.

'I didn't say yes, but I didn't say no. . . . Why don't you come out with it, say what you really mean, Alf Hodge.'

'All right. I can do better than a walk along the river bank, you need a peg on your nose in this warm weather. We could – well, go along to the music hall this evening – up in the gallery, o' course. You can see more from up there, anyway, and if you get there early you get the front seats. Mind, you have a long wait 'til the stalls are all filled, before they let you in, but it's worth it.'

'If you'll do the mangling, I'll do your washing – might as well, now me hands are all soggy, eh – then we'll peg it all out. Then you can come in our kitchen for a nice bowl of porridge. . . . *Then*, I'll make me mind up!'

'Ta. I'll see to Fred at the same time, that'll be in my favour, I know.'

'Oh,' Hester added, reaching for the scrubbing brush, 'I forgot to say, if I do agree to your proposal, you're to steer clear of *The Ship*. It'll be a sober night out, if you're with me.'

Alf deemed it wise not to tell her that most of the gallery boys had a bottle of beer tucked in their pockets, as well as visiting the nearby pub before and after the show.

Polly served breakfast to Harry, Fred and Granny Garter. This was their usual fare, whatever the time of year. The oats had been simmering in water for a couple of hours already and just needed bringing up to the boil. When Hester wasn't around Polly had sneaked the new tin of syrup out of the cupboard. She and Harry preferred that dribbled on the stodge to sugar. Fred had breakfast in his room, while awaiting Alf's ministrations. To the twins' surprise, Granny had deigned to join them in the kitchen, though she was still wearing her wrapper over her night attire, and she hadn't yet added her false hairpiece, so her faded fair hair hung in wisps. She'd evidently decided to recover from her malaise.

'I was thinking,' Granny said speculatively, staring hard at Polly.

'Oh, yes?' Polly was suspicious. What was coming next?

'My best clothes – I'll never wear 'em again – out of fashion now. Not that the folk round here bother much with the way they look.'

'They can't afford to, Granny,' Harry mumbled through a mouthful of porridge. 'Are you going to chuck 'em all out, or give 'em to the rag and bone man?' He'd be thankful to see the back of Granny's togs. That purple satin dress with the bustle, dangling from a hook in the box room ceiling was enough to give a lad nightmares, he thought. It looked like an avenging angel in the moonlight shining through the tiny window.

Granny ignored his remarks. 'Polly, it came to me in the night, I might take up my old profession. . . .'

'What was that, Granny?' Polly wondered, much too innocently.

'*Bookie's runner*. . . .' Harry said under his breath.

'I was apprenticed to a Court dressmaker, no less. Of course, I married young and well, so was able to give up work, but I made all those dresses and costumes upstairs, for myself, and baby clothes for Bess. My dear husband bought me a sewing machine. I haven't had time to use it since I had to look after you lot, but now you little tykes are bigger and can fend for yourselves, I might get it out of the washstand cupboard, and start sewing again. I could make you a decent skirt and jacket, Polly, from some of the material if I unpick my garments.'

'You'd have to let me choose the style and colour,' Polly said quickly, but she was flattered that Granny wanted to do this for her. 'And air 'em well before you expect me to try 'em on.'

'With your talent for twitching your nose, you'd make a good drains inspector,' Granny retorted sharply. However, she couldn't be riled with Polly for long. Being of ample proportions herself, she was satisfied she'd have plenty of material to work with. Maybe even two skirts from one!

'Well, clear the table, Harry, put the crocks in the sink for Hester to wash up. I'm going to get ready to go down the market.' Polly said.

The crowds already thronging the market, parted obligingly to allow Harry to push the wheelchair through.

'It's Fred!' old friends exclaimed, darting forward to wring his hand. 'Wotcher mate!' They noted the folded up trouser leg, but didn't comment on it. Fred didn't want their sympathy, he welcomed their repartee, their belly laughs. Anyway, *he* was about to entertain them.

There were already discarded cabbage leaves around the stalls, and other debris to steer through. It was a typical London market, busy and noisy, the entrance jam-packed with carts and stall-holders putting on a show while selling their goods. Chrisp Street was a good place to spend a Saturday.

'Oi! Ain't you got time to say good mornin'?' Purkiss called to Polly from behind the trestle table loaded with flat fish, spotted fish, brown shrimps and crabs, packed round with ice. 'Didn't you see me?'

'Smelt the fish,' Polly returned smartly, but she smiled, and paused for a chat. 'Hester said, have you got two pairs of kippers—'

'Where is she today?' Purkiss asked, reaching for the kippers with his cold, wet hands. He was a short fellow, with an oriental slant to his eyes, not surprising when you knew his grandfather had married a girl from Pennyfields, the old Chinese Quarter down West India Dock road.

'Wouldn't you like to know,' Polly tapped the side of her nose. Then she grinned. 'Hanging out the washing still, I reckon.'

'Should've thought she had enough of doin' the laundry – don't you help?' Purkiss's six sisters all pulled their weight at home. His little doll-like grandmother, whom all the family adored, saw to that.

'Got better things to do. You'll see – and hear – a bit later.

Harry and Pa are looking for a good spot this very minute. How much do I owe you for the kippers, Purkiss?' She loosened the strings of her bag.

'I got a given name, you know – Robert. I mostly get called Bobby. Ninepence to you. Fancy a stroll one night by the river?' He winked.

'Me pa would whack you with his crutch if he'd heard that! D'you know how old I am?' Polly demanded, but she was flattered to be asked.

'I'll invite you again in a couple o' years, eh? Unless I get round your sister first. See you again!'

Three pence change from the shilling she'd expected to pay: Polly wended her way to the haberdashery stall. A nice length of yellow moiré ribbon, she thought, for her hair – she couldn't abide hats. Also, she'd promised Granny to bring back a big reel of white cotton. Later on, she mustn't forget to buy the pork chop Granny had slipped her the money for, saying, 'I can't face no more fish', also, scrag end of mutton for Sunday dinner. Hester had counselled her to buy the meat later in the day, when prices were slashed to get rid of the cheaper cuts.

Polly caught up with her pa and brother by the Hokey Pokey Stall. The Italian ice cream sellers were doing a roaring trade, with customers sheltering from the hot sun under the striped awnings they had erected over their colourfully embellished handcarts. The Turnero Two, as they were known, on account of the way the ice cream was produced, were father and son, good looking fellows with ready smiles for the ladies.

Turnero junior was the centre of attention, with his sleeves rolled up so that his rippling muscles could be admired as he vigorously turned the handle of his ice bucket until the ice cream was thoroughly chilled and could be served up in the little glass cups. Papa Turnero, with his rakish neckerchief and impressive mustachios, was poised ready with his long handled spoon.

'Roll up!' he sang out. 'Hokey Pokey, penny a lump—'

'That's the stuff to make you jump!' the crowd returned.

Fred, Harry and Polly waited to one side until the crowd stood around, enjoying the delicious, cooling ice cream. Here they met up with Big Peg from the hospital laundry, carrying a bag with a small dog inside, poking out its wrinkled black face with cross-cut teeth to see who she was talking to. 'Like my little pug?' Big Peg had a rumbling laugh. 'He got left behind when my posh neighours done a moonlit flit . . . they weren't what they seemed to be. Old Boney's Josephine had a pet pug, so they say. This one don't like exercise. Where's Hester? Left her behind, have you, to the chores?'

'I hope you won't tell her what we're about to get up to,' Fred said.

'Depends what it is. I think a lot o' that gal.'

Then out came the penny whistles and Fred gave the signal to begin playing. 'Take a deep breath. . . .' Fingers in place over the holes in the tin whistle, the musicians placed the mouthpiece, the fipple, between their lips and blew gently. A low note was heard. A second deep breath, a more positive blow and a higher, true note was achieved.

Perhaps it was a trifle unfortunate that they began their repertoire with *'The Last Rose of Summer,'* as they received a few jovial cat-calls and the impatient remark: 'Blimey! It ain't even August yet!'

Resolutely, they carried on, with *'Cherry Ripe!'* Embarrassed, Harry put his finger over the wrong hole, and the audience winced. So did the pug dog. He let out an unearthly howl, followed by an explosive sneeze, causing everyone to stare at Big Peg and her wriggling bag.

'Better go . . . it ain't worth passing the hat,' Fred told the twins.

'Wait a minute! I got an idea,' Polly said. 'I'll sing and you can accompany me. What about *'I dreamt I dwelt in Marble Halls'* – not that I would like to do any such thing, it sounds all cold and draughty.'

She stuck her whistle in her bag, and boldly addressed the diminishing crowd, for some had sloped away in search of better entertainment. There was a man juggling bottles further up the market.

At the sight of a pretty girl holding up her hands for 'Quiet please!' the audience regained their interest.

Polly had a husky voice and was not too good on the high notes, but she sang with real feeling and the piping in the background was just right. She was so excited by the applause, she obliged with an impromptu cartwheel. The sight of her long shapely legs made the audience gasp. Harry snatched the cap off Fred's head and went round with it. It filled with pennies.

'Time for you to beat the retreat,' Big Peg said in Fred's ear. 'I reckon Puglet turned things round. That girl, she's got a gift, you oughter see she uses it. She might make all your fortunes. She could even do a dance like the gals-who-should know-better do, on the cellar flap outside the pub! By the way, the Turnero Two look fed-up – they haven't sold a single ice-cream for the last half hour.'

'Here you are, Pa,' Harry said, handing him the cap. 'Must be a few bob in there! Best not to tell Granny that Polly showed off her drawers, when her petticoats flew up over her head.'

To their surprise Hester was ready to go out with Alf, when they returned home. They couldn't wait for the kippers she said, but Alf was going to treat her to some supper. She thought it prudent not to tell Pa where she was off to. All she said when she heard about the cartwheel, was 'Well, thanks to me, at least Polly was wearing clean drawers!'

Four

Alf and Hester ate their supper outside the Queen's Palace of Varieties, while they waited to ascend to the Gods, with a good view of all the plaster cherubs of which there was a plethora. There were vendors walking up and down the long queue. A young mother with two ragged children in tow held out a basket of rather shrivelled oranges; a rival fruit seller touted bags of cherries. However, most of those waiting to see the show had brought food from home, hastily wrapped in newspaper, which they soon added to the litter in the street. They wiped their greasy hands on trousers, or skirts, and followed their meal with a swig of beer. There was a chorus of satisfied belching. Hester was glad Granny Garter wasn't around to observe such low-class behaviour, but although indisputably vulgar, it added to the atmosphere.

'There's more on offer in the winter, when it's cold hanging around outside,' Alf apologized to Hester. 'Hot 'taters and roast chestnuts to warm your cockles. But see, here's the fella with the goods – fancy a couple of ham sandwiches? He cuts the ham off the bone. Very tasty.'

'Yes, please!' Hester said.

The sandwiches were most satisfying, crusty bread spread with butter and thick slices of moist pink ham.

'I could do with a cup of tea,' Hester said, as she brushed the crumbs off her skirt into the gutter. She almost wished that Alf would produce a bottle from his pocket.

'Keep my place for me. I'll nip in *The Ship* for some lemonade,' he offered. Maybe he had time to quaff a small bottle of stout, he

26

thought. His pockets would be empty after he paid for their seats in the gallery, but he reckoned Hester was worth it.

While he was gone, a familiar voice addressed her from behind. 'Hester, you might have allowed *me* to bring you here!' It was Bobby.

She could smell his breath. 'You've been drinking, Purkiss!'

'What's young Alf doing in the pub, eh?' he countered.

'He's buying us lemonade. Not that it's any of your business.'

'You look right pretty when you get high and mighty. Your hair looks much nicer loose like that – shiny and black like my grandma's. Out to please him, are you?'

'To please *myself*! Alf's not my sweetheart, whatever you think.'

'Well, he'd like to be, and so would I,' Bobby insisted. 'Look out, here he comes. . . .'

'It's you what wants to look out!' she retorted, but she smiled; she didn't get compliments every day. Alf was certainly too bashful.

There was entertainment of the street variety to prevent the crowd becoming too bored, as well as the arrival of the better-off, like the local shopkeepers, who vanished smartly inside to the stalls. They masqueraded as real toffs in their Sunday best. Hester was quite taken with the ladies' fashions: big hats with nodding feathers, and tight-waisted costumes in silky materials. Here am I, she thought, ruefully, in my bunched alpaca skirt and best white blouse with a high starched collar and neat black bow at the neck. Like Polly, she was not one for hats, but Granny Garter had insisted she wear her old straw boater, with a band of artificial daisies. 'You won't be treated like a duchess, without a hat,' she warned.

'I've never met a duchess,' Hester couldn't help retorting – thinking, I bet *you* haven't either. But she skewered the proffered pin in place.

'Useful weapon for a girl when her honour's at stake.' Granny always had the last word. She knew exactly how to make a girl blush.

The merry fiddler bent over his cap, eagerly counting his takings. His rival, the crouching tom-tom player gave a last thunderous tattoo on his drums. He wore flowing robes, but that was not to say he came from foreign parts. In fact he called out in a cockney twang: 'Right folks, they're openin' the floodgates!'

There was more thunder, from heavy boots, as the crowd charged up the many stairs. 'Hang on to my arm!' Alf cried to Hester. She gave a quick glance behind. Thank goodness, she thought, Bobby Purkiss has disappeared in the crush. . . . There was no turning back, they were swept along in the stampede.

They managed to avoid sitting behind a pillar and being forced to crane their necks to see the stage. The heavy plush curtains were still in place, but they were fortunate enough to find two seats in the middle of the third row. Hester still clasped Alf's hand, as she suddenly felt giddy when she looked down on the audience far below. She couldn't tell Alf she hoped she wouldn't tumble down to join them, but thought, I'm glad we didn't get in the front row. . . .

It was definitely odorous and raucous up aloft. Cheap scent, peeled oranges, beery breath and hoarse voices.

The lights dimmed, the audience hushed and the curtain rose. The instrumentalists in the pit tuned up. Their musical director Mr Walter Loosely had arranged all the latest tunes to set feet tapping. A spotlight danced on stage. The backdrop was of a busy London street, similar to the one outside the Queen's Palace, but without the litter blowing about.

They hadn't got a programme, but that didn't matter for there was a regular Master of Ceremonies. The jovial, elegant Mr Frank Estcourt introduced the acts with much exaggerated aspiration, or lack of it, in rich, ringing tones, with: 'You h'all know 'Arry from 'Ackney!' and: 'H'order! H'order!' when the audience was too vociferous. He sat at the chairman's table to one side of the stage.

On came 'Arry from 'Ackney, a comic singer, in top hat and tails, with a monocle, who made the audience guffaw at his jokes, and sing along with his saucy renditions. Next, a beautiful, buxom young woman whose low-cut dress revealed her heaving bosom, sang with such verve she could be heard by those still lingering outside the theatre, with not even a sixpence for the gallery. Hester, averting her gaze, hoped fervently that the singer wouldn't burst out of her frock.

The acts came fast and furious. A ventriloquist, as inebriated as his dummy, was bombarded with cherry stones, by several youths with unerring aim, from the front row of the gallery, which made those in the seats below, look up, rather than at the stage. Unannounced, the snake woman, an acrobatic dancer, took the place of the unfortunate voice-thrower and then attention was riveted on her amazing contortions.

Just before the interval, the real stars appeared in an enthralling short play. This was a company who toured the country throughout the year, all members of the same family. They had been doing this for so long, the youngest member must have been pushing forty, but still made a credible ingénue. Her grandfather had a gouty foot, but did not let the supporting actors down. They carried him on in a sedan chair, to cheers from the entire audience. He played his usual part, that of the Squire. His son was the villain of the piece, out to seduce the maid with the golden ringlets. The cast had performed this drama so often they relieved the monotony, with a few humorous asides which were not in the script. Hester enjoyed the play so much, she was disappointed when it ended with the squire shooting his son and declaring he would 'marry the gel myself!' The ungrateful girl shrieked and fell in a faint. The curtains swished, then reopened to show the entire cast, including a revived villain and maid, bowing to the stalls and waving to the gallery.

When the lights went up, Hester blinked. Courting couples jerked apart, there was a concerted rush by most of the men in the gallery to the lengthening queue for the *Gents*.

'Would you excuse me please,' Alf mumbled, releasing her hand at last. 'Better join the lads.'

Hester didn't like to admit she felt unsafe because she was

perched so high up. She managed a smile. 'Hope you get back before the second half!' The seats along their row were almost empty now.

Five minutes later, Bobby slid into the vacant seat on her left. 'Found you!' he said, somewhat out of breath, because he had climbed over the seats from the back row. In his boots, too.

'Bobby! That's someone's seat – they'll be back – and so will Alf!'

'Just wanted to say – why him, and not me? I got a nice little business, I work hard and earn enough to give you a good time—'

'I've got plans for the future, Bobby. . . .'

'What don't include me, eh? Alf, I suppose—'

'He's a good friend, like a brother. That's all. Sorry, Bobby.'

'Well, if you've got a kind heart, you'll tell him the truth.' He got up and went off in a huff.

When the orchestra struck up again, Alf dared to put his arm around her shoulders and to draw her a little closer. Hester thought, Bobby's right, I must put Alf straight about things. I am fond of him, of course I am, but just because most girls of my age are thinking of marriage – and *that* – I don't want to give him the wrong impression. . . .

It was late evening when they emerged from the Palace. Some of the patrons, already tipsy from what they had imbibed during the show, made straight for the pub and a final draught of beer. Hester and Alf linked arms and began the walk home.

The lights were out in most of the terrace. They paused on the top step of Hester's house. There was no-one about. Alf's arms went round her and he hugged her tight. He pressed his lips to her cheek.

'Hester, did you like our night out?' he murmured.

'Yes . . . I did, Alf. Thank you for treating me to the supper and all.'

'Glad to oblige. Would you object to a real kiss?'

She turned her face impulsively, and their lips met – t was rather a hit and miss affair. Hester came to a rueful conclusion:

We are meant to be firm friends and nothing more. . . .

Alf obviously didn't think that. He said hopefully, 'Does this mean we're walking out together?'

She gently pushed him away. 'No, Alf. I'm sorry. I'm . . . not ready for any of that – I've got my responsibilities, as Matron said, when she told me about Pa's accident. I've got to see the twins through to being independent, and that ain't likely for a few years yet. Pa needs me – they all need me – I'm the breadwinner now.'

'I could help . . . well, I hope I do already.' It was obvious that he felt hurt and upset. Hester couldn't blame him for that.

'This is something I have to do myself. I've an idea how I might better myself, earn more, but I must find out if it's possible or not.'

'We can still be friends, can't we? Please, Hester. . . .'

'Of course we can. I hoped you'd say that. Nothing's changed in that way, Alf.'

'Well, goodnight,' he said sorrowfully. 'See you tomorrer.'

'See you then. You're invited to Sunday dinner as usual!'

Five

The mutton had to stretch to seven hungry people, not six, because the family had another unexpected visitor, Big Peg, wearing her Sunday costume and a big, flowery hat, with the pug in her bag. She'd been to church, and so had he. She said proudly: 'He's better behaved than most children during the sermon. Thought Fred might like to meet him.'

'You'll stay to eat with us, won't you?' Hester asked, after she invited Peg to 'step inside.' She added: 'There should be some scraps for your dog. Polly told me about him and his sneezing.'

'I suppose you could call him my dog, but I don't like the thought of leaving him all day while I'm at work. I might have to find him a new home – I wondered if Fred. . . .'

'Ask him! It could be the company he needs.'

'Puglet would be right for that – he don't like to run about much, just snooze. But he's a little clown when he's awake. I was told some people call 'em monkey dogs, because of their comical faces. I reckon though, that Puglet might be a rather ancient pug.'

While Fred was introduced to the dog, who settled immediately on his lap, Hester hurried down to the kitchen to dish up.

Young Polly's wiles at the butcher's stall had resulted in a decent piece of meat. Hester had rinsed it in vinegar the previous night, before she made her cocoa, then dried it thoroughly and dusted it with pepper and a little ground ginger, left over from Bess's gingerbread baking days, to keep any flies at bay. Then she wrapped it in butcher's muslin. At least it was cooler in the basement than on the ground floor of the house, which was why the kitchen was situated there.

After breakfast, she'd trimmed the joint removing excess fat, tied it firmly with string in a neat round, then placed this in a large saucepan of water. After bringing it to a rolling boil, she skimmed off the scum, then put it to simmer with a good dash of pepper and salt, on a low heat. Thanks to the Penny Whistlers' cap of pennies, there was a chip basket from the market of vegetables now in season, a bunch of carrots, big Spanish onions, new peas and potatoes, for Harry and Polly to pare, pop pods or chop, then add to the pot. The parsley sauce could be made later. They'd been able to splash out on a large jug of skimmed milk, keeping cool standing in a basin of cold water, and covered with a muslin cap with beaded fringe, also to deter bluebottles.

Despite it being a warm day already, Hester made that good old standby – suet pudding, rolled in a cloth, to steam beside the mutton pot. The family liked their pud with large dollops of Tate & Lyle's best.

Fred and Peg sat and talked in his room. He stroked the little pug's head, smiling at the wrinkles. 'Match mine, eh?'

'Fred Stainsby!' Peg exclaimed. 'You're still in your prime!'

'So are you,' he responded, with a wink.

Embarrassed, she changed the subject. 'I was glad to bump into you yesterday at the market. I didn't come to see you before, you know, not because I didn't care how you was doin', but your ma-in-law gets me all hot round the collar – she's so nosey.'

'She's only worried I might marry you and turf her out!' he grinned.

'Oh, Fred, you're jokin' ain't you?' She was hot all over now – her age she supposed. Had she betrayed her growing feelings for him?

'Well, I shouldn't have been so slow to ask you before I lorst me leg,' he said, serious for once. 'I thought . . . Bess wouldn't have minded, if you and me. . . . But I can't expect that to happen now – I'm an old crock, and I don't suppose I'll work again. O' course, we're not young romantics, and if you married me, you'd have to take on the kids, and Granny wouldn't budge an inch.'

'Fred, I get on well with 'em all, don't I? Specially Hester. I could relieve that gal of some of her duties here – oh, I'd have to keep on working too, but you could do your bit entertaining down the market, now and again eh? Why don't you try asking me proper?'

'Polly's going to be a handful, I can tell that.'

'Well, she takes after her granny, Victoria Garter, but *she'll* grow up – I ain't sure old Vicky ever has! Go on, ask me!'

'Will you,' he began uncertainly, just as Puglet stirred and gave one of his great sneezes. Then the dog turned round very precisely on his four little feet in Fred's lap before he settled down once more for another sleep. It was obviously some sort of ritual. Fred was instantly reminded of the time when, as a lad he'd gone to a magic lantern show in the mission hall. He said, 'He made me think of them picture slides of that famous circus elephant, Jumbo, balancing on a cube. I wondered how he could do it, on them four huge feet.'

'Puglet's made himself at home,' Big Peg said. 'I might as well join him here! Don't make no announcements yet. Not wise to hurry. . . .'

'I'll use me crutches to get to the dinner table – no, don't help me, I got to learn to do things again for meself. Will you wheel the chair? It's the only one I feel safe sitting in, and anyway, we've only got six chairs. Rise and shine, old gentleman,' he said to the dog. 'No begging at the table, mind. Hester'll scrape the plates for you later, I promise.'

'Time to lay the table, Granny,' Hester said. 'Alf'll move the sewing machine for you.' She was hot and flustered after stirring the gravy and waiting for it to thicken after adding the gravy salts.

'I've got an orange box at home, it's nice and sturdy – if you stood it on end you could put a curtain down the front and use the compartments inside for shelves to hold your sewing. The top would be a table for you to work at,' Alf offered.

'You're a kind young man,' Granny said, pleased at the results of her morning's work. 'Mind, my old mother used to say you shouldn't sew on the Sabbath, but my husband said that was *hand* sewing. You'll make someone a good husband, Alf Hodge.' She looked meaningfully at Hester, before she gathered up the blue cotton pieces she had unpicked from a voluminous skirt, and stuffed them into a tapestry bag.

'Well, get the cloth on and the knives and forks out,' Hester said quickly to Polly. 'Harry, you can help carry up the dinner plates today.' She hoped Alf would take his cue from her and act as normal, but she had lain awake for ages last night worrying that she'd hurt his feelings.

'Best dinner I've had in ages,' Fred said, as he finished his second helping of suet pud. 'Time for a bit of shut-eye, I reckon.'

'Yes, lovely meal, but I must be going. I'll leave Puglet with you, then, shall I Fred? He's made himself at home.' Peg smiled.

'*What?*' Granny demanded. 'Who said we'd have that animal?'

'I'm the head of the house,' Fred retorted. 'And I say it!'

'I'll see you out, Peg,' Hester said hurriedly.

As they went out of the door, they heard Fred suggest to Granny Garter: 'Maybe you can make the little dog a jacket, after all, he's going to join the act. . . .'

'What act?' Granny shrieked.

'Oh, didn't you know? Me and Polly and Harry – we're the Poplar Penny Whistlers!' The name came to him, just like that.

'That's how we could afford such a splendid dinner!' Harry added.

Granny Garter gave an ominous moan and put her head in her hands, but peered through her spread fingers to see what effect this was having on the others.

'Peace and quiet for five minutes, praise be,' Fred said cheerfully.

Big Peg was making ready to go to bed. She had a seven a.m. start at the laundry on Monday morning, so an early night was needed.

There was no gas laid on in the old cottage, or water on tap. It was one of many decrepit buildings in a crowded street. There were also several small corner pubs which barely made a living, but spilled the inebriated from their doors on Friday and Saturday nights. There had been rumours so long as Peg could remember, that all this would disappear when the long awaited Blackwall Tunnel was built. It was preferable to the local name for the river embankment, Bleak Wall, she thought.

Thomas had brought her to the cottage after the wedding; her first real home for she'd been brought up in the Foundling Hospital founded by the philanthropist Thomas Coram. The young couple had climbed the steep stairs, he with candle in hand, which he placed in the niche outside the single bedroom door. She still slept in the iron bed, with the flock mattress. Thomas had made the simple washstand and Peg added the bowl and jug she'd discovered abandoned in the coal hole by a previous tenant. She'd used them ever since. The bowl was cracked round the rim, but didn't let out water.

She sat on the edge of the bed and slowly drew out the hairpins from her topknot. She had no vanity, had never possessed a mirror. Thomas gasped that first night as the heavy chestnut hair cascaded down her back. She could still recall his husky voice, for even then he had a troublesome cough. He'd twined his fingers in her hair and told her: 'Oh, Peg, you're so big – so beautiful!' Sometimes even now she dreamed of what happened next, as he untied the strings of her chemise, which doubled as a nightgown, and gently lifted it over her head. She would never experience such passion, such joy again, she thought. Even if she married Fred, hadn't he said that they were past romance?

One brief year of marriage, she thought, and after three months had passed dear Thomas spent the rest of his short life lying on the settle by the fire downstairs. When they met, she'd been thrilled to find a young man taller than she was, for she was six-foot in height, and he was well-built, too. At the end, she could lift his frail, emaciated body with ease. She was his devoted nurse, but he forbade her to kiss him once the doctor had diagnosed the reason for his chronic cough. She was fortunate, she was robust and resisted the disease.

After he passed away, Peg returned to work full-time. She had to: it was either the laundry or the workhouse. No man had told her since that although she was big, she was beautiful.

Puglet had a cardboard box in a corner of his new master's room. Harry escorted him round the garden to snuffle at the odd snail, but wisely, the dog didn't attempt to chase a thin, stringy looking Tabby which soon disappeared into the undergrowth behind the privy, where Fred was at present ensconced.

'Settled in, Puglet?' Alf called from next door. He was having a smoke under a crabby old apple tree; his stepmother didn't approve of the habit. Privately, he thought it was preferable to Mother's Ruin, her favourite tipple. Although she had no time for him, or for his father, a burly docker who kept out of her way by spending all his spare time in the pub, Alf couldn't help feeling sorry for her. Not only had she lost her first husband, but he was aware that her entire family of five children had died in a diphtheria epidemic before he was born.

'Yup,' Harry replied. Then he was alerted by a rapping on the privy door. Fred needed his assistance: he hurried to his task.

Granny Garter was already in bed, well satisfied with her efforts that day. Polly would look really posh when she was all dressed up, she thought. She'd find that pretty parasol she'd twirled in her own youth, and give her that too.

Hester was wondering, as she brushed and braided her hair before getting into her own bed, if she would dare to knock on Matron's door and ask her an important question, or whether she would be rebuffed. . . .

Polly said, yawning, 'D'you think I ought to get Granny to sew lace on the legs of me other drawers?'

'Why? You thinking of performing more cartwheels?'

'I'm not revealing that. . . .'

'Well, it sounds as if you're thinking of revealing you know what!'

'Night, Pa, sleep tight.' Harry turned the lamp low, prior to leaving.

There was a grunting from the cardboard box as Puglet turned around and then buried his head in Fred's old jersey.

'Night, Harry. Spelling test tomorrer you said: get plenty of sleep.'

'Don't remind me, Pa. Been a good weekend, ain't it?'

'A good weekend.' Fred echoed.

Six

There had been sweeping changes in the hospital since Sydney Holland, the Director of the East and West India Dock Company visited earlier in the year. The long serving matron retired, and younger, more dynamic, staff were brought in. The new team benefitted from the dedication shown by the old brigade who had established the reputation of the hospital. Recently, the hospital had also acquired wealthy patrons, thanks to all the publicity.

The new matron, younger and slimmer than her predecessor, leaned forward in her chair behind her desk, with a reassuring smile at Hester, sitting opposite. She observed the girl's tightly clasped hands.

'Please tell me what is worrying you,' she said.

'I . . . wanted to ask you if I could train here as a nurse!' The words came out in a rush, but once said, Hester visibly relaxed.

'Ah. This is something you have been thinking about for some time, I presume. From what I have heard, you have the qualities, I believe, to succeed as a probationary nurse. A good character is valued above all.'

'I wondered – about wages. . . . I left school at fourteen, with a good report.'

'Your *salary*,' Matron emphasised the word, 'would be £12 for the first year; this would rise to £20 the second year. By the third year you would earn £25 per annum.

'You are intelligent, Miss Stainsby, I am aware of that, but in many ways the life of a young nurse is as hard as that of a laundry maid. The hours are long, with one day off every two weeks, and you would not always finish on time: the patients' welfare must always come first. There are one or two lectures each week, and these must be attended during off-duty time.

'Compassion, caring, dedication: I am told that you have applied these to your own family and I'm sure will continue to do so. Loyalty, punctuality, truthfulness and good manners: I believe I cannot fault you on those. Perhaps you are a little slipshod in your speech, but this can be rectified. Cleanliness – the nurse must be scrupulous in her personal hygiene before dealing with the sick; the wards must be kept spotless. The night nurse must not sleep while on duty: patients could be lying awake in pain, and need the nurse's help. A nurse remains calm. She accepts that the ward Sister's instructions are always to be obeyed. Do you understand?'

'Yes, Matron. I . . . think so. How long would I have to train?'

'We have recently extended the course to two years. The Sisters are highly educated: I have chosen them with much care and have personally supervised their nursing practice. You will observe that they manage the day to day running of their wards and the nursing staff. They are responsible only to me.

'I was fortunate enough to begin my career under Miss Eva Luckes, of the London Hospital – who is the author of a splendid book entitled *General Nursing*, which we regard as our hospital bible. Miss Luckes was trained by Florence Nightingale, who was the inspiration and founder of modern nursing. Due to the efforts of Miss Nightingale, it is now rightly regarded as a profession.

'The probationary nurses are like yourself, from good, if humble backgrounds. The best will rise above the ranks. You should fit in well. I expect you realize that you would live in. The dormitories which are at present in neighbouring houses will be replaced in time by staff accommodation within the hospital. For now, please be patient: this will take a few weeks to arrange, and then I will send for you.' Matron rose and held out her hand to Hester.

Back in the laundry, Big Peg was the first to be told. 'Oh, Peg, I'm going to be a nurse!'

Peg picked her up and whirled her round in her excitement. 'Your ma would have been so happy to hear that! And so am I. You're going to make something of your life Hester, but I know someone who'll be disappointed. . . .'

'Alf, do you mean? I don't like to hurt him, but marriage is not for me yet, perhaps never! I want to control my own life – like you!'

'Sometimes that's a lonely path, not the one I would have chosen,' Peg said simply.

'I'm sorry Peg – I didn't mean – you know I'm hoping you and Pa will have good news for us, one of these days.'

'You never know dearie, you never know.'

Hester's uniform was very similar to that of parlour maids in big houses, where there were many servants. Her skirt was long, but more practical than the style worn by society ladies, which still had the suggestion of a bustle and where the hem at the back swept the ground as they walked. She wore a voluminous apron, above which could be seen her high, detachable stiff collar. 'Chin up,' Hester muttered ruefully to herself. Her hair was plaited and coiled in the nape of her neck, and the only feminine touch was her cap, with its modest frill. The senior nurses wore more elaborate headgear to indicate their status. Her arms were covered by removable white cotton sleeves which were attached to shorter working sleeves. Out of the ward, or on the street, she was enveloped in a sturdy navy-blue cape. It was the cosiest garment she had ever possessed.

Hester learned that gloves were worn for various procedures, masks for dealing with infectious patients or septic wounds, and protective goggles when there was a danger of noxious fluids being discharged into the nurse's face.

It was some time before Hester was judged to be competent to deal with these complicated cases, of course; the trainee nurses were isolated from the general wards. She swabbed floors with a mop twirled in a bucket of scalding water and carbolic, with her fellow trainee and new friend Edie, a lanky, skinny girl with a worried expression. Edie followed where Hester led. The girls brought bed pans, and dealt stoically with the contents later. They soon became expert at stripping and making beds; they cleaned the bed frames after a patient had departed. Edie, who had nursed her younger siblings at home when they were poorly, was good at spoon-feeding helpless patients, and encouraging them to 'just have a little of this good broth'. Hester, with her small, capable hands, gently washed those too weak to do this for themselves. She soon progressed to bed-baths, ensuring that the patient was not too exhausted by this process, and was wrapped in warm towels. The young nurses went on to taking temperatures and marking charts. The patients were all male at this time, but there were proposals to build a ward for women injured at the docks and for a new isolation block.

Hester was glad to see a familiar face most days, even if she and Alf didn't have the chance to chat. There were no male nurses in the hospital, they were at that time employed only in the asylums, where a young female nurse might be in danger from unstable patients. The nursing staff in these sad institutions were sometimes ex-army personnel, who could understand those whose minds had been disturbed by war. Alf was a porter, and there was not much chance of promotion for him. He was proud of Hester's achievements, but he had to accept that his hopes of marrying her were fading fast. . . .

Their ward Sister was a superior being indeed: she gave little praise but pointed out any mistakes. Hester, having been used to the kindly supervisor in the laundry and the camaraderie there, sometimes despaired that Sister would ever unbend and be friendly. She didn't know that in fact Sister's reports on the new trainees, were positive. Hester and Edie had been probationary nurses for three months, and it was coming up to Christmas with important changes due in the new year: Hester would be moving into a cell-like room in the staff accommodation now provided in the old part of the hospital.

*

Hester had a rare Saturday evening and Sunday morning off, which meant she would be staying at home overnight. She joined Fred in his room before a late supper, because Granny was still whirring her sewing machine in the living room. Hester was grateful to soak her tired feet in a mustard bath, thanks to her kind brother Harry. She said, 'I know now just how hard the nurses worked to get you well enough to come home, Pa.'

'I'm worried *you* still work too hard,' Fred said. 'Harry and Alf, when he's around, give me a hand here, but I'm getting much better at managing things myself. I swing around on my crutches most of the day. Polly is doing a bit of cooking, but she don't make such wholesome grub as you. All them little cakes with jam in 'em. . . . Granny Garter, well—'

'She's at least doing something useful, Pa – making clothes for Polly and sewing for other people. I've never seen her so bright and cheerful before.' Hester withdrew her feet from the cooling water and wrapped them in an old towel. 'Dear Peg bought me a small bottle of eau de cologne,' she told Fred. 'Sister said to rub the soles of your feet with it, to harden them. If they get really sore, she recommends dusting them with boracic powder.'

'Doing your foot exercises?' Harry asked with a grin, as he stooped to remove the bowl of water. He'd shot up in height in the last few months, his voice had deepened and there was a smudge of dark hair on his upper lip. He also had pimples, which his twin seemed mostly to have escaped.

'Yes,' Hester arched her feet and then wriggled her toes. 'Thanks, Harry, I feel much better now!' She became aware of an appetizing smell wafting up from the kitchen. 'Oh, Poll must be making a special supper tonight!'

'With help from Peg – she said there was something to celebrate,' Harry said mysteriously.

I wonder what . . . Hester thought, then she saw the twinkle in Fred's eye. Oh, I hope it's what I think it is!

Alf arrived in time to help carry the supper plates while Hester, hastily changed out of her uniform, let down her hair in her old bedroom, then returned to sit next to Granny, while Peg slipped into the seat beside Fred.

Polly whipped off her apron and was revealed in her new outfit, the royal blue skirt and fitted jacket made by her grandmother.

'Ta ra! Wore these togs for my performance this afternoon down the market. Granny lent me her boa, as there was a cold wind. You oughter seen Bobby's eyes pop – I couldn't help thinking he looked like Puglet! You can thank the Poplar Penny Whistlers for the feast. Though it's Puglet, in his jacket, what draws the crowd.'

'What about your cartwheels?' Harry murmured. Polly gave him a pinch. Granny didn't appear to have heard, but unfortunately, Harry added: 'I ain't sure I like the dog wearing the same weskit as me, with silver buttons, too.'

Granny Garter certainly heard that. 'You ungrateful lad!' She thumped the table with her fist, making the cutlery 'jump'.

Peg quickly passed two steaming platefuls of food to Granny Garter and Hester. 'Ladies first, don't they say!'

'Kedgeree,' Polly said proudly, as Alf followed up with two more plates. 'Smoked haddock put aside by our friend Bobby. I told him it was Hester's favourite. He'd do anything to impress her!'

'Never had it before,' Hester smiled, 'I hear the toffs like it for breakfast!' She thought that Bobby likely had his eye on Polly now. She would be fourteen in February, but that was still far too young for walking out. If she got a chance she'd have a word in his ear. . . .

'Well,' said Polly, 'That's true, I believe, but Peg knew how to make it.' She recited: 'Cook fish, flake and bone; um, scrape skin off; then add a knob of butter and half a hard-boiled egg for each person—'

'Or one egg between two people,' Harry butted in. 'Even I could have made this – you just boil everything first.'

Polly ignored this remark and carried on: 'Chop the eggs up finely, then mix with the fish and butter – good shake of salt and pepper, add a pound of cooked rice – heat that all up in a pan, stir well and arrange on plates – don't you think it looks tempting?'

'We do,' they all agreed. Hester noted that each mound of kedgeree was topped with a flag of her home-grown parsley.

It was a good meal, if not very substantial. For pudding, there was one of Polly's wobbly jellies, with half an overripe pear for each of them.

When the table was cleared, Fred struggled up, leaning heavily on his crutches. 'I have an announcement to make.'

'Get on with it then,' Granny said, 'I was hoping for a cup of tea. You overdid the salt in that dish, young Polly.'

'Now, now, Vicky,' Fred admonished her. 'It was the best meal the gal's served up yet. You'll get your tea in a while – actually, it wouldn't hurt *you* to make it for once, would it? This is important. Maybe Peg'll put it better. . . .'

Peg rose and stood beside him. She was a good head taller than he was; handsome in a plum-coloured sateen skirt, one of Granny Garter's skilful renovations. 'Well, if you all agree – '

'What if we don't?' asked Harry, tongue-in-cheek.

'I'll be coming here to live with you all – and to keep you in order, Harry! 'Cos Fred and me have decided to get wed. You won't have to go performing down the market then, unless we hit hard times again. What do you say to Boxing Day?'

'Well, I say hooray!' Hester cried.

'Here, here!' echoed Alf, and then looked bashful. After all, it was nothing to do with him.

On cue, Puglet gave a tremendous sneeze under the table, where he sat by Granny, the most likely to drop a morsel or two.

'About time too,' said Granny Garter tartly, to Fred and Peg.

Seven

1892 was just round the corner – it promised to be a momentous year with work beginning on clearing the slum area to lead to the long awaited Blackwall Tunnel, designed by Sir Alexander Birnie. It was anticipated that the tunnel would be under construction for the next five years. Londoners would also see the erection of another enduring landmark, the statue of Eros, and the Queen was about to honour the Poplar hospital by becoming a governor and generous subscriber.

However, first there was bitter weather to be endured around Christmas 1891 with the arrival of snow. This made life very difficult for the workers and horse-drawn vehicles including the omnibuses. The outpatients department at the hospital was very busy dealing with minor accidents. The Poplar Penny Whistlers were firmly told by Hester that they were not to risk going to the market to perform in such conditions.

Big Peg thought she would be fortunate to leave all the coming confusion and noise of the tunnel excavations behind her when she married Fred and moved in with the Stainsby family; her little cottage would shortly be demolished. She'd shed a few tears in private, and then put the past to rest.

The family enjoyed a quiet Christmas Day, having opened their modest, mainly homemade gifts early on. Polly discovered that Granny had been aware all the time of her cartwheels down the market, when she unwrapped a ruched blue satin garter. 'If you must show off, do it in style,' was written on the accompanying tag. Polly beamed. 'You've given me a great idea – I'll take Polly *Garter* as my stage name!'

On the ward, Hester and Edie performed their routine tasks cheerfully for the sake of their patients and at noon served up a special meal for those able to eat it. Carols were sung, and the young nurses presented small gifts to everyone involved. They would have a light lunch themselves at the hospital and then continue with their duties until four o'clock, when they were free to go home, stay overnight, and return to work on Boxing Day afternoon.

At home, they waited for Hester to join them for their own Christmas dinner. Peg supervised the cooking of a large capon, which Fred promised to carve carefully, to leave sufficient for sandwiches for after the wedding the following day. There was also a hock of ham to eke this out, and crispy bacon pieces which had basted the bird. Polly and Harry peeled potatoes, carrots and turnips. They argued over who should tackle the onions for the bread sauce: Harry drew the short straw, or rather the half match when Fred settled the dispute. The alternative made Polly sigh, 'It ain't fair!' as she grated crumbs from a hard heel of bread. Granny Garter produced a small bottle of brandy which she said was: 'For the pudding. Remember to mark the bottle afterwards, Fred. . . .' She actually volunteered to make chestnut stuffing for the bird, and to twist fat pork sausages in half, making two from one.

'Leave a few chestnuts to roast in the grate later,' Harry whispered in Granny's ear. After all, he'd gleaned the nuts at twilight before the snow came, from a location a couple of miles away, known only to a few of the local lads, who were paid to collect them by the hot chestnut man who sold them outside the music hall.

Hester rushed in, the shoulders of her cape powdered white, with her face reddened from the cold air outside. She held out her hands to the fire, greeting the assembled family at the laden table: 'A Happy Christmas to one and all! If you can hold back for a few more minutes, I'll get changed quick, and then we'll all tuck in, eh?'

Peg was already ensconced in her new home. Harry and Alf had collected her belongings on Christmas Eve and pushed them on an old hospital trolley with a wonky wheel, which meant the neighbours had heard them coming. She'd not had much to bring, which was just as well, as they were already a 'full house' as Fred said. The washstand, basin and jug were now in Fred's room, her pots and pans in the kitchen, likewise her best china tea set with the bluebird pattern, her meagre stock of linen was in the cupboard, her few clothes in Bess's chest of drawers, and the old iron bedstead, much to Granny's displeasure, was temporarily in her big bedroom. After the wedding, it would be disposed of, as Peg would join Fred downstairs in the old parlour.

The Christmas dinner was a real treat, after all the hard times, which they hoped were now behind them. There were tiny dumplings – spoonfuls of batter dropped into the hot fat in the roasting tin after the chicken was transferred to the carving dish. These took ten minutes, then were served up in the gravy. There was white meat for the womenfolk; darker meat and a leg or wing of chicken for the men. The bread sauce was smooth, the stuffing delicious, the roast potatoes crisp and crunchy and the other vegetables glistened with melted butter.

Hester had contributed the pudding, having bought the ingredients one or two at a time, during the previous weeks. Harry and Polly well and truly mixed them all on Stir Up Sunday, as their mother always did, when they were younger. Now Polly proudly carried the pud to the table, dark with fruit and steaming, embellished with a holly leaf, removed from the wreath adorning the front door. She gave her usual cry of 'Ta ra!' Granny supervised the adding of the brandy and Fred lit it ceremoniously, before he scratched a mark on the bottle. This would go back under Granny's pillow, where it was kept for 'medicinal purposes.' It was the only strong drink in the house, in deference to Big Peg who'd signed the Pledge when she was in the foundling hospital.

'Mind you don't swaller the thrupenny bits,' Granny Garter warned them. 'Put them on this saucer, so I can count 'em all up.'

'Don't waste the pudding – lick the silver clean!' said Harry.

'Sorry about the lumps in the custard,' Big Peg apologized, 'I had to keep an eye on other things cooking at the same time.' She was having to adapt to feeding a family after being single for so long.

'I didn't think I could eat any more,' Alf admitted, 'But I find I can!' He'd had to work Christmas Day like Hester, but was back in time to share the feast. There was certainly strong drink in his house, he thought ruefully, and actually he wouldn't have minded a glass of beer. . . .

Late evening, the table flaps were let down and the table was pushed against the wall. The living room, since Fred slept in the other room, could only accommodate two easy chairs plus Fred's wheelchair. Younger family members relaxed on cushions on the floor, or sat on the hard dining chairs, in a circle around a crackling good fire, with the lights out. They were waiting for the chestnuts to cool a little in the hearth before peeling back the glossy brown skins, smeared with ash, to reveal the tender kernel within.

This traditional treat over, Fred cleared his throat. 'Time for a singsong, I reckon. Hope you're in good voice, if you're not playing the penny whistle?'

'That means Granny, Peg, Alf and me,' Hester said. 'We'll choose a carol in turn, eh? '

'*It came upon the midnight clear*,' suggested Alf.

'Not midnight yet – we'll have that later.'

'*O Little Town of Bethlehem*,' Granny put in. 'That seems fitting. It *is* very still outside today. . . .' This made them all recall these words in particular, which were always sang so fervently: *The hopes and fears of all the years are met in Thee tonight.* How true it was this Christmas.

A forgotten chestnut shot from the fire and frightened Puglet. He let out a yelp and hid under Fred's chair.

'No fighting over who gets it,' Fred said, but he was grinning. 'That one's got *my* name on it.'

The party ended with cutting the Christmas-cum-wedding cake and a small glass each of Stone's Ginger Wine, 'Suitable for young people,' as Granny remarked primly. She would have her usual nip of brandy later in the privacy of her room.

Around half-past midnight, Peg settled down for the last time on the flock mattress, which was as lumpy as the custard, she realized: she'd not really noticed the discomfort before. 'Goodnight Vicky,' she said, to the hump in the other bed. 'Another busy day tomorrow. . . .'

Granny Garter's response was unexpected. 'I think you should know Peg, that twins run in *my* side of the family, not Fred's.' She heaved herself over on to her other side, facing away from Peg.

This was just as well, because Peg was shaking with laughter, with the covers pulled over her head. How on earth could she reply to that?

They crunched their way through unsullied snow to the church, for there had been a fresh fall overnight. They kept to the middle of the road as there was no traffic that day, just a few others on foot, and it was impossible to discern where the path was contained by the kerb. It was fifteen minutes before eleven o'clock. Fred still referred to the church as the chapel, for it had been built in the last century for the East India Dock Company to replace a previous chapel, which was then over one hundred years old. St Matthias church was much bigger than the original and beautifully decorated within. It was said that the great columns were fashioned of material salvaged from the wrecked ships of the Armada. It was a refuge for those connected with ships, the sea and the docks.

Big Peg, being so strong, pushed her husband-to-be in his chair. She insisted he be wrapped around in a thick rug. Harry, as Best Man, walked beside her ready to help if the wheels stuck in a rut. Polly and Hester linked arms with Granny Garter. Alf was back on duty at the hospital, but Hester had been permitted the whole morning off. This would probably be her last Christmas at home for a long time, she thought, because she was moving into her hospital room that afternoon. She wouldn't see nearly as much of her family, or Alf, for men, even fathers, were not allowed to visit the nurses' quarters at any time.

Puglet was hidden under the rug on Fred's lap. Peg intended to transfer him to a bag as she had before, and Granny actually promised to look after him, while the girls, the bride's attendants, followed Peg down the aisle.

They didn't look much like a wedding party, being wound around with scarves and wearing woollen gloves which Fred, who'd learned to knit as a small boy, had made to while away the tedium of not being at work. Granny Garter had provided him with four needles and a large ball of grey wool, unravelled from one of her late husband's jerseys. She was energetic these days. 'I've come through the *Change* at long last – I'm a new woman,' she said. The youngsters wore smart leather boots, for Fred's old workmates had collected a Christmas box to help the family, and they'd been able to pay off the boot club held at *The Ship*. Hester and Polly sported tam o'shanters, and Granny had trimmed her own and the bride's round black straw hats with red ribbon. Fred and Harry wore their usual caps.

'Got a little surprise for you,' Fred said as they approached the church gate. After the joyous peals of Christmas Day, the bell ringers were having a well-earned rest, likewise the organist, although one of the congregation had offered to play the old harmonium with a choir boy to pump the bellows, on promise of a sixpence for his efforts.

The Poplar Penny Whistlers had made friends with most of their rival street musicians: The Heavenly Bell Ringer was happy to oblige with his campanology on this occasion. A small, wiry man, with rags wound round his boots and lower legs to keep out the cold, he was already setting up the bells on a taut wire, stretched between two yew trees. He had a stick in each mittened hand to strike the bells. The small procession halted to enjoy the melodious sounds, and to reward the Heavenly Bell Ringer with a florin. He played his favourite piece – *The Bluebells of Scotland*. Not quite apt, but somehow it sounded just right for a wedding. Then they walked into the quiet church, decorated with Christmas greenery, where they were greeted by the rector and his sexton, and the ceremony began. The harmonium wheezed, then gathered momentum, as Big Peg strode down the aisle to meet her bride-groom who leaned on his crutches, supported by his son.

There was only one hymn and the 23rd Psalm. The heartfelt responses and short prayers were said; the kindly vicar made the simple service special. He would not have dreamed of telling them that he had been told to hurry home by his family for they were having their hot Christmas Dinner a day late.

The bride and groom exchanged their first real kiss and the family crowded round them to wish them all the best and agreed it had been a lovely wedding.

Polly was tempted to do a cartwheel in the snow, but Hester put a restraining hand on her arm. 'Not here, Poll!' she whispered.

It was snowing again: time to hurry home, to ginger up the fire and to eat sandwiches and cake. They toasted the happy couple with cups of tea. The cups had bluebirds on them, of course. Then Hester gave them all a hug and departed for the hospital.

At bedtime, it was Big Peg who gently eased Fred into his side of the bed. She was well aware, although he never complained, that he still suffered with his 'good' leg, besides the phantom pain from the missing member. She went over to the washstand and discov-ered a new addition, a mirror in a swinging stand. It wasn't new and she guessed that it had belonged to Bess. She sat down and regarded herself shyly in the glass, then, as she had done twenty-odd years before, she loosened her hair and let it fall in a curtain around her shoulders and down her back. She didn't expect Fred to come up behind her, of course, as Thomas had done, and run his fingers through the chestnut mane. As she raised her brush to tease out any tangles before plaiting it for the night, she was startled by Fred's voice from the bed. 'Peg, leave your hair, I like it. . . ,' he said.

She rose, untying the strings of her old flannel wrapper. She wore a white silk chemise tonight, courtesy of Granny Garter. She had no illusions about the older woman, but she was relieved that she had accepted her into the family. Fred didn't say I was beautiful, she thought, but maybe he will grow to really love me, in time. . . . She touched the cheap ring he'd placed on her finger earlier. She glanced down at Puglet, already asleep in his box.

Peg slipped into bed beside Fred. He said softly: 'You don't mind too much do you, Peg, about me not being the man I was before I lorst me leg?'

''Course not,' she said stoutly. She put her arms around him, drew him close, and cuddled him to her comfortable bosom. What happened next was up to him. No hurry, she said to herself, but I hope it don't take another twenty years!

Eight

1894

The hospital had greatly expanded over the past three years, during which a new east wing with three floors of wards was added, with beds for women as well as children. Outpatients remained in the basement area, while the old building was adapted to accommodate the nurses. Matron was in loco parentis.

Hester's friend Edie was glad to escape the overcrowding at home to live at her place of work. Hester was happy she and Edie were still together, but she knew her family missed her, as she did them. How would they react when Polly flew the nest, which, she suspected, was likely to be soon? However, she thought that young Harry deserved a proper room of his own, now he was also sixteen and a working lad. Granny Garter could then take over the box room for her sewing. She had quite a business going now and made no secret of the fact that her modest earnings were to be invested in Polly's future career. For the moment, Polly had to bide her time in the laundry, like her sister before her. Harry, thanks to Fred's connection with the docks, had a clerical post in the dock's office.

'You might get writer's cramp, but you ain't likely to lose a leg,' Fred said bluntly.

Hester, now her probationary period was complete, was the proud possessor of the Hospital's Certificate of Training, and officially entitled to be called 'Nurse'. She wore a new cap, with ribbons at the back. She had just been assigned to the children's ward. Sister had talked at length to her young nurses and been convinced that Hester possessed the right qualities to become a good children's nurse; she was patient, gentle and very willing to learn.

'You brought up your younger brother and sister, and helped to nurse them, no doubt, through sickness,' Sister said. 'However, I believe that they were always well-nourished and in normal health thanks to the care of a good family. Some of the children you will come into contact with are so ill, they have little chance of survival. You will often experience heartache, but must always reassure your small patients and be cheerful. Each child is precious and deserves loving. The high mortality of the very young in our country is something that concerns us greatly. Those raised in poverty, with inadequate nutrition, are prone to rickets; limbs are wasted and deformed; disease is inevitable. Will you take on this challenge?'

'I will,' Hester said fervently.

Hester had been awoken as usual by the bell which rang every morning at six a.m. With the other nurses she had a light breakfast half an hour later, to keep her going until a second, more substantial breakfast was provided much later after the early-morning chores. The night and day staff merged at seven a.m. and she would be on duty until nine that night. The longest break was two hours at lunchtime. It would be a further hour before the night owls went off duty.

Hester sat near the fire, with the sick baby on her lap. Little Samuel had been slow to thrive following his premature birth, which had resulted in a haemorrhage for his immature mother, who arrived at the hospital too late to be saved. Samuel remained in the care of the hospital and despite the odds, survived. Although now almost six weeks old, the tiny boy was too frail to be bathed in a tub: Hester cradled him in a warm towel while she cleaned him all over with a soft flannel dipped in a bowl of warm water. It was vital that the procedure was quick, but thorough, so that the baby didn't become chilled. Fortunately he had no splints on his legs, as so many children did, but he was too passive, she thought compassionately. There was no resistance to her ministrations, no screwing up of the eyes and a mewling cry as with recovering infants.

She dried him with another soft towel and dusted the little bottom with soothing zinc powder, before pinning on a fresh napkin. A woollen vest was pulled carefully over his head and his arms guided gently through the holes. A nightgown completed the dressing process with cotton mitts to prevent the baby from scratching his face.

Hester had cared for Samuel since he came into the general children's ward. Until he was a month old and strong enough to be moved from the special nursery he had been cleansed with olive oil and kept warm with soft cotton wool padding. He'd been fed through a dropper. Even now he had not reached the average birth weight for normal baby boys, of seven and a half pounds. The day would come she knew, when she would be parted from Samuel, when he was fit enough to be taken to the Coram, as the orphanage was known affectionately after its founder, and Hester knew she would miss him. The hospital would ensure that he was vaccinated against smallpox. They were at last winning the battle against this deadly disease.

Another nurse removed the damp towels and the bowl of water, then brought the sterilized feeding bottle, one of two provided for each baby. The boiled, cooled cows' milk had been carefully measured then diluted with barley water. Hester remained by the fire, with the baby held in a semi-upright position against her shoulder as she had been taught. Samuel was fed two-hourly over the twenty-four hours.

Hester was only half aware of the rain beating against the windows of the nursery. Officially it was spring, but this was a room kept always at an even temperature. 'Fresh air and light are as vital as food to enable young children to grow' – Sister quoted this maxim most days. When the bottle was drained, Hester removed the teat from the baby's mouth and dabbed the little trails of milk trickling down his chin. Then she rubbed his back in a circular motion to bring up a satisfactory belch of wind. 'Well done,' she beamed.

When Samuel was tucked into his crib, she watched for a few moments the pulsing of the fontanel in his scalp as he resumed his sleep, before she went to help with the stripping of the beds, to spread clean draw sheets, then to bath the next patient. Many sick children were incontinent but the nurses were instructed that no young patient was to be reproached in this respect.

Another small boy, but this one was three years of age and could be a handful. However, this was a positive sign and the nurses were glad to see it. They'd learned to ignore the odd expletive from the child – it was not his fault, just what he'd learned at home, as Sister reminded them. His legs were in splints which must be kept waterproof. Dampness encouraged lice: the nurses were ever vigilant. All this before a proper breakfast, Hester thought ruefully, and my tummy is rumbling. . . . Hope I'm in the first sitting.

Hester and Edie were fortunate to have the same afternoon off and the two friends decided to go down the market.

'At least I won't come across my sister turning cartwheels in the rain,' Hester said, as they hurried along the wet street under a shared umbrella. Poor Polly, she's not cut out to be in the laundry, Hester thought. My bright and lively sister needs the spotlight!

The stalls were shielded by their canopies, but the Turneros and their ice-cream had obviously decided to stay at home. However, there was still a fair number of shoppers and the girls were poked in the back with a couple of umbrellas by women not looking where they were going.

They were hailed by a familiar voice: 'Fancy some cockles? ready to eat now.' Bobby feigned surprise, when they lowered the umbrella. 'Why, it's my favourite nurse! Want to see my whitlow, Hester?'

'I hope you've got it covered up, touching the fish,' she said primly, then she smiled. 'Nice to see you Bobby. It's been a year or two, eh? I'll have a plate of cockles please, how about you, Edie?'

'Well. . . .' Edie was embarrassed by Bobby's bold stare.

'Lin,' Bobby said to a small figure in the background. 'Serve my friends, will yer. No charge.' The young Chinese girl came shyly forward. 'Allow me to introduce my wife.' Bobby, although short himself, was taller than this solemn faced girl in traditional dress, protected by an apron the strings of which went twice round her slender waist, below which Hester's trained eye observed a barely perceptible swelling. 'This is Lin – don't worry, she can under-stand what you say, being born here. But she ain't one for chat, she leaves that to me.'

'When – did you get married?' Hester asked faintly. Big Peg hadn't passed on this snippet of gossip, as she usually would.

'Three weeks ago – guess what,' Bobby added proudly, 'We didn't waste no time, we're having a baby!'

Hester didn't say, 'I can see that,' but, 'Oh, that's good news!'

Lin handed them two of the small dishes and spoons.

'Anything else you fancy? A nice dressed crab to take home? Some plump herrings?'

'A crab would be nice, Bobby – a treat for the family. Want me to look at your finger, while you're not busy?' The nurses always carried a few items of first aid, like a roll of bandage – Bobby's digit was protected by a leather finger-stall, but Hester wondered what it concealed.

'Want me ter pay?' he joked, but, grimacing from the pain, he revealed a swollen finger tip. 'It burst this morning – what a relief. Lin made me a poultice with pipe clay. It was a splinter what caused it.'

'It usually is. . . . Here, take this new bandage, Lin, but bathe the finger and keep it covered until it has healed.'

'Thank you, Miss,' the girl said. 'I know what to do. Bobby's grandma tells me.' She appeared resigned rather than resentful.

'My name is Hester, and my friend is Edie – Bobby didn't introduce us properly! When is your baby due?'

'Sooner than Bobby thinks,' the girl smiled. 'Good to meet you.'

'The cockles were delicious. Thank you,' Hester said, as they were about to move on, after paying for the crab.

'Thank you,' Edie echoed.

When they were out of earshot Hester mused: 'Bobby, who'd have pictured him with a wife – and a baby on the way?'

'Seems to be what happens to most of us, Hester – but not me, I think. What about you? Alf still has hopes.' Edie sounded wistful.

Hester squeezed her arm. 'Perhaps he'll find the right girl one day, but I'm afraid it won't be me.'

It had stopped raining, and a watery sun was struggling through the clouds. Hester shook the umbrella and fastened the strap. 'I spotted some gooseberries on the coster's barrow – come on!'

After the girls parted company, each to her own home, Hester joined Fred for the afternoon. He was obviously pleased to have some company, apart from Puglet. Granny's sewing machine was being turned at a rate of knots, and the living room was awash with her paraphernalia. She paused to greet Hester: 'I forgot it was your afternoon off. You can get the evening meal under way, can't you?'

'I bought a crab – '

'We'll have that for our tea – it won't stretch to six – didn't you think o' that?'

'Can't say I did,' Hester returned, but she knew it wasn't worth arguing with Granny Garter – once a tartar, always a tartar.

'Come on,' Fred said in her ear, 'Let's go in the kitchen. I can get down them steps now on me crutches, though I ain't tried to get upstairs. I've taken over the cooking lately, to save Peg and Polly from setting to, after a hard day's work.'

'But Pa, you never cooked so much as a sausage before—'

'I got all day, as yer Granny tells me, and nothin' else to do.'

'*Stew*,' Granny said to their retreating backs. 'Any fool can make stew. Even Fred.'

Nine

1895

The country had somehow survived the worst winter for many years. The Thames was frozen over, the cold was relentless, every day was a struggle for the workers, which included those involved with the building of the Blackwall Tunnel. Then the floods came, with lives lost, businesses ruined. Boats rowed down the water filled streets to deliver necessities to the stranded. The hospital was busier than ever. Eventually, though, it was spring and spirits were revived.

Polly was having a bad day in the laundry. 'I don't know how Hester stood it for four years,' she grumbled to Big Peg when she staggered over with a load of wet washing for her stepmother to mangle.

Peg gave her a sympathetic look. 'You could leave, like she did.'

'I wouldn't want to be a nurse – she works even longer hours.'

'Look, Poll, she's doing what makes her happy, so should you.'

'What about you, Peg, stuck here all these years?'

'Ah, well I'm content at home, that makes a diff'rence.'

Polly flushed. 'It's not that I ain't – we all get on well. . . .'

'Course we do. But *you* need somethin' more, dearie.'

Her Fairy Godmother, or rather Granny Garter, was about to do something to help her beloved Polly. She decided to make a surprise visit to an old friend, now living in Brixton.

Vicky Lee as she was before she married the late Claude

Garter, was involved with the making of Louisa Penn's wedding dress when she married a member of the minor aristocracy. Lula, as she preferred to be called, was herself of humbler stock, but with an ambitious mother who had encouraged her talented daughter in her pursuit of a stage career: Alexander DuPont was a 'stage door Johnnie' with an appreciative eye for a pretty girl. This marriage was another step in the right direction. The two girls were the same age and instantly struck up a rapport.

Over the years since, Vicky read about Lula's marriage break-up in the Society columns, then her friend's debut on the stage, where she appeared in many varied productions, with accolades for her spirited dancing and singing. When Lula married again and moved to Madrid, she wrote to commiserate with Vicky when she was widowed. This was the last time the two corresponded, but recently Vicky had spotted an interesting advertisement in the *Stage* magazine, which she had purchased on a whim to give to Polly.

ELOCUTION, SINGING AND DANCING
LESSONS BY ARRANGEMENT WITH
MRS LULA DuPONT, (nee PENN) FORMER
DOYENNE OF THE LONDON STAGE

There followed an address in Brixton with a telephone number. Vicky had once or twice answered the telephone in the bookie's office in her old home, all those years ago, but had never made a call to anyone herself. She wasn't about to attempt to do so now.

'I'm going out and I shall probably be gone all day,' she informed an astonished Fred, one morning. 'You can prepare supper for the family.' She rustled out of the door in magenta taffeta, leaving behind her an aroma of face-powder and scent, with a hint of mothballs.

She descended from the omnibus having quite enjoyed the ride on the seats at the top of the vehicle, which were open to the elements. In inclement weather mackintosh lap covers were provided, but today the sun was bright, the gentle welcome breeze did not disturb her large hat or ruffle her elaborate false fringe of hair. The team of horses trotted gamely along the busy roads and she looked down on coal carts, laden donkey carts, bicycles and foolhardy folk risking life and limb in dashing from one side to the other. The baker's box handcart had a narrow miss with a loudly hooting horseless carriage which demanded right of way. No doubt the bread and the buns were all in a jumble inside the box container, but at least the boy hauling the cart had escaped injury, Vicky thought. Now that drainage was improving, a handkerchief held to her nose was sufficient: her smelling salts remained in her bag.

Brixton had an air of rather faded gentility. Off the busy main road with all the shops, were the residential streets with row upon row of tall, substantial terraced houses. These had been built as solid, middle-class homes for prosperous businessmen and their families, with domestic staff accommodation in the attics. The bathrooms were vast, chilly places with baths encased in mahogany boxes, but hot water gushed from the taps, due to the sterling efforts of the boiler man, and thanks to the regular delivery of coal down the chute to the cellar, when the ornate iron cover was lifted in the front garden.

In the past few years however, many of these houses had been converted into flats and rented out to folk from various walks of life, including some foreigners. The community was constantly changing. Enterprising widows, wanting to stay on in their homes, but worried about the upkeep, placed discreet notices in their front windows, advertising board and lodging at a few shillings a week.

Vicky puffed somewhat as she walked the length of the street in which Lula lived. She'd put on too much weight, she realised ruefully, during her idle years. Ah! She'd come to the right house at last. There was an imposing sign near the gate: ACADEMY FOR THE ARTS. PROPRIETOR MRS L. DuPONT.

She dabbed her brow with her handkerchief, stood for a

moment by the high brick wall, then opened the clanging iron gate. She walked to the front door and pulled the bell peering through a coloured glass panel into the hall beyond. Footsteps, then the door swung open.

'Yes?' A heavily built man, dark in complexion with silver hair, inquired politely. He was unrolling his sleeves after buttoning his waistcoat over a portly stomach.

He's not English, Vicky realized.

'Please inform Mrs DuPont that her friend, Mrs Garter is here,' she said primly. She experienced the discomfort of a trickle of sweat under her arms. Thank goodness, she thought, I sewed in those dress preservers last night. . . . She felt nervous – what if her old friend was not overjoyed to see her? After all, Lula hadn't contacted her since her return to London. Lula could have been here some time, she realized.

'Step inside Madame,' the manservant indicated a chair by a small table in the hall. 'Mrs DuPont is taking a class, but I will advise her of your presence. Excuse me, please.'

'And you are?' she called sharply after him. He turned, before entering a door to the right. He left it ajar.

'You may call me Carlos, Madame.'

Someone inside the room was playing a piano loudly. Vicky heard the thumping of feet on an uncarpeted floor. A shrill voice: 'That's enough for this morning. Leave the barre. You all have two left feet. Get changed and join my niece in her room for your elocution lesson.'

Four flushed girls wearing Grecian tunics and scuffed pink ballet shoes came out of the room. One of them managed a smile as they filed past the seated visitor, before they ascended the staircase and vanished out of sight.

Vicky heard Carlos making his announcement. 'You have a visitor, Madame, Mrs Garter. Shall I show her in?'

'Mrs Garter. . . . Oh, yes, do so, Carlos. Will you bring a tray of coffee to us, please? A cup for Miss Blom, too.'

'Certainly, Madame.' Carlos backed out of the room.

Vicky thought: as if she is royalty! Lula hasn't changed!

But of course she had, they were both middle-aged women now. However, Lula was stick-thin, whereas Vicky had recalled her with a lovely, supple body as one who'd danced since early childhood. Her black hair was drawn back from her high forehead and the lines on her face carefully disguised by makeup. She was smoking a cigarette in a jade holder. She looked searchingly at Vicky, who immediately felt overdressed, for Lula was wearing a practice tunic like her pupils, over footless tights and satin pumps.

Vicky was lost for words for once. What could she say to this old friend? It was so long since she had last seen her. She was conscious of her own matronly figure – the bookie had declared his approval of her growing girth by enthusiastic squeezing of her flesh. He would have described Lula now as 'thin as a starched fart on a hat pin,' in a disparaging tone. Vicky had often been pained by his vulgarity.

'Well, well,' Lulu broke the silence. 'This is a pleasant surprise. Let me introduce Miss Blom, my pianist. Like me, she used to perform on the professional stage. In her case, in Germany. Come and sit by the window and tell me how things are with you, Vicky.'

Miss Blom, another willowy woman, gathered up her music, piled it on top of the piano then closed the lid. She merely nodded in response to her employer's introduction.

Carlos appeared with the coffee, which he placed on a small table in the recess of the bay window. 'Cook hopes you enjoy the little cakes, still warm from the oven.' He poured coffee into three small cups, offered cream from a jug, and indicated silver tongs for the lumps of brown sugar. Then he left the room once more.

Cook! Vicky thought. Lula must be doing well, to employ servants.

Lula said: 'Carlos and his wife run my household very smoothly between them. I can't afford parlour maids or even skivvies. Our elocution teacher is my niece. She works for me in return for her board. I rescued her from the life she was reduced to, after her parents died. My second marriage was a mistake. He married me for my money, not the other way around. Another divorce, I'm afraid to say. I had to start all over again. I took my former name.'

Vicky glanced at Miss Blom: she had hoped for a private consultation, as she thought of it, with her friend. This was not possible with someone listening in, even if they were not contributing to the conversation.

'I can guess what you are thinking,' Lula said, not bothering to whisper. 'Emmy is stone deaf, due to suffering meningitis in her twenties, which is why she had to give up her stage appearances. When she performs, she hears the music in her head, although sometimes she plays very loudly. This is no problem for me, or the students. She can read my lips, my instructions, even when she has her back to me at the piano, for as you will see there are mirrors on all the walls. Emmy is my companion, we set up this business together.

'Now, tell me what has been happening in your life since we were last in contact? I remember you went to live with your daughter Bess, of course, after Claude passed away.'

'Bess died a few years ago. . . . I am still with her family, the Stainsbys. I am Granny Garter to them all. The children are now grownup and working, Fred remarried – a nice woman, Peg, we get on well – and I have taken up my dressmaking again.'

'I am glad to hear that, but I am sorry to learn of your loss. *Granny Garter*! Doesn't that make you feel *old*?'

'I like it.' Vicky surprised herself when she said that. 'My younger granddaughter Polly, has decided on Garter as her stage name—'

'Polly Garter – I don't think I have heard of her. . . .'

'Oh you will,' Vickie said in a rush, 'If you agree to take her on as a pupil!'

'How old is she?'

'She's seventeen, and a born performer: she already has a following as a street singer and musician – she can dance, she can turn the most amazing cartwheels – please say you will see her, Lula!'

Lula's raised eyebrows at the mention of street singing made Vicky think she should perhaps not have mentioned that. However, Lula put out an impulsive hand to pat her friend's arm. 'She sounds rather like you, Vicky, at that age. She is in employment, I presume? Bring her here on her next afternoon off. If I approve of her, think she has talent, we might have a special arrangement regarding fees. I have pupils who come daily; some part-time for particular courses, like elocution; but up to four full-time students can be accommodated on the premises. I assure you that Emmy and I take good care of them, though they might tell you I am too strict at times. I can't put up with airs and graces either.

'I don't wish to hurry you, but we must drain our coffee cups, and you should go home and tell Miss Polly Garter that I look forward to meeting her soon. Emmy and I must supervise a young singer, who is due to arrive shortly.'

Polly sat on the edge of the straight-backed gilt chair, while Lula bent over her, turning her face this way and that, scrutinising every detail.

'You have a good complexion, Polly, a tendency to blushing, but I can show you how to deal with that. Your eyelashes and brows need to be darkened, to show off your beautiful blue eyes. These ringlets – it must have taken you ages to put your hair in rags last night! – are far too ingénue. You must arrange your hair off your face in a classical dancer's knot.'

'I don't propose to be a classical dancer,' Polly ventured.

'You must let me be the judge of that, my dear. Is it the music hall or the legitimate stage you intend to grace with your dancing?'

'I – I'm not sure,' Polly floundered, receiving a sly pinch from Granny Garter on her other side. 'I just want to, well, dance and sing.'

'You will need to improve your diction if you are to be a musical *actress*,' Lula stated. She released her grip on Polly's chin.

'You think I could act as well?' Polly could hardly believe her ears.

'You have the personality. You need training. I am prepared to take you on. You would be able to join other like-minded girls in their dormitory upstairs. Carlos will take you now to where they are play-reading with my niece Mira, who is in charge of drama. I wish to discuss business with your grandmother.' She rang a hand bell and Carlos appeared, obviously listening for such a summons.

'Now, Vicky, I imagine you are anxiously waiting for me to reveal my terms,' Lula said, with a smile. 'I have a proposition to put to you, which I hope very much that you will accept.'

Big Peg whirled Polly round in her embrace – she didn't lift her up as she had Hester when she announced that she was to become a nurse, because Polly was taller than her sister and not as slight in build.

'Miss Polly Garter, we'll see your name in lights!'

'Not for a while, I reckon,' said realistic Harry. He was pleased for his twin, but maybe he was a trifle disgruntled because he would now be the main support of the family, along with Peg. There must be more to life, he thought, than being a clerk in the docks office, dealing with endless bills of lading, and officials from the Port of London Authority seemingly intent on disapproving of young employees. . . . He would rather have gone to sea, but he couldn't disappoint Fred in that respect. It had upset him when Fred, urging Harry to take on the job, added: 'Look to the future, my lad. You'd be able to take on the house, when I'm gone.' Seeing his alarmed expression, Fred had reassured his son: 'But I ain't goin' yet – no fear!'

'How are we are going to pay for all this?' Fred worried now.

'Well, here's more good news! My friend Mrs DuPont has asked me to be her wardrobe mistress! I shall be busy sewing all the dancing clothes and mending and altering 'em too. I'll get to design costumes and I'll be able to continue working from home – mind, what with my regular clients as well, I won't have time to do anything in the house.' She added, before anyone dared to comment on that last statement, 'Any payments due to me from

Mrs du Pont will be kept for Polly's expenses in Brixton. Now! You will see I am making a sacrifice for her sake, and not thinking of myself, eh?'

Fred cleared his throat. 'Well, Polly, what d'you say to your granny?'

'*I love you*, Granny Garter!' Polly declared. She turned a neat cartwheel in the confined space of the living room then she flung up her arms and cried: 'Three cheers for Granny!'

Ten

A Sunday morning in September. After a hazy start, the sun appeared from behind drifting small clouds and it promised to be warm. Alf had the whole day off from work and was on his way to meet a young lady for a stroll along the riverside and a picnic lunch. The covered basket he carried was full of carefully selected treats: cold sausages, chicken drumsticks, buttered rolls, pieces of cheese, two giant Chelsea buns and a bottle of beer. This particular young lady was not averse to a drink in moderation, he was glad to know. His friends next door were eager to encourage this sudden interest in someone other than Hester. Granny Garter had hemmed two pretty napkins – 'You must use these, even for a meal outdoors – you can't wipe greasy fingers on your best clothes.' Big Peg contributed the buns, and Fred slipped him the beer bottle when she wasn't looking. 'Take a corkscrew, lad,' he said, 'and don't forget the cups.'

There were plenty of folk about, some making their way to church or chapel, others to the Sunday market. This was also the destination of the Salvation Army, who, like the Pied Piper attracted their followers with rousing music as they marched. They hoped the crowd would join them for their open-air service shortly.

The pretty girls in their demure bonnets, rattled their tambourines, the bugles blared, and all joined in the hymn, *Bless His Name*, to the familiar music hall tune of *Champagne Charlie*. As their founder William Booth said: 'Why should the Devil have all the best tunes?'

Alf was entertained as he waited on the corner for his friend.

He joined in the singing, improvising the words, and was so enjoying himself, he didn't immediately spot the girl in the moss-green skirt with matching shoulder cape over a ruffled white blouse, making her way through the crowd towards him.

Edie had grown in confidence since she began her nursing career: she didn't seem so tall and awkward now that she had filled out due to all the nourishing food dished out at the hospital. She'd been used to going without at home quite often while feeding the family when her mother was confined once a year. The nurses were even offered a small glass of beer with their supper, because it was considered safer than water, supplies of which were still not as pure as they should be. It was emphasized that it was vital to boil water and allow it to cool or make hot drinks, the nurses were told.

Hester had encouraged Edie to make the most of her fine, pale hair. She showed her friend how to wash her locks with melted soft green soap, then to rinse thoroughly with warm water. Regular baths were one of the perks of being a nurse. 'Press waves in your hair while it is damp with your fingers,' she advised. 'That's something Granny Garter does. Though she also used to say if you stroked your nose between your finger and thumb every night before you went to sleep, you would have a lovely, straight nose when you were grown up. It worked for Polly, but not for me, I'm afraid.'

So now Edie, in a stylish outfit she would never have been able to afford three years ago, walked up to Alf and startled him with: 'Here I am, at last! The band held me up. May I take your arm?'

'Oh, please do,' he said gallantly. The weather still being summery, he wore a straw boater, like all the other young men walking out with their girls. He thought, I'm glad I found the nerve to push that note under her door, inviting her out. . . . It was now or never, with future plans in mind.

'I'm wearing sensible shoes, as you suggested,' Edie lifted a foot to display her brown elastic-sided boot and neat ankle. She had on white stockings today. They made a nice change from black, she thought.

'Ready for a long walk, then?' They would take the main path behind the many large buildings overlooking the river, and then Alf planned to follow one of the winding footpaths worn by the feet of men over the centuries: short cuts from riverside cottages, or maybe, as he now remarked aloud: 'Trod by the Vikings, so they say.'

'Oh, d'you love history, too?' Edie exclaimed. There had been only two books in her crowded home, the Bible and a copy of *The British Empire*, a treasured school prize.

'Yes – and we'll be part of all that one day, I reckon.' *I've just said something to her*, he realized, *that I never have before. I've always been too bashful – that's why I didn't make friends at school – apart from Hester.*

Later, they paused by an open stretch of the river, to watch a steamer go by. There were busy barges, under sail, with men with seamed, tanned faces, puffing on clay pipes and yelling at friends on other boats. Gulls swooped and quarrelled in the muddy shallows by the banks. Behind them was a tangle of scrubland and a few ancient trees, beginning to shcd the first leaves of autumn. A bony cow surveyed them over a rickety fence and a pair of geese flapped and spread their wings as they raucously defended their territory.

'Along this track, watch out for nettles,' Alf advised Edie, as he led the way to a small clearing, which had recently been used for wood chopping, judging by the debris left behind. He put down the basket, then spread his jacket on the dry grass. 'Sit down – and we'll have our grub.' He waited for Edie to smooth out her skirts; she leaned back against a tree stump. Another stump made an improvised table to set out plates and cups of by now, rather warm beer.

Alf handed Edie one of the neatly folded napkins. 'Tuck that in your collar,' he said awkwardly.

'I think I'll take off my cape, it's warmer than I thought it would be – you look more easy in your shirt sleeves,' Edie told him.

'Mind if I take off my titfer too?'

''Course not. I didn't notice before, you know, how red your hair is,' Edie instantly realized she had said the wrong thing.

'I wish it weren't,' he said vehemently.

'Oh, why? I'd give anything to have that colour, it makes you look,' she had a sudden inspiration, 'like a *Viking*, Alf!'

'No wonder Hester likes you so much.' he said, smiling.

Edie didn't comment on the coating of fat on the cold sausages, which had shrunk considerably during cooking, or the rather tough texture of the drumsticks. The bread rolls were a trifle stale, because they'd been purchased yesterday, but the butter made them palatable. Edie made good use of her napkin, as they were using their fingers, there being no knives and forks. She enjoyed the cheese – strong cheddar – more tasty than the mild variety at the hospital.

'More beer?' Alf inquired. 'We might as well finish the bottle.'

Edie nodded. 'Not too much – I'm used to one glass at a time.' I need something, she thought, to wash down that enormous bun! Also, she didn't want the embarrassment of having to bob behind a tree. . . . She gave a sudden squeal. 'Oh, something bit my ankle!'

'What was it?' he asked, concerned. He should have thought of stinging insects – you always got those near the water. 'Take your boot off, roll your stocking down – I won't look, I promise.'

'Oh, don't be so silly,' she cried. 'Pass me my bag – I came prepared, as we nurses always do. I made up a solution of alum and water in a little bottle. I'll have to use the napkin to dab it on.'

He watched openly, as she pulled up her skirt, deftly rolled off her stocking, then examined the red swelling on her foot. She dabbed it with the fluid, then re-corked the bottle. 'Ouch! That stung too, but it should work, I hope.' Edie quickly replaced her stocking and looked around for her boot, which she'd flung aside.

Alf retrieved it, knelt before her, and eased the boot back on. He resisted a sudden urge to span her ankle with his hand. He rose quickly and moved back. 'I think we ought to go back,' he said, glad the basket would be lighter. 'If you feel like walking, of course.'

'Don't fuss, it wasn't a wasp. An ant, I reckon, look, there's a lot of 'em running about! Thank you for a good meal, I enjoyed it.'

He slung his jacket round his shoulders and replaced the straw hat. He assisted Edie to her feet and carefully brushed the twigs and leaves from her skirt, while she put on her cape.

They walked hand in hand, talking as they went.

'I haven't told anyone else yet,' he said suddenly, 'but I'm leaving my job at the hospital at the end of the month. I've been there since I was fourteen, and I'm twenty-one now – I'll soon be twenty-two.'

'I'm older than you, then – I'm twenty-three. I started later at nursing than Hester. Where are you going, Alf – not leaving Poplar, I hope?'

'I'm joining the river ambulance service which ferries patients to the hospital ships moored at Long Reach. I'll be helping the sick and injured like I do now, but I'll have some more to learn. You know about them ships, I suppose?'

'Course I do. The seamen's hospital ships at Deptford creek which took smallpox patients during the big epidemics twenty years or so ago, were moved out there weren't they?'

'Yes. There's the *Dreadnought* too, the first-aid post for workers injured in the new Tunnel. The Long Reach ships are used mainly for convalescent patients now. I always wanted to go to sea, but the river boats will do – they carry food and other supplies as well as patients.'

'You'll meet up with lots of nurses there,' she stated.

He gave her hand a squeeze, laughed. 'Why I think you're jealous!'

' 'Course I ain't,' she retorted, reverting to her old way of talking.

'The rules are just as strict on the ships as in the hospital, they say. *Keep your hands off the nurses!*'

'That's not very nice – not like you, Alf.'

He stopped, and so did she. They looked at each other for a long moment. 'Any other lad would've kissed you by now, Edie.'

'Well, why don't you?'

'I didn't think you were – like that, either,' he faltered.

'Alf Hodge, just because I've never walked out with a young man before, don't mean to say I ain't thought about what might happen,' she said daringly. 'Or do you still have hopes of Hester?'

He shook his head slowly. 'No. But I don't want to rush you, Edie.'

'Didn't you hear me earlier? I'm twenty-three – and I want you to know, well, I'm agreeable, Alf.'

He glanced quickly around: just the boats on the water; no one else on the footpath. He set down the basket, and edged nearer to Edie. They were much of a height, so really it was easy to first kiss her on the cheek and follow that up with a lingering kiss on the lips.

Edie gave a happy little sigh. 'That wasn't so hard was it?'

They both dissolved into helpless giggles as a gust of wind caught Alf's boater and deposited it on the water, where it floated rapidly out of reach.

'Come on, I don't want to lose my hat, as well as my head!'

'Oh, look,' Edie exclaimed as they walked along, this time with his arm around her waist, 'There's someone with a boathook leaning out of that barge – he's hooked your hat – now he's waving at us.'

'Oi!' the boatman hollered. 'Is this your hat, Ginger?'

They paused, while Alf cupped his hands round his mouth, and called out: 'Thanks – but keep it – I don't need it.'

'Now the world can see you've got fiery hair,' Edie smiled.

'I don't care any more about that!'

'Oh, why not?'

' 'Cause *you* like it!' he said, hugging her trim waist tightly.

Eleven

November 1895

'You have done extremely well in the children's ward over this past year,' Matron said, having summoned Hester to her office. 'However, I feel it is time for you to move on. You will report to the men's accident ward tomorrow, they are understaffed at present. The influenza epidemic is responsible for that.'

Matron had spoken, and like the good nurse she was, Hester did not dream of questioning her decision. Later, she would discover that she and Edie would be reunited on this ward, which pleased them both. Edie had been on the women's ward and was glad of the change.

'I shall miss all the little ones, of course,' Hester said, as they ate their supper that evening. She knew that she had become too attached to some of her small patients, and she often shed a few tears in private, when they were parted, especially if the patient had not survived, but she told herself sternly she must be happy to see them go, when the outcome was good, and be glad at the part she had played in that.

'I shan't miss some of my lot on the women's ward.' Edie was always honest; Hester, and now Alf, admired that trait in her. 'Mothers of large families don't make good patients, they grumble because they can't wait to get home – they don't appreciate the chance to have a rest from all their responsibilities.' She was thinking of her own worn-out little mother when she said that.

Sometimes she felt she had deserted the family by leaving them to become a nurse, but her mother had urged her to do so. 'You deserve a better life, dearie, than what I got.' Her father had as usual been too drunk to care. She gathered that she and Alf had that in common, but they were both rising above their backgrounds, she thought.

'Heard from Alf lately?' Hester asked. Edie was reticent regarding this burgeoning relationship. Hester suspected this was because Edie thought she might wish she hadn't told him that she could never marry him.

Edie flushed. 'Yes,' was all she said.

'You really like him, don't you?' Hester persisted. She was fond of them both, but hoped that Alf would concentrate on Edie in future.

''Course I do. But he's got to keep his mind on his new job at present. Like us, eh, we've got to do the same, from tomorrer—*tomorrow*,' Edie corrected herself.

'We have a new patient,' Sister informed them as she gave them details of their duties for the day. 'An engineer from the tunnel. The accident, we don't have full details of that yet, happened in the capsule inside the tunnel, which was designed to protect the workers and has definitely kept the accident level low. The patient was taken first to the *Dreadnought*, then transferred here for further treatment. The *Dreadnought* doctor diagnosed a compound fracture of his right femur.

'Nurse Stainsby, I require you to take his temperature, then you should encourage him to complete this admission form. He was sedated when he arrived last evening, but should be coherent this morning.

'The patient is in bed six. Pull the curtains round the bed. When the form has been dealt with, you should make the patient comfortable with a clean temporary dressing. Remember that it is imperative that swabs are discarded after a single use. Have all the equipment ready before you begin this task.'

Sister turned to Edie. 'You should assist the night staff with the washing of patients. I'm sure I don't need to explain the procedure in this case. That's all for now.'

An elderly night nurse had already provided and removed immediately after use the patient's urine bottle. This was a strict rule: no chamber pots under beds because of the risk of infection. She had also freshened the patient's face and hands with a flannel and warm water.

'Good morning,' Hester greeted the patient with a smile. She popped the thermometer under his tongue, rested a finger on the pulse in his wrist and studied the watch pinned to her front. 'Your temperature is still a little high, but better than when you were admitted. Now, before I change your dressing, I need to ask you a few questions, if I may.'

'I am capable of filling in the form myself,' the patient said.

Hester was struck immediately by his deep, well-modulated voice: he was obviously an educated man, she thought. Although he was grey-haired, she judged him to be around forty years of age. His face was drawn and pale, but he managed a smile, revealing unexpectedly good, white teeth. These, with very blue eyes, which he blinked now and then as a result of the pain in his leg, meant he was a good-looking man.

'I am sure you are, but it is usual for the nurse to fill in the details, especially when her patient is unable to sit up. You will be expected to sign the paper though, of course. Is that all right?'

He nodded. Hester pulled the curtains round the bed, sat in the chair beside him, pencil poised, for the details could be inked over later: 'Your name? And your nationality, please.'

'Nicholas Van der Linde. My father was a Dutch sea captain, but my mother was English. I have dual nationality, however, I don't suppose you need the added information?'

Hester said before she thought about it: 'No. But it makes my task more interesting! Your date of birth?'

'November 17th 1853. I shall be forty-two years old next week.'

'Place of birth?'

'Ah . . . at sea, on a dark and stormy night. . . .' Again, that heart-warming smile.

'I'm not sure I can put that—'

'Well, my mother could never recall which ocean it was, because she accompanied my father on many of his voyages. He may have made a note of the event in his log book, but he died at sea when I was only a small boy, so. . . .' She guessed he was teasing her now.

'Well, *you* must explain that one to Sister, I think. Oh, your address, I missed that earlier.'

'We lodge in a house called *Cottonia*, what else? in Cotton Street, Poplar. I've stayed there, on and off, because I was so often at sea, for more than twenty years. We are looked after by Mrs Dingwall, a widow.'

'You are an engineer?'

'I was a mariner, but now I use my skills on dry land. Yes, I am a marine engineer.'

'Your next of kin? Wife's name?' She'd noted the 'we' earlier,

He explained: 'I share my rooms at present with a young friend. I have no wife. My mother died last year. She founded a school for girls in Surbiton, with my two unmarried sisters, they are older than me, who still run the school. I disappointed my mother when I decided to go to sea, like my father. My sister Lucy Van der Linde is my next of kin. I apologize, I'm talking too much, aren't I?' His voice trailed off; his hands clenched on the bedclothes.

'Don't apologize, it's a natural reaction. I can see you are in some discomfort – we need details of your accident, but we can complete the form later. Do you need some relief from the pain, Mr Van der Linde?'

'I should be grateful, Nurse.'

'Put your arms around my neck,' she said a little later. 'Do not try to move by yourself, I need to adjust your position. I know the mackintosh and the draw sheet are not the most comfortable, particularly when you have a high temperature, but they are necessary, because of the danger of bleeding from the wound or seeping from the dressing. I am now going to give you an injection – you will feel a sharp scratch, hopefully just that.'

When this was done, Hester eased him on to his back, removed the supporting pillow. 'I shall dress your leg when you are feeling more relaxed. It is important for you to lie as flat as possible. I will return in ten minutes. Meanwhile, relax and doze, if you wish.'

Hester passed Edie on her way to collect the items needed for her next task. Edie was assisting the night staff with giving out medicines, renewing compresses, sponging of feverish patients and taking temperatures. The night nurses were not finished yet, but would hope to go off duty before 9.30 a.m., when they could take a bath themselves before their dinner and then retiring to bed. The day staff would then have to sweep the wards and wash all surfaces.

'Your lucky day Hester,' Edie whispered ruefully, as she paused for a brief moment or two.

'What d'you mean?'

'Looking after the hero in bed six.'

'I don't understand. . . .'

'A truck with some heavy equipment became out of control, in the tunnel capsule, apparently. Your patient saved the life of another chap by shoving him out of the way; he was knocked down himself. Alf was with the team who delivered him here from the *Dreadnought* – he told the porter here.'

The Sister taking over for the day shift, appeared in the doorway, looking in their direction. 'Must go,' Hester told her friend.

Mr Van der Linde was conscious, if in a dreamy state. 'They cut my clothes off me in *The Dreadnought*,' he murmured. 'This hospital nightshirt is rather inadequate, I feel . . . I am unable to adjust it.'

This was not surprising as the injured leg was suspended in a cradle above the bed. Hester did her best to ensure as much decency as possible.

'I'm afraid cutting is the best way to remove clothing in the case of a fractured femur. Don't worry, I'm sure your garments can be mended: the nurses are taught to cut along the seams. Your boots are another matter. I'll pull the curtains around you again.'

Be gentle, but firm, Hester silently recited to herself. The patient must be reassured at all times. Sister had already told her quietly that the leg would be in traction for the next three months, and that as this was a compound fracture, the open wound would have to be scrupulously cleaned to prevent bone infection, and possible amputation. The receptacle for soiled dressings was to hand. She dipped the first swab into the solution of dilute carbolic acid, aware that the patient had closed his eyes. 'I hope this will not be too much of an ordeal,' she said quietly.

The procedure was over. Mr Van der Linde was made comfortable, lying on his back as before. He managed just three words: 'Thank you, nurse.'

She wheeled the trolley of equipment away, towards the swing doors. The night staff had gone; Edie, with the other day nurses, was still busy with the cleaning of the ward. Sister was at her desk. She looked up. 'Well done, Nurse Stainsby. Mr Van der Linde will benefit I am sure from your special attention while he is a patient on this ward. By the time you have dealt with the trolley, the general cleaning will be complete, so you may go straight to your main breakfast.'

'Thank you, Sister.' Hester glowed from the praise. Best of all, she had earned the right to be responsible for a special patient.

Mr Van der Linde had a visitor the next day, who waited patiently for his friend to return from theatre, where the surgeon was deciding on further treatment for his injury. Hester, changing the bed while the patient was away, spoke to the fair-haired young man, offering him a chair.

'He won't lose his leg, will he?' was the anxious question.

'The surgeon is very skilled, we have every hope that Mr Van der Linde will make a good recovery, but it will be some time before he is fit enough to return to his work.' Hester smoothed the sheets in place, then topped the covers with the scarlet day blanket.

'He saved my life, you know,' the young man said. 'I had to come to see how he was. Van, that's what the men call him, is one of the engineers in charge of the tunnel construction – he is my boss, but he is also a good friend of my father – they were at boarding school together. Van kindly arranged for me to stay with him when I arrived here, not knowing the area or anyone else.'

'My father lost his leg in an accident in the docks: the hospital was so good to him—' Why was she confiding in a stranger, she wondered? 'That's what made me want to be a nurse, I think.'

'I am Arthur Winwood by the way. Has Van mentioned me?'

'Not by name. He is still mostly sedated for the pain.'

'May I know who you are?'

'I am Nurse Stainsby.'

'That sounds too starchy, like your apron. Your first name?'

She knew it was against the rules, but the young man was staring at her with obvious admiration and she was flattered. 'Hester,' she said.

There was the sound of a trolley being wheeled the length of the ward. Arthur Winwood rose and stood expectantly, as Hester and the porter dealt with the transferring of the patient from trolley to his bed, and the adjustment of the pulley. She pulled the curtains with a swish! 'Excuse me, Mr Winwood, while I settle the patient: he is not round from the anaesthetic yet. Please sit down and I will call you when Mr Van der Linde is able to talk to you.'

As she measured the beat of his pulse, the patient stirred, but did not open his eyes. His fingers suddenly curled round her hand, gripping it firmly. Hester was instantly reminded of how little Samuel in the children's ward, had unexpectedly clasped her hand in just such a way. The baby was so weak, yet she had marvelled at the strength with which he clung to her.

She gently disengaged herself, aware that she was trembling. How foolish I am, she thought. Mr Van der Linde isn't conscious of his actions – he's not a young man to stir me like this. I don't understand. . . . Perhaps it's just as well, her sensible inner voice advised her.

Twelve

Big Peg had just pushed a heavy blanket through the rollers of
her mangle, when she suddenly felt giddy. She opened her mouth
to call out, but no sound emerged. The floor, cold and slippery
with spilled water, seemed to rise up to smack her on one side of
her head as she fell. She slumped, unconscious on the unforgiving
flagstones, with blood trickling down her face.

The laundry workers were suddenly galvanized into action.
Big Peg was too heavy in her inert state to be lifted by one, or
even two of the women. The supervisor called for help; it took
two porters to lift her on to a trolley and wheel her away to
Outpatients. The nurses there took one look and summoned the
nearest doctor.

Big Peg's first words when she regained consciousness were the
classic ones: 'Where am I?' Her eyes focussed on a familiar face.
Hester, in her uniform, sat beside her, holding her hand.

'In the women's ward,' Hester told her. There were unshed
tears in her eyes, but she managed a tremulous smile. The thought
of losing Big Peg as she had her mother, was just too awful to
contemplate.

'What – happened?'

'You fainted – I suppose – in the laundry. I was at breakfast,
but the porter fetched me, so you wouldn't be alarmed when you
woke up.'

'My . . . head hurts.' Big Peg put up a wavering hand and touched the pad covering the wound to her head.

'I'm not surprised, Peg. You banged it on the floor. Actually, it's only a minor injury, but it bled a lot.' This was not the moment to tell Peg that the nurse had to cut a clump of hair before applying the dressing. The swatch of chestnut hair would have to be incinerated.

'And my other arm?' Peg looked, bemused at the sling.

'Badly bruised, but not broken, thank goodness.'

'Does Fred know? He mustn't come out in the cold. Anyway, he can't manage without someone with him—'

'We haven't told him yet. It may be that you can be taken home later today, to rest up at home. Doctor will be along to see you shortly.'

Peg was in a small private cubicle off the main ward. A knock on the door, then it was pushed open, and the doctor appeared. 'Mrs Stainsby? I am here to check that you are recovering from your recent fall.' He smiled encouragingly at Big Peg. 'Has this happened before?'

She shook her head, then murmured 'Ouch!' as the movement set the wound throbbing. 'No, sir . . . well, sometimes I am short of breath and I do get hot and bothered a lot nowadays. I suffer from heartburn,' she indicated the centre of her chest, 'but it don't last long. I never passed out before. I've been a mangle woman for thirty years,' she added proudly.

'You can help me, if you will, nurse,' the doctor asked Hester. 'Unbutton her shift, so I can listen to her chest, front and then back. You will need to support her shoulders while I do that.'

The chilly touch of the stethoscope, then another reassuring smile. 'Well done, Mrs Stainsby. You can rest back on your pillow now.' He looked down at Peg. 'Your heartbeat is irregular. You may have had a slight heart attack. It is unfortunate this happened where it did, with nothing to cushion your fall. I have no objection to you being taken home as long as you go to bed and keep quiet. We will make you an appointment in Outpatients for three days' time. We need to investigate further. Is there someone at home to care for you?'

'My husband . . . but he is disabled. His mother-in-law will be there,' Big Peg said hopefully. She had a sudden thought: 'How long will I be off work, doctor?'

'It will depend.' His voice was guarded. 'We shall see. Your strenuous work could have caused this. You may have to settle for lighter duties. I will arrange for the ambulance to deliver you home this afternoon.'

'I'm afraid I must go now, too,' Hester told Peg. 'I have a special patient who needs me. I have a day off at the end of the week – I was planning to spend it at home – so I will see you then, if not before.' She stooped to kiss Peg's cheek. 'You'll be all right, dear Peg. We can't do without you, you know.'

Fred was speedy on his crutches nowadays. However, he looked at Granny Garter when he heard the thump on the door, but she was in her own little world, busy guiding a froth of pink net under the sewing machine needle. Puglet, as befitted his obvious vener-able status, though they'd no idea just how advanced the little dog was in years, snored intermittently beside her, festooned with discarded scraps of material. Sighing, Fred swung his way to the front door. His own heart skipped a beat at the sight of Big Peg in a wheelchair balanced on the top step, and in the street below, the hospital ambulance.

The young man accompanying her asked: 'Would you open the door wide please, so I can push the chair into the hall? Your good wife has had a fall; I will explain more when we are inside.'

Fred hardly took in what he was being told. He was only concerned that Peg was all right, despite the evidence to the contrary. They moved into the living room, where he requested sharply that Granny move some of her clutter, to accommodate the wheelchair.

'What's up then?' she demanded, in a huff. She looked at the bandage round Peg's head. 'Been through the mangle, have you?'

This joke was not appreciated. Fred glowered at her. 'Can't you see poor Peg's too shocked to speak? Make a pot of tea,Vicky!'

Granny bustled out of the room with a martyred expression on her face. Peg remained silent in the chair.

'I won't wait for the tea, thank you,' said the hospital attendant, 'I'll leave the chair here, and collect it when I fetch Peg for her hospital visit. I'll see myself out, Fred.'

When they were alone, Fred gave Peg a careful hug. 'I'll look after you, don't worry about anything, Peg. It's a pity the gals ain't living at home no more, but we'll manage. You get well, that's what matters.'

'The doctor hinted,' Peg said in a small, far-away voice, 'I might have to give up work. Well, I can't – how would we manage with just your pension and Harry's wages? Twenty-five bob a week don't go far.'

'I'll speak to Vicky. She's lived here scot free for far too long.'

Granny Garter overheard Fred's comment when she was about to re-enter the living room. As she handed them their cups, she said, 'I got something to tell you. I was considerin' it but now I've made up me mind. It's too much for me going over to Brixton twice a week with all them costumes. My friend has suggested I move in with her and work on the premises. It makes sense, don't it? As well as meaning I can keep an eye on young Polly – she must miss her Granny Garter.' She looked at Fred with a glint in her eye. They ain't going to make no nursemaid of me, she thought.

'Makes sense?' Fred repeated. 'I should say.'

'We'll miss you, of course,' Peg put in, revived by the hot tea.

Granny Garter played her trump card. 'You might let my big room upstairs to a lodger – a gentleman, not a lady, seeing as young Harry's got the room next door. Boys of that age are easily tempted. Peg could give up the laundry – you get more rent for full board. Still hard work, but that never hurt nobody so they say, and *you* can do with an occupation Fred, 'stead criticizing others. Don't say I don't have bright ideas.'

'When are you thinking of goin'?' Fred asked bluntly.

'End of the week, when Harry's around to carry the heavy stuff downstairs.' She added grandly, glancing at Peg, 'No wheeling a barrow with me belongings to Brixton, like *some* do; I'll hire a carrier.'

'I wouldn't say no, to another cup of tea,' Peg said. She was feeling better by the minute.

Hester was back on duty. She shook down the thermometer, and marked the chart with the result. Mr Van der Linde observed: 'I thought you'd run away Hester, I missed you.' He smiled at her as she bent over him to straighten the bedclothes.

'How did you find out my name?' she demanded, but she smiled back at him.

'Can't you guess? My young friend Arthur, I guessed he'd know. He has a winning way with the ladies, goes with his name, Winwood, I tell him. By the way, he asked me to find out when you were next off duty, he fancies taking you out.'

'Oh does he? Well, tell him we're not well enough acquainted for that! Anyway, I'm going home on my day off – my stepmother had a fall today, and my family comes first. She is a good friend of mine as well as being married to my pa—father,' she corrected herself.

'I'll tell him. Are you really trying to say Arthur isn't your idea of a beau?'

'I'm not trying to say anything of the sort,' she retorted. 'There are hospital rules, Mr Van der Linde. Nurses should not become personally involved with patients. I suppose that goes for visitors too.'

'Ah, does that mean that, when I am walking again and out of here, you will forget *me* instantly?' He caught hold of her hand as she smoothed a wrinkle in the draw sheet beneath him.

'How could I forget you?' she said lightly, with a shake of her head. 'If you are comfortable, I must go. I will be back later.'

Big Peg was in bed, reluctantly following the doctor's recommendation. She'd discarded the sling, but she wouldn't lie on that side, she thought. There was a dull ache in her head. I'll live, she told herself wryly.

Harry came in with her supper on a tray. 'Granny insisted on gruel – I said that was for invalids. You'll be all right soon, won't you Peg?'

'You're a good lad, Harry. I'll be all right, I promise. But there's going to be a few changes round here – did your pa tell you?'

He grinned, sat on the edge of the bed. 'He did! Can't say I'm sorry, I've never been Granny's favourite—'

'You're mine, dear boy, along of Hester. I want you to know that.'

'Thanks, Peg,' he said awkwardly.

'How are you getting on at work – like it better, do you?'

'I'm like Alf, I'd rather go to sea or even up the river. He loves his new job. But I reckon Pa would be disappointed if I did – he wanted to make a scholar of me. I do enjoy writing and reading, but I need an adventure or two before I get too old. Most of the other clerks are grey – or bald – with whiskers!' He fingered his downy upper lip ruefully. Much to his chagrin, it had not yet developed into a real moustache.

'We don't want to lose you too, Harry – not yet – but if you wait a while I'll get round your pa. Now, if you'd like to cheer me up, how about a serenade on the old penny whistle? Tell your pa to join you. You must miss goin' down the market now winter's on us.'

Harry said, 'We don't draw the big crowds anyway now Polly ain't turning her cartwheels, and the dog is past performing. I need to keep up with the latest tunes: sailors enjoy a bit o' music at sea, don't they?'

'Well, you can't do better than give us a taste of *Miss Marie Lloyd*!' Her tone was wistful. Fred had never suggested a night out at the music hall, but she'd heard all about it from the girls at the laundry. When the supervisor was not around, they sometimes burst into a song, full of saucy innuendo. '*A little bit of wot you fancy does yer good!*'

''Night, Harry,' Fred said later, when Peg lay back on her pillows and closed her eyes.

She murmured dreamily, 'Thanks Harry, I really enjoyed the music. Hope Granny hasn't left the washing-up for you to do. . . . She went to bed in a huff, I guess, as she never looked in to say have a good night, eh?'

'Not worth taking a bet on it,' Harry grinned. 'The sink will still be full of crocks, I reckon. You don't have to help, Pa, you look tired too.'

Fred retired to the commode corner and thence to the wash-stand. He slipped his baggy nightshirt over his head, hooked the crutches to the bottom rail of the bed, before hopping over to his side. He turned the lamp off, then reached out cautiously to Peg. 'You laying right for comfort, Peg? Got a kiss for your old man?'

'Not too old, I hope, for what I have in mind,' she returned, for she usually made the first move in that direction. Whether his diffidence was because of his missing limb, she could only guess.

'Peg – d'you reckon we ought to – you being not yourself,' he ventured.

In answer, she seized his hand and thrust it inside her bodice. The contact with her firm, warm breasts had the desired effect. He was never rough with her, but sometimes she felt he was a trifle tentative. He fumbled with the cloth buttons at the neck, eased the simple shift free of her shoulders, being careful not to twist her sore arm. 'Are you sure?' his voice was muffled as his lips traced the contours of her well-rounded body. It would be hard to stop now, he thought.

Peg knew what she wanted, more than anything. This could be their last chance to make a baby. She said to herself, I'm forty-four years old, and time is running out. Fred doesn't make love to me very often. Bess had been gone some years when we married; he got out of the way of it, I guess. I'd gladly give up work if I had a little one to care for. Fred's family is grown up – surely it's *my* turn now?

Thirteen

Polly was stretched out on her narrow bed in the large front upstairs room she shared with three other boarders. It's not fair, she thought, Granny Garter wheedling her way in here to keep an eye on me. She needn't worry, we're all females here – well that's if you count Miss Blom who Granny reckons is too fond of Lula – except for old Carlos.

She was wearing her practice tunic and warm, footless tights, for there was very little heating in this big house. 'Exercise generates heat,' as Lula told them often. '*Sweat*, more like!' the girls muttered back. Polly sucked the end of one of her plaits, a childish habit which surfaced whenever she had a fit of the sulks.

Laura, resting on the next bed, after a punishing work session at the barre, rebuked her: 'You'll finish up with one side of your hair shorter than the other, Polly. Don't you approve of your grandmother being here? She brought us those lovely pink tutus, didn't she, for the show we're putting on next month. My grandmamma can't sew, nor can my mother.'

Polly didn't deign to reply, but she thought, I bet she's got maids at home to do all the mending and sewing: her mother is a lady of leisure – well, Madame calls her 'a lady of the night', which, when I asked, straight-faced, what she meant, she said that Laura's mother went out to dine in posh places most nights. I reckon Madame thought that up quick, but I wouldn't mind doing that. . . .

Laura, a small, plain girl with a frizzy mop of hair and olive skin inherited from her unknown father, possessed a pliable body: she could perform acrobatics with ease. Polly, so proud previously of her own exuberant cartwheels, envied Laura the backbends, the contortions such as legs tucked behind the ears and expert backflips. She was not encouraged to try to follow suit: Polly, Madame said, was to concentrate on her singing and drama; Laura, however, had a talent for comedy and comical songs. Laura was the nearest Polly had to a friend, although she was younger than Polly, only fifteen, as the other girls were sisters who hoped to become stars in stage musicals. Tansy and Maybelle Cole had good, carrying soprano voices and could act. They thought they were superior to Polly and Laura, not surprising, as their mother was a West End actress. However, her daughters had adopted another surname, because Miss May Weston had been thirty-two years of age for some time now, and they certainly had not been born, one when she was sixteen and the other when May was seventeen years old. The sisters had been boarders here for four years already and would stay until they were ready to launch on stage.

A tap sounded on the door to remind the girls that it was time for their elocution lesson with Miss Palmira Penn.

Polly liked Mira, as she allowed the girls to address her. Fortunately, so did Granny Garter, which was just as well, because they now shared a double room next to the dormitory. Mira was the House Mother, responsible for the girls when tuition was over for the day. She certainly earned her keep. Lula and Emmy Blom were well out of earshot in the room they shared alongside the bathroom on the mezzanine below. There was a short flight of steps to the other bedrooms then more stairs to the servants' quarters, occupied by Carlos and his wife.

The name Palmira had become popular, like Florence and Alma, following the Crimean War between 1853 and 1856. She was blunt, and popular with her charges, informing them when they first met: 'You can guess how old I am from my name – Palmira was much in the news of the time as there was a 349-day siege of the hotel there.' She must be at least forty, Polly guessed, but she was one of those women who never really looked young when they were, but actually aged well. Mira was also interested in palmistry which intrigued the girls. 'Inspired by her name, I reckon,' Polly said, when Granny Garter found this out and passed it on. However, Granny said firmly that you didn't dabble in that sort of thing if you had any sense, certainly not until you were over twenty-one! Polly thought that Granny was probably going to have *her* hand read sometime – that wasn't fair.

Now, the four girls went next door to Mira and Granny's room. There were twin beds at one end, and a walk-in cupboard which held their clothes and clutter, but the far end, by the bay window which looked down over the garden, was furnished with a desk and stool for Mira, a bookcase, a blackboard on an easel and a row of chairs for her pupils, two of which were already occupied by day girls.

Granny did her sewing downstairs in the old butler's pantry; every part of this lofty old house was used for Lula's enterprise. There were no sitting rooms for relaxation, or idleness, as Lula termed it, and those who lived on the premises ate meals together in the big kitchen along with Carlos and Rosa, the cook.

'No gazing out of the window,' Mira said as usual, handing out a sheaf of papers, rather as dealing a pack of cards. These were extracts, handwritten by herself, from the chosen book of the day, *Childhood, A Hundred Years Ago.* She had almost perfect diction which she was determined to pass on to her charges. Mira had high hopes of Polly, who was also determined to succeed.

'I was given this book when I thought I was too old for it,' Mira continued: 'The only thing I liked about it then were the coloured plates of pictures by Sir Joshua Reynolds, on which the text is based. I have come to appreciate it since, and I recommend these sentiments to you. Polly, will you begin? Each of you to read a paragraph in turn.'

Polly stood up reluctantly. Skimming through the words she thought it appeared rather dull, being reminiscences of the late eighteenth century. She enjoyed declaiming Shakespeare, the sonnets or more contemporary romantic poetry.

> *To prove what a serious matter travelling was, where children and old people were concerned, a hundred years ago, I quote from Lucy Aikin. 'The earliest event which dwells in my recollection was a journey. In those days it was indeed an event. I had just completed my third year when my father decided on a removal from Warrington to Yarmouth in Norfolk. My grandmother, her maid, my little brother and myself were packed in a post-chaise. My father accompanied us on horseback. It was Christmas week; the snow deep on the ground. The whole distance was two hundred and forty miles across the country, and we were six days in accomplishing it. The last night we arrived at my Aunt Barbauld's house in Palgrave, where my grand-mother remained behind. She died in a few days of the cold and fatigue of the journey.'*

Mira commented, before Laura continued: 'You mispro-nounced Palgrave. I could tell, when you began reading, that you were wondering why I should choose such a piece: however, when you read that last poignant sentence, with such expression, I knew that you understood. Now, Laura. . . .' Polly, she thought, might well become a dramatic actress. She must take care not to show favouritism, but she allowed herself to direct a small smile of approval at her protégée. She hoped for much more for Polly than she had achieved herself. She thought: I must lend her Lucy Aikin's four-part poem *Epistle on Women* – it might influence Polly as it did me, at her age. The difference between Polly and me though is that she is beautiful, which I could never claim to be. Men will be drawn to her, as they never were to me.

'I am feeling much better, thank you, sir,' Big Peg told the consultant at the hospital.
'I am glad to hear it, Mrs Stainsby. Your wound is healing

well, and the rest has obviously benefitted you; your pulse has steadied. We have come to the conclusion that there is no underlying serious cause for the symptoms you suffered, the giddiness, the hot flushes. . . . We believe you have begun your menopause.'

'Sir?'

'Your change of life. Perhaps earlier than you expected, but to many women of your age, particularly those with a large family, this could come as a relief. It can also be a warning to lessen your work load. In time, your life really will change, for the better, I assure you.' He was a kindly, elderly man, and when he observed tears in her eyes, he was concerned. 'This is unwelcome news? I assure you, it has its problems but you are a strong woman and with support from your husband will come through.'

'Oh, sir, I had hoped, you see – it was not too late. . . .'

'Ah. You have no children, I understand; you married for a second time only a few years ago. It is not impossible, but unlikely, I must tell you. I would not advise it. If you can find a less taxing job than the hospital laundry, you can still feel fulfilled and be happy, I am sure.'

Big Peg declined the offer to take her back home in the ambulance. She didn't want to return until she'd had time to collect her thoughts, as the last thing she wanted to do, was upset Fred.

There was the new Temperance coffee house near the docks; she decided to walk there and see an old friend from the foundling hospital days whom she'd met again at church, who was running the place. Maybe Winnie would have some ideas about life in general, she thought.

The coffee house was a welcome refuge for sailors on shore leave who had either given up the 'demon drink' or might be helped to do so, within its portals. In winter it was a warm place to be, and the staff were always willing to listen to tales of woe, and to offer practical comfort. There was a private room where they could talk, help with letters home for the illiterate, reading matter such as daily newspapers, and for those who showed interest, a few religious tracts. Or the customers could just be quiet and contemplative, over a steaming cup of fragrant coffee.

There was a tantalizing aroma of freshly ground coffee beans, as Big Peg approached the door. She could glimpse through the front windows of the building a big room with long tables and settles, but it was still morning, and there were more women than men at this time of day. She spotted Winnie, a little woman with an unsteady gait, due, Peg was aware, to a leg iron, concealed by her full skirts. Winnie carried a laden tray. Peg couldn't hear this from outside the coffee house, but she could tell the cups were rattling; she hoped they were empty. Winnie was a determined soul, she thought, very independent. The two of them were alike in that respect, only Winnie hadn't been fortunate enough to find a good man like her Fred.

Big Peg suddenly felt hungry. She hoped there was something to eat here, as well as coffee, a taste she had not yet cultivated.

In less than five minutes, she was ushered into the quiet room and sat opposite her beaming friend. 'What brings you here?' asked Winnie. Before Peg could reply, Winnie spotted the bandage under her hat. 'What's happened to you?'

'I had an accident – well, a funny turn, you could say, and fell on me head in the laundry – don't worry, I missed the mangle!'

'You poor soul – what d'you mean, a funny turn?'

'Oh, just my age – you know,' Peg said airily. A large cup of coffee was placed before her by another small helper, who scuttled back to the kitchen to the washing up. 'Anything to eat, dearie?' Peg called hopefully after her retreating figure. She took a gulp of hot coffee.

'You need more sugar,' Winnie advised, noting her wry expression.

'I need a job – Doctor says the laundry is too much for me now.'

The helper was back, with a plate of thinly buttered split scones, which Peg almost fell upon. 'I couldn't face breakfast earlier!'

'The sailors prefer a cheese sandwich, whatever the time

of day,' Winnie told her. 'I could do with a part-time helper to make them. Can't pay much – most of the staff are volunteers and Temperance members. I recall you told me you signed the pledge while you were at the Coram? You need to be a good listener to folk's troubles, and hand out the tracts. Interested?'

'Oh, I am,' Peg nearly spilled her coffee in excitement. 'It's something I believe in, after all. Could I bring Fred with me?'

'Why not. He can play dominoes – no gambling, mind – and chat to his old pals, eh? Maybe entertain with his penny whistle. When do you want to start, Peg?'

'Soon as I get rid of this bandage,' Peg said.

She hurried home with a spring in her step. I don't know about the coffee, she thought, but Fred will feel useful again, and get out of the house, and it's a job that will tie in very nicely with looking after lodgers, so long as they are out at work all day. I ain't about to lay in bed and moan all day, like Granny Garter did for so long.

She paused for a moment, suddenly aware of a familiar nagging pain in her insides. No baby then; she was glad she'd said nothing to Fred. The doctor was right, a pregnancy was unlikely at her time of life, but she could still be busy and happy.

Fourteen

Spring, 1896

Van was learning to walk again after coming out of traction; a few steps at a time as both legs were wasted and weak. He had lain in bed for four long months and was still reliant on Hester's help and support. She had been encouraging throughout his stay in hospital, and had understood when he lapsed occasionally into depression.

Hester was aware that Sister was watching her, as she supported him firmly with an arm around his waist as he slowly placed one foot and then the other. This was their new routine before the visiting hour.

'Would you like to sit in your chair while your friend is with you?' she asked.

He nodded gratefully. 'Please, Hester.'

'Nurse . . .' she reminded him softly.

She was tucking a blanket round his lower half, after easing a plump pillow behind his back, when Arthur Winwood arrived.

'Good to see you out of bed,' Arthur beamed. He fetched another chair for himself. 'Oh, do you have to go?' he asked Hester.

'I do. The night staff are taking over, and my supper awaits. Then I'm off duty from tonight until tomorrow, when I'll be on night patrol myself, so I'm going home to see my family.'

She went to report the patient's progress to Sister at her desk.

'You're doing splendidly,' Arthur said to Van. 'You'll be back at work in no time at all.'

'I don't think so. Another month, at least, here, and then I have to convalesce. My sisters have invited me to stay with them. How are you faring at Mrs Dingwall's?'

'Well, I was going to ask your advice with regard to that. It's a dull old life without you there. The widow feels the same: she's mentioned that she would like to travel abroad for a month or two with her daughter, somewhere warmer than London. I'm looking for new digs at the moment, but I don't like to let you down.'

'Don't worry about that. Mrs D will store my belongings as usual, and no doubt I'll return there eventually. I'm fond of my sisters, but don't want to be a burden to them.'

'You might return to your sea-faring—'

'My dear chap, I don't think my legs will stand up on a rolling deck.'

Arthur passed over a bundle of magazines. '*The Strand* – I paid your subscription as you asked. Plenty of good reading there. A new Sherlock Holmes story. I wouldn't mind becoming a detective. . . .'

'Don't tell your father that, he'll think I'm a subversive influence. Time you found a nice girl and settled down, Arthur.'

'The only one I've fancied recently, apart from a girl I saw once, turning amazing cartwheels in the market – but she seems to have vanished into thin air – is your little Nurse Nightingale. But I reckon you've got an eye on her yourself, eh?'

'Oh, I'm far too ancient for Hester. And you are rather worldly wise, despite your youth, for such a proper young lady.'

'I can't resist a challenge! Despite your protestations – well, may the best man win!'

'I don't know whether it's wise to tell you this, but Hester mentioned that her parents have a vacancy for a lodger. . . .'

'Thanks, Van! When I leave you, I'll loiter outside for a bit and see if I can ask her about it when she comes out of the hospital.'

Hester was eager to see her family and hear all the news, so she moved at a brisk pace, unaware that she was being followed.

'Hester, do you mind if I walk you home?' Arthur asked as he caught up with her.

'Really, Mr Winwood—'

'Now, you know my name is Arthur. Don't tell me we can't be friends when you're off duty?'

'I – think – well, why not. But I can't discuss your friend's progress with you, you know.'

'Oh, I can see that he is doing very well – I won't beat about the bush, Van told me your family are on the lookout for a suitable lodger. I am asking you now if I might see them regarding this, because it seems to be my only chance to speak to you.'

'Don't be silly. You engage me in conversation whenever you visit your friend.'

'With Sister's eagle eye watching me all the time?'

Hester couldn't help laughing. 'Come on then, I don't imagine our home will be at all what you're looking for, but if you want to be entertained – well, it's the right place for that.'

'Take my arm,' Arthur offered, 'and allow me to carry your bag.'

Hester was actually glad of his company. She was always uneasy when she walked alone in the evening; you never knew who was lurking round the next corner, she thought.

They chatted of this and that. 'I ought to tell you,' she said, 'that ours is a nice house, but we don't have an indoor WC or a proper bathroom – but there's a tub in the wash-house and the copper heats the water. It must sound old-fashioned to you.'

'Not at all,' he returned. 'Anyone who has been in boarding school like me will remember all too well cold baths and hard beds in the dormitories. Mrs Dingwall, my landlady, believes that too much bathing is not good for you, so I have taken to visiting the public baths. All you need is a big bar of soap and an adequate towel.'

'Mr Van der Linde – Van – was also at boarding school, I understand, with your father?'

'The same establishment. Old-fashioned is the word for that. My father was in the sixth form and a prefect when Van arrived. He was my father's fag—'

'What's that?'

'Slave. Usual in such places. Fortunately my father was – is – kind-hearted, and they have been friends ever since. Oh, is this your house?' She had paused outside the houses on the rise.

'Yes. Remember, they are not expecting you.' She sounded anxious now.

'I'm looking forward to meeting them,' Arthur said.

Harry opened the door, obviously surprised to find his sister accompanied by a young man, a gentleman, by his clothes.

'Harry, this is Mr Winwood – he's come to see about the lodgings.'

'How'd you do?' Arthur responded politely, as Harry moved back to allow them to step inside. He added: 'I've met you before, haven't I?'

'Not that I know of,' Harry said. 'Pa and Peg are expectin' you are they?'

'Not that I know of, either,' Arthur grinned.

'Follow me – they'll wonder why we're lingering in the hall,' said Hester.

Big Peg was sitting by the window with her sewing basket, darning socks. Her needle, threaded with grey wool, twitched in and out the heel of the sock, held taut on a wooden mushroom. Fred was enjoying the new paper, the *Daily Mail*, bought for a ha'penny by his thoughtful son. There was the latest from the new Olympics now taking place in Athens: this was inspiring other nations, including Britain, to see the Games continue in venues all round the world.

They looked up in surprise to see that Hester had a companion.

'My pa, Fred,' Hester said proudly. She knew Pa wouldn't like to be called 'father'. Then, 'My step-ma, Peg.'

'Usually known as Big Peg, a name they give me when I was young, because I had a friend called Little Peg.' Peg put down her sewing, got to her feet, and held out her hand. 'And who might you be?'

'Arthur Winwood, a friend of Hester's – well, I hope she thinks of me like that. I am very pleased to meet you.' He shook her hand, then turned to Fred. 'Don't get up, sir. Now, this is strange, but I feel I know you from somewhere, too. . . .'

Fred had the answer. 'You might have seen me, my son and my other daughter Polly down the market – they call us the Poplar Penny Whistlers.'

'Of course, that's it – but that was some time ago, wasn't it?'

'Well, Harry's a working lad now, and Polly's gone to a h'academy, I think they call it, to train for the stage. Peg won't let me perform on me own, and the dog's past it, too.' The dog was curled up on his lap. He'd placed the newspaper inadvertently over Puglet's head, and at mention of his name, the dog emerged, scrabbling and crumpling the newsprint as he did so. Fred tickled him affectionately under his dewlaps. 'What can we do for you, young sir?'

'Arthur, please. I hear you have a room to let? I'm a junior engineer in the Blackwall tunnel – I met Hester when I visited my boss, she's his nurse in the hospital, he had a nasty accident a few months ago – you might have heard?'

'I heard, but not from Hester – she don't discuss the patients outside o' the horspital – it ain't allowed. Sit down Arthur, make yerself at home. For I reckon you'll do very well with us.'

Arthur was rather taken aback. 'You'll need references, of course, from my current landlady, and from the company I work for, I reckon. . . .'

'If Hester invited you here, that's good enough for me.'

'And me,' Peg added. 'Would you care to see the room now?'

'Yes, I would, please, if it's convenient.'

'You got two choices – meals in your room or with the family – full board, at any rate. Good, plain cooking. When you want to shut your door, you can be as private as you want.'

'With the family sounds good. You haven't told me how much

you intend to charge? I pay Mrs Dingwall one pound a week – would that be sufficient for you?'

'More than we expected,' Peg said, honest as always.

'Let's shake on it.' Fred proffered his hand, again. 'Hester'll show you upstairs. When d'you want to move in?'

'As soon as I can. I have to tell my landlady first, but she already knows my intentions.'

'All right if I pop next door to see Alf? I said I'd let him know when Hester was home next,' Harry asked his pa. Fred nodded.

'Our neighbour's about your age, Arthur, he's an attendant on the hospital boat. Nice young chap – his father died a while ago and his stepmother got carted off to the asylum, poor thing. Alf thinks of us as his family now, I reckon.'

Now, why did Pa have to say that? Hester wondered, as she escorted Arthur upstairs to Granny Garter's refurbished room. But she knew the answer: the family still hoped that she and Alf would tie the knot one day. She suppressed a small sigh.

After Arthur had approved the room, he asked: 'I hope I am not taking the room you use when you are at home, Hester?'

'Oh, no, dear Harry lets me have my old room back, the one I shared with Polly, next to this one, and retires to the box room and the cobwebs,' she said lightly. 'You go downstairs and give them your verdict, while I just change out of my uniform and tidy up, eh?'

When she appeared again, Arthur saw a transformation from the prim young nurse in her all-concealing uniform. Here was an attractive girl in a blue Holland dress with a lace collar and long dark hair, crimped from braiding, loose round her shoulders. He couldn't help thinking he was one step ahead of old Van, seeing Hester like this. Also, there was now the possibility he might get to meet her beautiful younger sister.

She obviously read his thoughts about herself. She said in his ear as she passed him, 'I still smell of carbolic, you know. . . .'

Fifteen

'We've got a lovely young lodger,' Big Peg confided in her friend Winnie, as she poured a stream of coffee from the big jug into a row of cups. You need muscles, she thought, lucky I've got 'em, to lift that up when it's full to the brim. There was a crowd in the coffee house that morning, and this was the first chance she'd had to chat to Winnie.

'Oh, yes?' Winnie was fanning her face with her apron, after a blast of hot air from the oven when she removed a tray of scones.

'He's a real gentleman, perfect manners, but he's easy-goin' and our Harry's cheered up as they went out and about together at the weekend, and Alf, you remember our neighbour, Alf Hodge? tagged along because he had a day off and no-one to spend it with.'

'Alf – he was in here a week or so ago, with a young nurse from the hospital – a friend of your Hester's, she said.'

'That'll be Edie. We had hoped that Alf and Hester – you know – but Hester turned him down. I'm glad he's found someone else. Poor lad's all on his own next door, now.'

'He looked happy to me, and so did she. Suited, I should say. Watch out, that cup's overflowin'!'

A customer was banging a spoon on the side of his empty cup. 'Service!' he called hopefully.

'Ignore him,' Winnie told Peg. 'He's a trouble maker, I reckon. He don't look sober to me. There's somethin' I was goin' to say to you – now, what was it? Oh, yes, is your lodger much older than your Harry?'

'About five years older I'd say, same as the diff'rence 'tween

Hester and the twins—'

'Well, then, you want to watch out he don't lead the lad astray.'

'Whatever d'you mean?'

'Look at the notice, DOWN WITH THE DEMON DRINK! No doubt your gentleman will be acquainted with that, and young females, but as for Harry, he's young and innercent, ain't he? '

'I wish I hadn't told you about the lodger,' Peg was in a huff. 'He's a *gentleman*, as I said.' She'd forgotten how bossy Winnie could be.

'Well, *they're* too fond of gamblin', drinkin', gals and such.'

'Not our Mr Winwood, I assure you.' Peg looked over at the spoon banger. 'Comin'!' she called. She was having one of her hot flushes, and it was Winnie's fault, she thought, for riling her. However, maybe she'd ask Fred to whisper a few wise words in his son's ear.

'Sorry I upset you,' Winnie said when Big Peg returned to the coffee pot. 'I ain't been married like you, and you must admit we had it drummed into us when we was young to behave proper like. D'you forgive yer old friend?'

''Course I do,' Peg said. 'Still, you made me think, y'know.' What she was thinking now, with a stray tear trickling down her cheek, was: I have been married – twice – but what do I know about other folks' children growing up? I love them kids like me own, but the fact is, they ain't. . . . She mopped her damp brow and surreptitiously blotted the tear.

Alf had cleaned the house from top to bottom, which occupied him every evening one week in early May. He had big plans for his next Saturday afternoon off, when Edie would also be off-duty. He'd also disposed of all the old gin bottles, the legacy from his step mother. He'd visited her twice since she was taken away, but she no longer recognized him, so he knew she was in the best place. He missed his dad, but his father had been an unhappy man and not always too kind to his son after his mother died. Alf was the man in the house now and had something to offer a prospective bride.

Edie felt guilty as she slipped quickly past the Stainsby abode and then rapped on the adjacent front door. It opened instantly and she was pulled inside. 'See anyone?' Alf asked anxiously. He didn't like deceiving his kind neighbours, but he thought that they wouldn't approve of the two of them, alone in the house.

'I did tell Hester where I was going,' she said. 'We don't keep secrets from each other.'

'She won't tell anyone else?'

'Alf Hodge, don't you know her better than that? Well, aren't you goin' to show me round your palace?'

'You keep it very nice,' she said approvingly later, after traipsing up and down stairs. She was rather intrigued that he had not showed her his bedroom, but merely indicated the door with, 'My room.' Then it came to her: he don't feel it's proper to take me in there. . . .

'Too big just for one I suppose, but in the future. . . .' he hinted. 'Now, how about tea? I bought fresh cakes, not what the baker had on his shelves at the end of the day. I hope you like egg and cress sandwiches? I cut the crusts off. '

'I'm always hungry, you know that. Make a good strong pot o' tea, we get weak and watery at the hospital.'

They sat regarding each other across the table, laid with a rather crumpled cloth which Alf had washed, but not had time to press with the flat iron. She was wearing the green skirt she'd worn on the day they first walked out together, along the riverside, and a white muslin blouse embroidered with French-knots, with full sleeves to the elbow and long buttoned cuffs. The material was so fine he could discern the outline of her chemise and the peachiness of her skin, despite the high ruffle round her neck. He was also aware that she was breathing fast, like himself. They were both nervous, he realized.

'When are you expected at your home?' He hoped she wouldn't say it was time to go when they'd finished their tea.

'I haven't told them I would be off-duty after the morning shift, so we can spend the evening together, I hope that's what you had in mind,' she said demurely.

'That's good. Let's go into the parlour, eh?' He'd arranged a row of cushions along the sofa, so she wouldn't be troubled by twanging springs. He'd invested in one new piece of furniture, with the unexpected windfall from his father, given to him when he knew the end was near. Twelve pounds, in small change, apart from three florins, collected in a large bottle hidden inside an old sock. He had something to offer Edie now, he thought. Especially since he had been granted the tenancy of the house with the proviso that this was a dwelling for a married man, with the prospect of a family.

They were just making themselves comfortable, and Edie had kicked off her shoes, when they heard the back door being opened, and a voice called, 'Anyone at home?'

'Harry!' Alf whispered in consternation. 'Quick – go upstairs, while I speak to him. I'll fetch you when he's gone.'

On stockinged feet Edie padded up the staircase, suppressing a giggle. Alf was such a worrier! She paused at Alf's bedroom door, then, on impulse, opened it and went inside. What she saw made her eyes widen in surprise. She sat down abruptly on the edge of the big double bed and discovered that the mattress was plump and soft. She swung her feet up. What bliss, she thought, a feather bed. . . . Her eyes closed: it had been a difficult morning on the ward, with a patient suffering an epileptic fit. This had involved restraining and comforting the patient and reassuring his neighbours. She was exhausted by the time the drama was over and hadn't really felt like changing her clothes or going out for the rest of the day. She mustn't fall asleep, she reminded herself, with a huge yawn.

'Oh, there you are. You took your time,' Harry said, following Alf into the parlour. Alf closed the living room door in passing, as he suddenly remembered the table hadn't been cleared: two plates, two cups would give the game away.

However, Harry spotted the shoes and his eyes sparkled with mischief. 'New shoes, Alf? Bit small for you, I reckon.'

Alf's face was as red as his hair. 'I – had a visitor,' he mumbled.

'What? She rushed off without her shoes? I didn't see no-one leaving here when I come.'

'All right, no sneaking, mind. It's only Edie—' He felt guilty, it must sound too casual.

'Where've you hidden her?'

'I haven't – she sort of – vanished.'

Harry laughed out loud. 'I'll leave you to your hide and seek, then, I can tell you ain't about to accept my invitation to join me and Arthur down *The Ship* tonight. I might play my penny whistle.'

'You guessed right. Well, don't keep your new friend waitin'.'

'I won't. Cheer-ho then. Give my regards to Edie.'

This time, Alf locked the door after Harry departed; he didn't want any more intrusions. He went in search of Edie.

He looked in the other rooms before he realized Edie must be in his bedroom. He called her name, but there was no reply. He discovered her lying on the coverlet, on the new bed, sound asleep. He lowered himself cautiously beside her, rested his arms behind his head, and regarded her solemnly. He'd planned to keep the bed and its heavenly mattress a secret until the day he dreamed of came to be, their wedding day, so he'd been sleeping in his father's old bed.

Being relaxed, he succumbed to slumber himself.

A couple of hours later, when it was becoming dark outside, and the curtains remained open, Edie awoke, refreshed from her sleep, to the sound of gentle snoring close by. She put out an uncertain hand, and gathered she had a companion. Her eyes adjusting to the shadows, she was relieved to find that it was Alf. Her panic was groundless: they were both still fully clothed.

'Alf,' she said softly. As there was no immediate response, she leaned over him and kissed his cheek. 'Wake up, there's a good chap.'

The next thing she knew, his arms went round her and he was kissing her as he never had before. It quite took her breath away.

She was aware that she ought to put up some show of resistance, but her attempts to pull herself out his embrace were perfunctory. He fumbled with the waist of her skirt, slid it down over her slender hips. She allowed him to remove her blouse and toss it to one side of the bed. They were both in a hurry now. She rolled down her stockings while he tore off his own top clothes. Laughter bubbled up in her, spilled out. 'You look funny in your shirt tails, 'specially with your bow tie and socks!' She clung to the final vestige of her modesty, her chemise.

'This was to be our wedding night bed,' he whispered huskily, as they slipped with one accord under the covers. 'I was . . . going to ask you to marry me, this evening. . . .'

'Yes!' she murmured. 'The answer's *yes!*' She wriggled free of the chemise, while he struggled with the buttons on his shirt.

There was a long night of loving ahead. They were oblivious to a raucous version of *Nellie Dean* rendered outside at midnight when Harry, supported by Arthur, arrived back from the pub. Fred was waiting up, and Harry was about to receive a right royal ticking-off. Arthur made himself scarce, hoping Fred wouldn't guess it was he who'd treated Harry to extra pints of beer. He'd looked after Harry in another way, stopping him from 'going outside' when invited to do so by a buxom widow. However, he thought it best not to mention that either.

The morning was the time for questions in both houses. Peg tried to smooth things over in the Stainsby house; next door Alf asked Edie if she was willing to sacrifice her nursing career? The hospital's policy was not to employ married nurses. She couldn't answer that immediately. However, Edie assured him that she had no regrets about the events of last night. Alf was a good man, he loved her, and she loved him. That was all that mattered for now, though she affirmed: 'We *will* be wed, I promise you.' What would Hester say? This rehearsal for their wedding night was a secret she must keep from her best friend, she decided. From her mother, too, who'd advised her so often not to follow her example.

Sixteen

May 1896

Miss Lucy Van der Linde arrived at the hospital to make arrangements to take her brother home to Surbiton. His recovery had taken longer than expected and he had been on the ward for almost six months. The hospital doctor explained that tall, well-built patients sometimes had problems with weight-bearing on the injured limb when they began the slow process of learning to walk again.

Lucy was big-boned and handsome, smartly dressed in a tailor-made suit in fine navy wool, despite the summer weather. Under the bolero-style jacket she wore a shirt-waist blouse in crisp blue-and white striped cotton, with a floppy blue bow at the neck. Like her brother, she had prematurely grey hair, swept up into an elaborate coiffure, to which her feathered hat, the only frivolous touch to her rather severe appearance, was firmly anchored.

She caused quite a stir when she swept into the men's ward and spoke to the first nurse she saw: 'Where may I find my brother, Mr Nicholas Van der Linde?'

The nurse happened to be Hester, for Sister had requested she be available for his sister's visit. 'Miss Van der Linde has a proposition to put to you, Nurse Stainsby, to which I am sure you will be agreeable.'

Hester was tempted to bob, as she had been taught to do at school when there were visiting inspectors, but she smiled and said: 'I will take you to him – I presume you are his sister? He expects you.'

Miss Van der Linde was not as formidable as she looked. She smiled back at Hester. 'Thank you. May I, in turn, presume you are his nurse, Miss Stainsby?'

'I was assigned to his care, yes, but naturally the other nurses have played their part in his recovery.' Hester had been rather upset to learn from Edie that she was regarded with envy by a couple of the older nurses because of the responsibility she'd been given by Sister. She had been new on the ward at the time, after all.

'Nicholas sings your praises in his letters home. You may well be wondering why I haven't visited him before this?'

Hester had wondered, of course, but she shook her head.

'I will tell you anyway, I don't want you to think badly of me. My sister Dora was unwell – she suffers from periods of depression. I cannot leave her at such times; Nicholas understands.'

'Here we are,' Hester said, as they arrived at his bedside.

Van was sitting out of bed, fully dressed, with his stick hooked over the back of his chair. He levered himself up to greet his sister. 'Lucy, it's good to see you – did you have an uneventful journey?'

'Yes thank you. Mrs Dingwall made me very welcome and helped me pack your bags. We leave tomorrow morning. Dora is holding the fort at school, but I suspect there will be uproar, as she was excited to be left in charge.' She didn't sound too serious, for she smiled at the thought, adding, 'Dora sends her love.'

Hester pulled the curtains to ensure privacy for the two of them to talk. 'I should go now. . . .'

'Not just yet,' Lucy insisted. 'I have spoken to Matron, and the ward Sister, Nicholas, as you requested, earlier, and they have kindly agreed that Nurse Stainsby, if she is agreeable, may accompany us on the train from Waterloo to Surbiton station, and from there by cab to the school, to enable your settling in, for a few days. I have also given, in your name, a donation to the hospital in appreciation of the excellent treatment you have received here.' She paused. 'I suggest you ask Nurse Stainsby yourself, Nicholas.'

'*Are* you willing, Hester?'

Looking into those blue eyes, she was disarmed, as she had been the first time they met, so made up her mind instantly. 'I should be happy to oblige,' she said. 'Now, I have other patients to see to, if you will excuse me.'

She hoped she'd have a chance to tell Edie her amazing news.

'You have all the luck,' Edie sounded doleful. She appeared pale and tired. Seeing Hester's disappointment at her reaction, she said quickly:

'I'm sorry, I didn't mean to snap.'

'You don't look well, Edie, what's up?' They were alone in the sluice room, so could talk.

'I can't keep it from you, Hester . . . . I believe I'm expecting a baby.'

'Edie . . . how? Not Alf!'

'It wouldn't be anyone else!' Edie was indignant now. 'Don't worry, he's eager to marry me, and I've said yes, but it means I'll lose my job here, and Sister will be shocked, I know. She'll say I'm letting the hospital down, after all my training.'

'She'll be sorry to lose you, I know I will – we've been pals for five years now. You're like another sister to me. This might be a false alarm—'

'I'm two weeks late, and this morning I was sick first thing. I've seen my mother like that too often to be mistaken.'

'You've told Alf, I gather. What did he say?'

'He couldn't say anything for a while, then he said it was just what he wanted, to be part of a family again. Please don't say "how could he" because it was as much my fault as his, but really, how can it be wrong when you love someone?'

Hester put down the receptacle she was holding. She hugged her friend tightly to her. 'You'll be a wonderful wife and mother, I know; Alf is a dear, loyal chap, and I'm happy for you both.'

'What's all this?' Sister had entered, unnoticed, and was now waiting for an explanation.

Hester gave Edie a nudge. Get it over with. . . . She said: 'Edie

– Nurse Brown, will tell you – it is not really my business, Sister.'

'Off you go, then, but I will see you later to discuss your temporary role in Surbiton.' When Hester left, Sister closed the door behind her. 'I'm waiting, Edith,' she said, and at the unexpected use of her Christian name, tears gushed from Edie's eyes. 'Sit down. When you've composed yourself, will do,' Sister added kindly.

The words spilled out. 'I'm sorry, Sister to let you down, and the hospital after all they've done for me, training me to be a nurse and that, but it seems likely I may be expecting a baby – oh not for months, but—'

'Is the man concerned standing by you? Will he marry you?'

'Oh yes! It's Alf Hodge, Sister – you remember him? He left to work on the hospital ferry – and he has a house, and can support me.'

'A very nice young man, as I recall. Hard working and thoughtful. You realize that you cannot continue nursing here after your marriage?'

'I know. That's what upsets me. I love my work, Sister.'

'You are an excellent nurse, Edith. You will be much missed. However, if I may make a suggestion, it is possible that you can continue nursing later on if you have the time, or feel the need, in a private capacity. You will receive excellent references from the hospital. You did well in Midwifery, didn't you? There is always a call for a trained midwife, too many of the other sort. Most babies are still born at home.'

'You're not angry with me, then, Sister?'

'My dear, I'm sure you regard me as a hard taskmaster, but I have respect for my young nurses. A great deal is expected of you including the sacrifice, in most cases, of a normal life outside the hospital. I wish you well. This conversation will remain unreported by me, until it is time for you to leave. Now, wash your face, and I will excuse you from further duties for a couple of hours. Rest in your room until lunch time.'

'Thank you, Sister, for being so understanding.'

'A baby is always a blessing,' Sister said so quietly that Edie wondered if she had heard aright. She added briskly, 'A larger uniform —' she was about to say 'will cover a multitude of sins', but instead continued: 'will conceal all. I'll see about it today.'

Van could bath himself now, with Hester hovering discreetly outside the bathroom door in case he should slip, and also get dressed without help, although this took him longer than normal.

He took Hester's arm as she escorted him to Sister's sanctum where he would sign himself out of hospital care. A porter had already fetched his luggage, and Hester's small bag to the waiting cab, where Lucy was ensconced. It was ten a.m.

'You are still in your uniform,' Van observed. Even through the starched layers she was vibrantly aware of his close proximity as they moved in unison.

'I am on duty,' Hester reminded him. 'In any case, I shall wear it for the journey. I am, after all, still officially your nurse.'

'Oh, you do know how to put me in my place! But I must admit I am looking forward to getting to know you much better than is possible here,' he said daringly, for they might well be overheard.

Hester hadn't travelled on a train before, as she had never left London, all parts of which were accessible by omnibus. She enjoyed the short ride in the hansom cab, where Van sat between the two women, linking arms with them both at his sister's request, in case of any jolting on the journey. Lucy did all the talking and Van made the occasional light-hearted comment but Hester watched the world go by from the window. She started, when he gave her a discreet nudge. 'We're here.'

The bustle and noise in the vast station made Hester's ears ring, after the quiet of the hospital. She was clinging to Van now, worried about moving too near the edge of the platform as the train, emitting clouds of smoke steamed towards them. Lucy directed them to follow the porter wheeling the luggage to further up the train, and all the while, doors slammed until they were jostled aboard by other eager passengers.

In the first-class compartment, there were comfortable uphol-
stered seats, with lacy antimacassars to rest the head against; a
luggage rack and windows which pulled up and down with a sash
cord. There were bright posters along the corridor, advertising
places of interest.

'It's not a lengthy journey,' Lucy said, adjusting her skirts. The
carriage was spotless, but she didn't wish the hems of her clothes
to touch the floor. She sat by the window, and Van settled in the
seat opposite, with Hester beside him. 'I expect,' Lucy said to
Hester, 'you have heard of Surbiton?'

'Is it . . . another name for the suburbs?' Hester ventured.

'No my dear, it is a place in green and leafy Surrey, in the
borough of Kingston, so you will still be not far from the great
River Thames. If you are wondering why our station is in Kingston
and not Surbiton itself, well, when it opened in 1838 it was called
Kingston-on-Railway. Kingston turned down its own station
fearing it would affect the busy trade from coaching. The line
was routed further south in a cutting in the hillside of Surbiton.
When the new Kingston railway station was built in 1869, our
line was renamed Surbiton. Kingston must regret postponing their
own railway station because it has remained a mere branch line,
whereas *ours* is the link with London, and much further.'

Hester took all this in. 'How interesting,' she said, meaning it.

Van grinned at his sister. 'What about the famous artists,
Lucy.'

'You've heard of John Everett Millais, Hester?'

'Yes, we did famous people at school. . . .'

'Well, he painted the Hogsmill, we'll point it out to you on the
last part of our journey, as the background to his beautiful picture
of *Ophelia*, and another artist, Holman Hunt used the fields
beyond this landmark in *The Hireling Shepherd*.'

'Oh.' Hester recalled that Lizzie Siddal, the beautiful model
for *Ophelia*, had caught a severe chill and almost expired herself
after posing uncomplainingly in a bath full of cooling water on a

freezing day in November, while the artist was engrossed in his painting. The model's dedication had impressed the young Hester more than the print of the picture shown to her class.

Van gave her arm a little squeeze. 'I know you've read Thomas Hardy, because you told me so, when I asked which books you liked. Well, *he* once lived for a brief time in St David's Villa in Hook Road.'

It sounds awesome, Hester thought. I'm not sure I will fit in.

Seventeen

The school was in a wing connected to the main house, which was built of red brick with ivy spreading its tendrils up the walls and round the windows. It was surrounded by land, mostly down to grass, with a few flower beds, but to one side there was a flourishing kitchen garden and a long glasshouse, where Hester glimpsed rows of pots along the shelves, with a rampant vine which looked as if it would burst through the glass if it got half a chance. Behind the house was an orchard with apple, pear and a few plum trees. There was a tethered billy goat which Hester was warned to steer clear of, and a fat cat sunning itself on the front step.

The house, it was obvious, was a home, and from what Hester could tell from the outside, glancing through the windows at the girls at their desks, scratching away with their pens, the school was a pleasant place to be, too. Dora perched on the teacher's high desk, swinging her legs, as she talked animatedly to the pupils. She waved when she saw her sister, brother and his nurse.

Hester relaxed. Perhaps, after all, she would like it here.

The interior of the house was as reassuring as the exterior. The furniture was comfortable rather than ostentatious. In the main reception room to which Hester was escorted by Van, there was an upright piano with faded rose-pink silk panels, brackets on either side for candles, and sheet music piled haphazardly on the piano stool. A round table was in the window recess with chairs grouped round it; a mound of exercise books on top, a blotter and a pen and ink stand. There were plant pots and ornaments, mostly from foreign parts, armchairs covered in faded chintz, a barometer hanging on the wall, alongside a tall bookcase and a grandfather clock. Hester took it all in; it was a living room, a family room, she thought, not a musty parlour, and she liked that.

Two portraits hung side by side on the wall attracted Hester's attention. 'Your mother – and your father?' she exclaimed to Van.

'Yes, can't you see the likeness to Lucy in my mother?'

'She must have been about the age your sister is now. And the captain looks very distinguished – because it's a painting and not a photograph, I can see he has the same blue eyes as you!'

'He was younger than I am now: he died at thirty-eight,' Van said.

'We brought the captain's chair down from the attic for you, Nicholas,' Lucy said, as she came into the room, removing her hat and tossing it on to the table. 'Sit down, you must be tired. Mrs Long will bring us coffee directly.' She turned to Hester. 'Mrs Long is our housekeeper and good friend. She was Nicholas's nanny until he went off to boarding school. Dora and I joined Mother's pupils, of course. I took over the running of the school some years ago, but have been teaching the Three Rs here since I was seventeen. Dora helps out – music, French and art are her forte – but we have a teacher who takes the girls for history and geography, and supervises games. Some of the girls are learning tennis this year. We acquired a second-hand net and have marked out a grass court. We would have preferred to have installed a proper court, but the cost was prohibitive.'

Hester couldn't help thinking: she is making sure I know they are not as wealthy as I might suppose . . . . Why?

'Is this a day school?' she ventured, after seeing Van ensconced in the upright chair. Fortunately, it had a padded seat, she thought. Otherwise the hard wood could cause him discomfort.

'Yes. We have grown since Mother's day. She started with eight pupils, including us. We have twenty local girls from seven to eleven years of age. Ah, here is Mrs Long with the coffee and biscuits! Don't indulge in too many, because it will be lunch time in an hour.' Lucy paused, while the elderly housekeeper passed the cups around the company, then added: 'Thank you, Mrs Long. Please will you return in fifteen minutes to take Miss Stainsby to her room?'

Mrs Long nodded, smiling at Hester. 'I will show her the dining room, as we pass, and the bathroom upstairs.'

When she had departed, Lucy said to Hester. 'We have our lunch in the dining room with the girls. This consists of soup – we always have a stock pot on the stove – rolls, and a choice of fruit. Mother considered that a heavy meal at one o'clock contributed to afternoon lethargy – we have our main meal of the day at seven p.m. in peace! I hope this suits you? Naturally, Nicholas is familiar with our routine.'

Although she was used to substantial hospital lunches, and evening meals, Hester agreed, 'Soup would be nice,' even as she privately thought a salad would be preferable on a warm day.

'I'll go upstairs with you, if you don't mind,' Nicholas said to Hester. 'I shall be glad of your help, Hester.'

'That's what I'm here for,' she replied, guessing that despite the horsehair cushion he found the chair too rigid. He still suffered pain in his gammy leg and was aware he would always have a limp, because this leg was now shorter than the other. 'I think you should have a rest on your bed before lunch – don't you agree, Miss Van der Linde?'

'Lucy, please! I shall leave such matters to you whilst you are here. By the way, I will be teaching this afternoon, so after the girls have returned to the classroom, and are not romping around on the grass, why don't you both sit out in the sun then. It will do you good, Nicholas, after such a long stay in hospital.'

Hester's room was the old nursery, next door to Van's bedroom.

'Mother insisted I had my own quarters whenever I came home,' he said. 'The rocking horse is still in the corner, but now it is the guest room. You can lock the door which connects with my room.'

'What if you need my assistance in the night?' she joked. 'I am

119

still on duty, after all.'

'The only thing I might call on you for would be to raid the larder downstairs! I'm afraid my sisters follow a Spartan diet.'

'Now, you know I can't do that – they might think I was a burglar! Look, I'll get you settled, before I unpack – not that I brought much with me, as I shall only be here a few days.'

'I wish it could be longer, climbing those stairs exhausted me. I didn't realize I was still so weak. I hate being incapacitated!'

'You must try not to go up and down them unnecessarily,' Hester advised. 'But gentle exercise is what you need now. We'll walk round the grounds this afternoon before we sun ourselves. Shall we go into your room through this door, then?'

He stretched out on his bed and closed his eyes. 'Call me in good time for lunch. Hester—'

'Yes?' She paused at the open door.

'Could you change out of that starched uniform? It makes me think I am still an invalid. . . . Lucy will lose patience with me, if I behave like one, I know. She found me a tiresome small boy to have around when we first came here; she's always been a bossy elder sister. Believe me, I admire her spirit, and appreciate both my sisters, different though they are. You'll like Dora, I think.'

'I only packed one dress,' she said, 'However, if it pleases you. . . .' She closed the door behind her.

There was a bunch of mixed flowers picked from the garden, in a jug on the windowsill. Beside it was a coil of ribbon, left perhaps by a previous guest. On an impulse, after discarding her uniform and changing into her blue dress, she brushed her loosened hair and tied it back in a bow. The dressing table had three mirrors and she regarded her reflection in each one in turn. She looked so solemn, she made herself smile. Am I pretty? Will he think so? A smear of Vaseline on her eyebrows, and on her lids, then she bit her lips to redden them, and made a little face at herself this time. You are vain! she told herself. It seems he's a confirmed bachelor, and anyway, I'm not in his class, though I know he wouldn't dream of thinking of it like that. It's just that, well, I can understand why Edie allowed Alf to make love to her even though she was well aware what might happen, and did, because of how I feel when Van looks at me. . . .

Hester did indeed like Dora, who was as giggly as the girls who followed her into the dining room and sat down obediently at the table waiting for Lucy to say grace. Dora was a will o' the wisp, small and restless, with a dimpled face and sparkling blue eyes like her brother's. It was obvious that she couldn't sit still for more than five minutes, for she jumped up and down to pour water for her charges and to help carry the bowls of soup to the table. She appeared childish in many ways, despite the fact that she must be well into her forties, for she was older than her brother.

'Do stop that, Dora,' Lucy said sharply at one point.

The soup, Hester found, was lumpy, with chunks of vegetables in a colourless fluid – the stock pot had obviously been well diluted with water over several days, Hester thought. She could imagine forthright Polly, if she were here, saying, 'You need a knife and fork, not a spoon!' Van looked over the table at her, and raised his eyebrows expressively.

The meal was soon over: the girls, some small, some large, spilled out into the garden and their laughter drifted through the open windows. Mrs Long cleared the table, sighing over the wasted food. Hester would liked to have helped her with this task, for it had become obvious she was the sole domestic help in the house. The sunbeams showed up the cobwebs on the ceiling and the dust on the sideboard in the dining room.

'We'll take coffee in the other room,' Lucy said to the others.

After she rang the hand bell to summon the children back to lessons, and Dora led them into the classroom, Van and Hester went for their stroll around the grounds.

Once out of sight of the classroom windows, they linked arms and talked as they walked.

'You will have guessed,' he said wryly, 'Why I have been an infrequent visitor here. I find my sisters a little . . . overwhelming

121

at times. Of course, I am very fond of them both, but this has always seemed a houseful of women to me. Lucy was in control of everything, even in my mother's day – I wouldn't dream of interfering, but I suspect that the school doesn't make much money. Dora – she was the brilliant one of the three of us, but . . . as a nurse, you must have noticed that she is not *quite* right. . . .'

'I took to her immediately,' Hester replied, sidestepping his question.

Van opened the glasshouse door and they went inside among the profusion of plants. She asked: 'Has Dora always been the same?'

'Let's rest on this bench for a moment,' he said. He moved a few broken terracotta pots to one side. 'Mother didn't want any of us to marry, or leave home, but accepted that I had to go away to school, then Dartmouth naval training college and later, off to sea. Lucy played her role perfectly, but Dora was a rebel. She eloped before she was twenty with a chap from the village. I was home from school at the time, fifteen years old, but I was sent in pursuit on my bicycle after they were spotted walking to the station. I caught them up before the train arrived, but Dora refused to return with me.'

'You had to go home without her?'

'Yes. Mother told me then that I must always be responsible for my sisters. She said it was my duty as the only male in the family.'

'That wasn't fair!'

'Dora came back after several months. He hadn't married her, in fact, he already had a wife and two children. How they became acquainted, I have no idea to this day. Dora was pregnant, but Mother refused to acknowledge the fact. I was unaware of this, being away at school, but when I returned for the summer holidays, Dora was studying for her music grades and was, as she is now, unpredictable and sometimes moody. I only heard about the baby much later, when Dora told me, one day, when she couldn't stop crying. When I asked her why, she said, 'My baby was taken away.' Adopted I suppose, but neither Mother nor Lucy ever spoke of it. Are you shocked, Hester? I know how compassionate you are.'

'Poor Dora.'

'Don't think too harshly of my mother. She was a wonderful woman, who brought us up on her own and provided well for us, but she had a strict moral code. No doubt she thought she was protecting Dora from being ostracized in society. Women speak up for themselves now.'

Hester was silent, thinking of Edie, and how the hospital Sister had reacted surprisingly to her news. Poor Dora, indeed.

'It's too warm in here,' she said eventually. 'We are supposed to be walking, you know.'

Later, when Van needed a further rest, rather than sunning themselves, they sat in the shade of a willow tree, the branches of which hung over to their side, from the adjoining meadow where two horses and a donkey grazed. The goat was pulling at his chain, and Hester smiled at the thought that if Granny Garter had been with them, she would have been sniffing her smelling salts, for there was a distinct whiff in the air.

He obviously thought the smile was directed at him. 'Nice and private here. I always felt the ward Sister was watching us together, in the hospital.'

'She was only following the rules,' Hester retorted. 'She cares about her nurses.'

'I was hardly capable of seducing any one of you,' he said ruefully.

'Was it what your mother said to you – didn't you ever want to be married?'

'The thought had crossed my mind... I have to say that there have been one or two ladies in my life, though not recently, and I admit I believed I was past all that, until. . . .' He took her hands in his, turned them palm up, then back again, as if inspecting them. 'Well-scrubbed.'

She said: 'What do you expect from a nurse? Or from a former laundry maid?'

'I – don't understand.'

'That's what I was, before I bettered myself! I'm not ashamed of it, either – I had to work hard especially after my father lost his leg. I expect Arthur has told you about my family, and our home. I'm proud of where I come from, because the people I love most live there.'

'Hester, don't tell me you think I am a snob? That's hurtful.'

His reproachful look made her regret her outburst. 'I'm sorry.'

'So am I. I thought you'd guessed that I was attracted to you. I didn't want to say anything, though, until after I found employment in another field. There is also the fact that I am much older than you and no longer as able bodied as I was. It would not be fair of me to make any promises or expect any from you, when my future is uncertain.

'Lucy wants me to stay on here; she says I don't need to work because I have a small, private income, and the house was left to me by my mother, with the proviso, of course, that my sisters can stay here for their lifetime. It is not my wish to retire at forty-two! This is their house and rightly so. Do you agree with my sentiments?'

'Oh, Van, I do.'

'Perhaps I should ask you how you feel,' he said. 'Have I misinterpreted your concern for me?'

He was still holding her hands, and now she leaned impulsively towards him and kissed him on his cheek. 'No,' she whispered.

'Is that the best you can do?' he teased 'Would you like me to show you?'

'I'm your nurse – remember. This is not the time, or place to get carried away. But, I *do* care for you. '

'Here you are!' Dora came upon them suddenly. 'I've been looking everywhere. Don't worry, I won't say anything to Lucy. There are some ripe strawberries in the hothouse, shall we go and pick them for tea?'

That night, when Hester looked in on Van to enquire if there was anything he needed, he grinned. 'A goodnight hug, if you're willing?'

She turned the light low first, while she considered his request. When she bent over him to brush his cheek with her lips again, he deliberately kissed her full on the mouth. He stroked back her hair, his fingers gently caressed the nape of her neck. Nothing more. After a few moments, she resolutely pulled away. 'Goodnight, Van.' She was shaking, as if she'd received a shock. It was her first real kiss, after all. Certainly not his, she thought wryly.

She went through the connecting door, which she locked on her side. It wasn't that she thought he might come to her, it was more that she wasn't sure she could trust herself. . . .

Eighteen

Hester didn't let her hair down again, and she wore her uniform on the following two days. On her final morning in Surbiton, she watched as Van managed to descend the stairs without help. It was a laborious process, but she had to be sure he could achieve this before she left.

'No more hazardous than going below deck in wild weather,' he said cheerfully.

It was Saturday, so Dora offered to accompany her to the station. Hester said, more confidently than she felt, that she would be all right travelling on the train by herself. She promised to catch a cab to the hospital after she arrived in London.

'Tuck this in your bag,' Lucy said, passing her an envelope. 'No, do take it, I promised to pay your expenses. '

'I will be on hand,' Dora said cheerfully, 'to help Nicholas if necessary – I've learned from watching you.'

Hester and Van did not have the chance to say goodbye privately. Maybe, she thought, it was just as well. He had made his intentions clear already.

They shook hands. 'Thank you for all you have done for me, Hester,' he said. They were both aware that Lucy was watching them keenly. He added: 'I hope to say hello when I come to the hospital in a few weeks' time to see the consultant. Have a good journey!'

'The cab's here!' Dora had been looking out for it, in the drive. 'I gave the driver your bag, Hester. You'd better hurry, you have to get your ticket at the station, remember.'

'You must visit us here again sometime,' Lucy said affably. 'Well, goodbye, and thank you for looking after your patient so well. It is much appreciated.'

Once in the cab, Hester couldn't help dabbing her eyes with her handkerchief. Why had he not said he would write and tell her how he was getting on? That omission hurt.

Dora patted her arm, whispered to her: 'I know how you must be feeling, Hester. He couldn't say anything in front of Lucy. . . . She hopes it will be the three of us together again. Oh, she took to you, I can tell, but she is like Mother in that respect. Please don't cry. I – had a disappointment once – did Van tell you I ran away years ago?'

'Yes,' Hester admitted, 'but he didn't condemn you for it.'

'Lucy never mentions it. I know it would help if we could talk about that time, and I could explain that I very soon knew I'd made a mistake, but she has been a good sister to me, and I'm grateful for that.'

They were entering the station forecourt. The cabbie hailed a porter to carry Hester's bag, and then waited for Dora to return after seeing Hester on to the train.

'I'll write to you, if I may, I knew we'd be friends, the moment we met – I do hope my brother doesn't break your heart,' Dora said as she stepped down on to the platform. 'Close the window, you don't want a smut in your eye.' She waved, as the train rumbled away.

There were two other passengers in her compartment, but they were already engrossed in their newspapers. Hester sat back; she would count the stops anxiously until she reached her destination.

She'd suddenly realized she missed her own sister, when Dora had been so friendly. Her visits home had not coincided with Polly's for ages. I should have written to her, kept in touch, she thought. I must see her soon. I'll go to Brixton the next day I am off duty.

Hester reported back to Sister at the hospital and was told that she was being transferred to the women's ward. 'I think you need a change,' Sister told her.

'Will Edie be with me?'

'Nurse Brown will stay where she is, as she is leaving the hospital in six weeks' time. She is marrying Alfred Hodge then. We will miss her.' Sister paused. 'I hope you have no romantic notions, Nurse Stainsby? We do not want to lose you, too.'

'No, Sister, not at this moment.' She managed to smile.

'I'm relieved to hear it. I wish you all the best in your new duties, you are an excellent nurse.'

Hester didn't meet up with Edie until supper time. 'Did it all go smoothly?' Edie asked, as they sat down to steak and kidney pudding.

'Yes, it did. How are you feeling now, Edie – up to all this food?'

'I'm still sick most mornings, but by this time I'm really hungry!'

'So am I. I imagined those who live in big houses had kedgeree for breakfast, and several courses after that, but the Van der Linde family have gruel to set them up for the day!'

'Well, I can see you're not going to tell me anything,' Edie said.

'It's not that, Edie, there's nothing to tell. How about you?'

'I'm to be wed the eleventh of July. The Henley Regatta day, so two important events, eh? My mother's come round to the idea, but my father don't want to know. Your dear pa is giving me away, and Big Peg is in charge of the food – we're going back to your place for that. I want you and Polly to be my attendants, with my little sister Floss. Granny Garter's offered to make the dresses.'

'I'd be honoured to be your bridesmaid. Who' s best man?'

'Harry, of course – he appointed himself!'

'Alf's always seemed to be part of our family, but I'm so glad he'll be with you now, and before you know it—'

'Shush! Sister told me not to say anything about *that*.'

*

Hester and Edie walked to Alf's house from the hospital, and Granny Garter and Polly arrived by cab first thing on Edie and Alf's wedding day. Edie's mother and sister came along a little later.

The ceremony was arranged for late morning, so Granny Garter had time to insert a gusset in Edie's green skirt, to accommodate her thickening waistline. 'It'll be covered up by your jacket, ' she hoped.

'If I can do the buttons up,' Edie said ruefully. She'd insisted that she didn't want to buy anything new. 'After all, I wouldn't be able to wear it again, would I?' Anyway, she was sentimental about the outfit she'd worn the first time she and Alf walked out together, and later, when she came to this house. She smiled happily at the thought. She was feeling much better, having worked through the first three months of her pregnancy; her skin was glowing and the extra weight suited her, though she guessed she wouldn't feel the same about this when she was nearer her time.

The womenfolk gathered together in the bedroom in Alf's house, apart from Granny Garter who'd gone next door after completing the emergency sewing, and was telling Big Peg what to do in the Stainsby house. The bridegroom, best man and lodger, who was to be the usher, wisely kept out of sight.

Floss was sitting on the much admired new bed, wearing a sulky expression, having been warned not to get in the way, or to 'muss up your new frock' by her mother, who looked very presentable herself in Hester's blue dress, which she'd washed and pressed for her, as well as replacing the lace collar. It was fortunate they were both small and slight, so no alterations had been needed. 'It looks so nice on you,' Hester whispered in her ear: 'Please keep it.' She hadn't worn the dress herself since she was with Van.

Hester glanced at Polly. She'll outshine us all, she thought, particularly me, even though she, young Floss and I are wearing identical muslin dresses with sashes. I couldn't say that the style

129

doesn't suit me now I'm over twenty. Still it was good of Granny to make them, the muslin was a market bargain, and Alf forked out the wherewithal.

Polly was in charge of hair and a little discreet face paint for those who needed it. Edie's little mother submitted to a touch of rouge on her face and to having her hair brushed through with a dash of eau de cologne then arranged in a more becoming knot.

'Here,' Polly said to the bride, 'a token from Granny Garter.'

Coyly, Edie positioned the ruffled garter above her knee. It was expected of her, but they all knew Alf had already seen much more of her than that. . . .

Hester tucked a spray of rosemary under the pleated ribbon of Edie's new hat which matched the colour of her costume. The hat was small, barely covered the crown of her head, and tilted at a jaunty angle. 'Rosemary for remembrance,' Hester remarked. The scent of it made Edie sneeze. 'Thanks,' she said, dabbing at her nose. 'I'll remember today all right.'

'Ain't goin' ter sit 'ere much longer,' Floss sighed ominously.

'Right,' Polly inspected them in turn. 'We're ready, I reckon.' She looked out of the window. 'Your carriage awaits, Edie. Fred's already aboard. The groom, best man and usher must already be at the church. The rest of us will walk down there now with Big Peg and Granny.'

The donkey cart, newly painted with the name R. PURKISS & SON, FISHMONGERS, was festooned with streamers, and the driver, Bobby, wore a well-brushed second-hand top hat. He helped the bride aboard; the neighbours and wedding party cheered as he called 'Giddup!' The donkey pricked up its ears and moved off at a steady pace.

'Bobby's come up in the world,' Hester observed as she and Polly linked arms with Granny to help her on her way, while Floss's mother and Big Peg held grimly on to the smallest brides-maid, already scuffing her new shoes.

'That's what marriage does for you,' Granny said. 'Makes or breaks you! Hope the bride don't pong of fish after her ride!'

*

Fred's pals at the market had planned a surprise, as they had for his wedding to Big Peg. *The Turneros*, complete with ice-cream cart, were also turners of the hurdy gurdy. They stood outside, respectfully to one side of the church gates, surrounded by well-wishers. The rousing music made the nervous bride smile and Fred to exclaim: 'What ho!'

The Turneros were now dispensing ice cream, very welcome on a hot day, and business was brisk. 'We'll save some for you, when you come out,' called Papa.

'Good luck,' Bobby said, doffing his hat, 'I'll wait out here if you don't mind, I ain't much of a one for churches.' He helped the bride down from her carriage, then Fred, with his crutches. Edie, reverting to her role as nurse, supported him as they walked to the church door.

'The rest of our party must already be inside,' Fred said.

Edie was reassured by Alf turning his ginger head to watch her progress down the aisle, somewhat halting with Fred doing his best to swing smoothly along beside her. She carried a little posy of mixed flowers, which she would hand to Floss when they reached the altar steps. The older bridesmaids were holding the smallest one in check until that moment.

The organist was here on this occasion, and the choir. The bell ringing had been somewhat eclipsed by the hurdy gurdy, but fortunately the ringers up in the belfry were not aware of it.

'We are gathered together, to celebrate the marriage of Edith Brown, spinster of this parish and Alfred Hodge, bachelor of this parish,' the vicar began.

The congregation leaned forward in their seats. Floss began to pick petals from the posy and received a poke in the ribs from her mother. The door at the rear of the church closed, and the usher tiptoed down the aisle to his seat. The best man fingered the ring in his breast pocket. The organist pulled out the stops for '*Love Divine, all loves excelling*,' and all sang their hearts out.

131

They emerged from the church to brilliant sunshine. The local photographer, with camera set up on its tripod, was about to duck his head under the cloth and to click the camera. First the bride and groom, then the entire wedding party posed for photographs. It was a shame the photographer missed out on the best picture of all – the happy couple in the donkey cart, enjoying their ice-creams. Bobby had to move off smartly, for he was going on to the market as usual, where Lin and his small son were waiting for him.

Back home, the guests sat out on chairs in the back garden and ate the dainty sandwiches, pork pies and cake handed round by the three girls in their demure muslin gowns with satin sashes.

Arthur caught Hester's attention, beckoned her to come over so he could confide: 'Van was sorry to miss you when he came up to the hospital for his check-up.'

'I know. Dora wrote to tell me that. He didn't bother to write himself,' she said flatly.

'Oh, don't think too badly of the old boy! He believes he has very little to offer you and it's best he stands back. . . . He wished me all the best if I wanted to woo you myself—'

'Oh, did he! Well, I've been aware you've had eyes for no-one other than my sister today!'

Arthur looked sheepish. 'I never thought I'd meet her, but she's been on my mind ever since I saw her singing one day at the market.'

'You'll get a chance to see her performing later on – the Poplar Penny Whistlers are planning a surprise for Edie and Alf.'

Fred, seated, with Puglet in his little weskit sitting on his lap and his twins standing either side of him, gave the signal. 'Blow!' The trio played a medley of tunes. When they paused, the call came: 'Ain't Polly goin' to sing?'

'Clear a space for the gal then,' Fred urged the company, knowing how she would end her solo.

The boy I love is up in the gallery
The boy I love is looking now at me,
There he is, can't you see, waving his handkerchief
As merry as a robin that sings on a tree.

Polly could see out of the corner of her eye that there was indeed a handsome young man waving a large white handkerchief in her direction. They'd been introduced earlier, of course, but she'd been puzzling since over where she had seen him before. In the market, she realized, when he cheered so loud at my cartwheel, I blushed all over!

'Well?' Fred whispered, 'They're all waiting, Poll.'

Polly not only performed her cartwheel, she hoisted her skirts and followed it by the splits. The scrubby grass was not the best place to do this, as she discovered. She dusted herself down with a grin.

The applause was deafening. Polly took a bow, then so did the Penny Whistlers. Puglet obliged with a sneeze and shake of his jowls.

'Who's for another cup of tea?' asked Big Peg. Everyone, it seemed.

'I'll help,' Hester offered. She saw Polly moving toward Arthur. The late afternoon sun haloed her bright hair. Oh, her sister was a star!

'Will you be next?' Big Peg gave Hester a hug in the kitchen before they began the tea brewing.

Hester shook her head. 'I'm wedded to my work, Peg dear,' but she sounded just a trifle wistful.

It was past midnight and Edie and Alf were alone at last, snuggled up together in their lovely feather bed. She tucked the now wilting sprig of rosemary under her pillow.

'Oh, Alf, what a wonderful day we've had,' she yawned.

'We're penniless now,' he joked. 'Well, not quite, eh? And we've so much to look forward to.'

Nineteen

It was time for the end-of-term concert and Lula had booked the large reception room in the town hall. Family and friends would naturally be present, but she also advertised the event in both *The Stage* magazine and the local paper. Lula had high hopes that influential folk connected with the theatre and yes, the music halls, would be looking for fresh talent and she was determined the girls should follow-up any offer. She was also angling for more pupils, preferably boarders, as the Cole sisters were ready for their debut, and their mother had intimated she would ask for a refund of this past term's fees if they were not selected by a theatre manager soon.

Lula's niece Mira insisted that Polly needed more tuition in elocution and singing if she were to join a repertory company. Polly had other ideas, which she'd confided only to Laura, who'd already appeared in the chorus in the spectacular local pantomime, *Sinbad and the Great Bird* last Christmas. Laura reported ruefully that Belli's Troupe of Performing Sea Lions, were the biggest attraction. 'They can do back flips too – and I can't swallow a fish in one gulp!'

Polly thought that Granny Garter might disapprove, when she discovered her plans, even though Granny herself was established as wardrobe mistress, with a permanent home there. Polly was eager to become a working girl once more. *She* had her sights set on the music halls. She knew that would disappoint Mira, but she was a Poplar Penny Whistler at heart.

*

Lula's pupils were ready for their graduation show. The four boarders had the advantage of extra practice sessions after the day girls went home. Each evening Emmy sat at the piano and stoically played the set music, with many repeats; whenever Lula shrieked, 'Stop! That's not good enough – you must get that right!' the dancers gamely obliged.

Mira was there to listen to the singing: she clapped her hands over her ears, looking pained at any forced notes. Polly was chosen to recite a Shakespearean sonnet and received a brief nod of approval. Mira had taught her well. However, Polly enjoyed more the comical, rather than the dramatic, sketches which came between what Granny Garter called 'the warbling' and the dancing.

This year Lula was taking a gamble. 'Who would like to provide a surprise act of their own, as a finale to the show? A chance to show what you are capable of, without being told what to do?'

Polly's hand shot up. 'I would – if I can work with Laura.'

'Laura? Are you agreeable?' Lula asked.

Laura grinned. 'Yes. We could be the Garter Girls!'

'You'll need to work hard, practice by yourselves. There is plenty of floor space in the kitchen when Carlos and his wife retire upstairs. He can shift the table back for you. You won't be disturbed there. You can start tomorrow. Right! That's enough for now. Goodnight.' Lula swept out, followed by the faithful Emmy.

'I hope you've got some bright ideas,' Laura said to Polly.

'My head's full of 'em,' Polly assured her cheerfully.

'What about costumes? Granny Garter's got enough to do—'

'That's no problem. I've everything we need, you'll see.'

It was an early evening show, to accommodate those travelling to Brixton from further afield. The dress rehearsal was held in the afternoon, and timed precisely. There was a small stage, with new electric spotlights, replacing the old gas-lit ones, and much safer than limelight, which was still a feature of the picture houses.

There were red velvet curtains, and a crowded dressing room at the rear.

Screens unfolded into entrance and exit wings at either side of the stage. Most props were minimal, often cardboard cut-outs, painted by the students, but no backcloths.

Polly and Laura's secret was well-kept, though they had to explain to Lula that they had borrowed their large, anonymous prop, covered by sheeting, from a friend, and please would she tell the girls not to investigate and spoil the surprise? This item had been delivered shortly after their arrival at the venue by Bobby Purkiss, in his donkey cart: 'Always willing to oblige', as he said. He and his wife Lin had been given free tickets to the show, in return.

Lula organized a team to put out the chairs. Carlos and his wife had come along to sell programmes at the door, and to provide refreshments in the interval – there was no licence for alcohol.

All the seats were occupied by five-thirty. The lights were dimmed and the curtains were drawn back for the first performance. Lula, in a black satin robe with sequins scattered on the bodice and skirt, together with a matching turban, came front-stage to announce: 'Welcome to you all! Please put your hands together for the Military Parade!' She nodded at the faithful Emmy, also, in black, with a multi-coloured shawl round her shoulders. As the pianist played, the 'soldiers', in red jackets with gold braiding, plumed hats and white knee breeches, marched on stage in their shiny black boots, and formed a line, standing to attention. Each dancer was linked to her neighbour, with a hand placed firmly on her shoulder. At commands from Lula, the line of dancers rotated round in a snake-like movement, then turned to high-kick in unison, to enthusiastic applause.

Each act followed swiftly, literally on the heels of the one before. The Cole sisters sang a soulful duet, looking demure, which they certainly were not, in short dresses with old fashioned pantaloons. Polly, in a black wig and extravagant makeup, thrilled the audience with her interpretation of Lady Macbeth's 'Out damned spot!' This was a late substitution for the sonnet, when Polly had insisted that this was something that shouldn't really be recited by a girl: 'Shakespeare's writing from a male point of view,' she pointed out. Mira wiped her eyes, in the wings: her protégée had risen to the occasion. Then Laura danced a lively polka with a taller girl. Laura was more comfortable in the male role, with a willowy partner and the unusual pairing was a comical success. The music set the audience's feet tapping. They sang along with the dancers: '*You can see me dance the Polka – you can see me cover the ground. . . .*' When Laura's partner sank into a graceful curtsey at the end of the dance, Laura bowed, and then slapped her thigh in unconscious imitation of a principal boy in pantomime. 'Encore!' came a chorus of male voices from the audience, led by Bobby and Harry. Alf was restrained by a warning pinch on the arm from Edie, and Fred was shushed by Big Peg, who nevertheless, was smiling, as she was enjoying every moment of her evening out. Laura's mother had let her down as usual and not put in an appearance, so the Stainsby lot had adopted her for the evening as one of them.

There was a sketch, which involved the entire cast of ten girls, prior to the interval. This is where Emmy really came into her own; improvising with atmospheric accompaniment. Recently, not altogether with Lula's approval, she'd played the piano at the new cinema when the hired pianist was too inebriated to perform one Saturday evening. This was the ideal medium for her, interpreting the silent pictures.

The title of the musical sketch was *Oh! Mr Porter*, yet another of Miss Marie Lloyd's favourites.

A sign on a stand proclaimed 'The Station'. Another sign indicated 'Platform 2'. A cardboard facade of a railway carriage was transported on stage by the passengers who were glimpsed through the 'open' windows. These were the backing singers.

As the music began, a diminutive porter, Laura again, with a bristling moustache and oversize cap, wheeled on a trunk, followed by Polly, wearing a huge hat and white-gloved hands which she waved to good effect. She positioned herself in front of the painted carriage door, and addressed the porter thus in song:

Oh! Mr Porter
Lately I spent a week
With my old Aunt Brown;
Came up to see the wond'rous sights
Of old London Town;
Just a week I had of it
All round the place we'd roam
Wasn't I sorry on the day
I had to go back home?
Worried about with packing
I arrived late at the station
Dropped my hat-box in the mud
The things all fell about;
Got my ticket, said 'Goodbye';
'Right Away!' the guard did cry
But I found the train was wrong
And shouted out:

(Chorus) sung by all:
Oh Mr Porter, what shall I do?
I want to go to Birmingham
And they're taking me on to Crewe;
Send me back to London
As quickly as you can
Oh! Mr Porter, what a silly girl I am. . . .

The porter twiddled his mustachios, then walked across the platform on his hands, losing his own hat in the process.

Polly came front stage and addressed the audience: 'Mrs duPont decided that the second verse is too risqué for us innocent girls, so why don't you all join the company in a rousing rendition of the chorus – you know the words, I'm sure!'

This brought the house down. The lights went up, and it was time for tea and shortcake biscuits.

The second half was as enjoyable as the first, except for the non-appearance of the Garter Girls, who were preparing for their big moment at the end of the show, with Granny Garter fussing round them, trying to find out what exactly they planned to do. The costumes worried her: 'Whatever do you want to wear them old togs for?'

'You'll find out shortly,' was all Polly would say. The secret prop was finally unveiled: a small, old-fashioned handcart, with trays of cockles, mussels and fat, pink shrimps. There was a neatly printed placard: GARTER GIRLS – FISHMONGERS.

'I wondered where that fishy smell was comin' from!' Granny gasped. 'And what a cheek – using my name!'

'Take it as a compliment, Granny,' Polly sauced her.

Lula was aware that the manager of the Empress, sitting in the front row, was peering at his gold hunter watch. It would soon be time for the curtain up in the music hall – so it was time to announce the final act, before he left the assembly rooms. . . .

'Now for our mystery item: the Garter Girls!'

The empty stage was revealed and a squeaking sound was heard from the wings. On came Laura, wheeling the cart which she displayed to the audience. 'Ain't got no oysters, but you only need a pin for the winkles, my dears.' She was dressed in a short skirt, which revealed wrinkled stockings and down-at-heel boots, with a top hat to add height, also borrowed from Bobby, and an apron tied twice round her tiny waist.

Polly appeared, also in shabby old clothes with a pudding basin hat clamped on her head. 'Can I stand beside yer, an' entertain the customers?' she asked Laura. 'I got just the tune ter suit yer.'

In the wings, Mira buried her face in her hands – all those hours of coaching Polly with her diction, and how swiftly she could revert to an exaggerated version of her speech, as it had been, when they first met. Had her efforts been for nothing?

139

From her pocket, Polly produced her penny whistle. 'Come on, ain't there one or two who can 'elp me aht? Stand up, let's see yer!'

Harry rose, to the surprise of his family, and held up his own penny whistle, then blew a tremulous note.

'Pa? You brought your's? You can stay sittin'!' his daughter called. She turned to Laura. 'They call us the Poplar Penny Whistlers dahn the market. Right, here we go – blow!'

Cockles and Mussels, Alive, Alive Oh!

The audience sang and clapped along with the tuneful whistling. Requests followed, including *When The Boat Comes In* and *My Bonnie Lies Over the Ocean*; the *Hornpipe*, performed by Laura, who pulled on invisible ropes with a will, then *Dashing Away with the Smoothing Iron*.

'You sounded as if you meant them last words,' Bobby whispered in Arthur's ear.

'I did,' he said. 'She stole my heart away, all right.' He was gazing at Polly, waiting for her to cartwheel across the stage. She obliged, of course, but Laura's irrepressible back flips had everyone cheering even louder. Laura had an admirer too, bashful young Harry. Lula was waiting for an approach too, and was not disappointed. When the crowd dispersed outside, saying what a jolly good show it had been, worthy of a professional airing, Lula was talking terms to the manager of the Empress. He wished to book the Garter Girls in the act he had just seen – the one improvised by themselves. A month's trial was agreed.

Mira shed more tears when she heard that. So did Granny Garter. It wasn't what they'd hoped for. Polly, though, was over the moon, as she hugged Laura: 'Music hall – I'd rather that, than a West End play!'

Fred and Big Peg were waiting to have a word with Polly. 'Alf's popped out to find a cab for the four of us – Hester's so sorry she couldn't get time off to come along, but sends her love. You was wonderful, both of you.'

'So were you, Pa – thank you – I do love you – you and Peg!'

'There's a couple of young gentlemen here,' Fred said, 'waiting their turn to ask you both out to supper. Pie and Mash, I reckon. You remember Arthur – and your brother Harry?'

'Who could forget *him*! We must get changed quick, Laura, and get permission from Lula to go out, I suppose.' Polly winked at Arthur. 'Come and help with the packing up backstage, why don't you?'

'Be back by ten o'clock,' Lula said firmly. 'If your father approves, so do I. By the way, your friend has taken the cart, but said we can have the fish for our supper – think what you're missing, eh?'

'Oh – pooh!' the girls said with feeling.

Fred's prediction proved right: the four young people walked to the nearest Pie and Eel shop, with its gleaming tiled walls, long counter, and fast service. The girls sat down at a table for four, surrounded by cheerful, noisy folk enjoying a cheap but nourishing meal, illuminated by bright electric light, which didn't allow for canoodling. Anyway, most of the patrons were middle-aged, or so it seemed to the girls.

Plenty of material here for more sketches, Polly thought, taking it all in and making mental notes. Laura was a trifle disappointed. 'I hoped we'd get taken to a posh place – the sort my mother goes to.'

'I expect Arthur's used to those, but Harry doesn't earn much, I know,' Polly told her.

'He's a good-looking fella, your Harry.'

'I can't get over that he's taller than me, now! He dresses smarter, now he's friends with a toff.' In fact, Harry was in borrowed togs – at Arthur's tactful suggestion.

Arthur placed a steaming pie, mash and mushy peas on a large plate before Polly, and slid into the seat beside her, after depositing his own dish. 'Eat up! You must be hungry after all your exertions!'

Harry followed with full plates for Laura and himself. 'All right if I sit by you?' he asked diffidently.

''Course it is! Thank you – what a treat,' she said, picking up her knife and fork and stabbing at the pie, which oozed thick gravy. 'My, this smells good, Harry.'

'We've got a booking at the Empress,' Polly said, through a mouthful of mash. 'We'll have to stay on with Mrs duPont, of course until we are in regular work – she's already told us we'll be paying for our keep in future!'

'Let's toast your success then,' Arthur lifted his mug of strong tea. 'But it'll be champagne in the years to come!'

Twenty

Hester was rushed off her feet in the women's ward, dealing with two bad cases of ulcerated legs. This was definitely not one of her favourite tasks, but she tackled such cases with her usual compassion and as gently as possible, for she knew the pain was excruciating. This morning she bandaged both patients' affected legs from the toes up, with gauze bandaging, avoiding the ulcerated areas which would be covered by the prescribed dressing. The gauze was then painted with a brush using a melted solution of oxide of zinc and gelatine and allowed to solidify, thus forming a good support. Then the whole was covered with ordinary bandaging to keep it clean. The relief shown by the patients was Hester's reward.

All this endeavour meant that she didn't find time to read the letter from Dora which had arrived in the morning post until lunch time. She pushed her plate to one side. She'd lost her appetite after her onerous morning.

Dear Hester,

I'm sorry not to have written for some time, but you will see I have a good excuse! We have a new member of staff, our cousin, recently returned from many years in Africa where he taught in a mission school. His wife died two years ago in childbirth, when Maurice was still recovering from malaria. He was left with a seven year old daughter, Ida, to care for. The Missionary Society decided that for his health's sake, he should return to England. He is an excellent teacher and has taken over geography and religious studies in the school.

Now here is the exciting part! I thought that Maurice and Lucy were eminently suited and encouraged their friendship – however, Lucy confided to me that she did not wish to change her single status, that she liked things as they were. She said that Maurice was more interested in getting to know me better, which seemed unbelievable. However, he has now told me this himself, and actually asked me to marry him and to be a mother to young Ida! We are engaged! I know you will be happy for me. I think Lucy is relieved that someone else will be responsible for her sister! He is a calm and kind man, and knows of my past problems.

I wonder if you have heard from Nicholas since he returned to London? He recently became an assistant master at the Greenwich Royal Naval College, and has rooms close by. His old landlady has retired and gone to live with her daughter. I think Nicholas was glad to make his escape when Maurice arrived – we have a man about the house now who will take care of us! And another new pupil in Ida.

Maurice and I plan to be in your vicinity (Garford Street) shortly to visit the Scandinavian Sailors' Temperance Home – Maurice promised a young sailor he met on the voyage back here that he would look up his uncle, who is there. Could we meet, do you think? I think you would be interested in the good work they do at the Home. If you agree, please advise us when you next are off duty on a Saturday.

Love from Dora.

*

'Your lunch is getting cold, Miss,' the girl collecting the plates reminded her. Hester placed her knife and fork together. 'Sorry, I can't manage any more, but it was very nice.' The girl sighed, scraped the plate, then piled it on top of the others. She wasn't surprised, with that reek of carbolic from the nurse's hands.

Hester tucked the letter into her pocket. Six months, she thought, it is six months since I was with Van in Surbiton. He hasn't contacted me once since then. When did he come back to London? Arthur hasn't mentioned it, maybe Van told him not to do so. She felt hurt by his silence. If he had decided that nothing could come of their relationship, it would have been kinder of him to write and say so. She sighed inwardly. I wish I had never admitted I had feelings for him. Another thought struck her, it will be his birthday next week – it's a year since we met. I never got around to telling him that it's *my* birthday four days after his. . . . He'll be forty-three and me – I'm twenty years younger, and always will be. That's my first Saturday off in ages, the twenty-first, and it would be a birthday treat to have an outing with friends. . . .

She would write back to Dora that evening.

Hester had been waiting by the Sailors' Home, which was only a short walk from the hospital, for some fifteen minutes, in the mist and drizzle, thankful that she'd decided to add an extra layer of warmth by wearing her nurse's cape, before the cab drew up alongside. The cabbie gave a hand to Dora, as she stepped down, waving to her friend. A rather tubby little man with a muffler wound round his face against the damp, chill air, followed her. Hester moved forward to greet them, even as the cabbie assisted another passenger to alight, a tall, grey-haired man, who leaned on a silver-knobbed stick.

'I hope you don't mind,' Dora said with a mischievous smile, 'But it seemed a good ruse to get the pair of you together again!'

Van had a square parcel tucked under one arm. 'Dora told me it was a special day for you: it's good to see you, Hester.'

145

She was still speechless, so Dora said quickly, 'Let's go inside, it's too cold to stand out here, don't you agree? By the way, this is my fiancé Maurice – and Maurice, please allow me to introduce our friend Hester, whom you have heard so much about.'

'I am impressed by this place – the atmosphere is very good. It is obviously a real home as well as a refuge for the sailors who live here,' observed Maurice. With his muffler unwound, his smiling face was fully revealed, with twinkling eyes behind his wire-framed spectacles. 'I heard from my young acquaintance on board ship, that a missionary from the Swedish free church, Agnes Hedenstrom, began her work among the Scandinavian seamen in Whitechapel, nearly twenty years ago. When bigger premises were required, £1,200 was raised to buy the plot of land here from the dock company. This five-storey building was opened in 1888 by Prince Oscar of Sweden.'

They had been shown into a reception area after passing through the gatekeeper's lodge, where they studied a large map on one wall showing the extensive layout of the Home, while awaiting the arrival of the old sailor they had come to visit.

'Bagging store, boathouse and stables,' Dora pointed out.

Van was reading from an information booklet. 'Two hundred beds for ordinary seamen, with separate apartments for officers . . . dining room, reading, writing and lecture rooms . . . and, naturally a temperance bar – but a smoking room, I see.' He turned a couple of pages. 'This is interesting – there is temporary accommodation provided for Scandinavian emigrants en route to Australia. Back in 1891 I visited friends, at Blackwall Pier Emigrants Institute, which was overcrowded, but it must be much more pleasant here.'

An elderly man came into the room and introduced himself. 'I'm Axel, and I am very pleased to meet you all. I will take you to the coffee room, where we can sit and talk. I heard from my nephew that you were coming, but he did not know when.'

Hester found herself bringing up the rear with Van. She felt she must say something to him now. 'You are managing very well with just a stick now, that's good.'

'Thank you. It has been a long process of recovery, as my nurse told me it would be.'

She glanced at him to see if he was poking fun at her, but he looked solemn.

'As for the stick,' he told her, 'This was a birthday gift from my sisters – quite fashionable with men about town, I believe. I hope it impresses my students.'

'You enjoy your work, I hope?'

'Why are we being so formal?' he asked softly. 'Yes, as a matter of fact, I do. I feel fortunate to have secured such a post. I have already made some good friends, including one who I never expected to meet.' He passed her the parcel, 'Please put this in your bag. It is not quite new, being a book which I wanted to read myself, but I thought you might like it for your birthday. Ah, now you can tuck your arm in mine, if you wish; this is a never-ending corridor of closed doors, it seems.'

Hester took his arm because she could tell he was tiring.

'And whom are you nursing these days?'

'I won't say, no-one special, as all my patients are that when in my care. However, I still seem to be concentrating on gammy legs,' she said ruefully.

'Your defences are up, I can tell. Will you forgive me, Hester, for not keeping in touch with you? Though I could say the same of you.'

She changed the subject swiftly. 'Who wrote the book?'

'Joseph Conrad. I'm sure you have heard of this wonderful writer? He was a seaman himself for many years – English is not his first language, but his descriptive powers mean the reader is – *transported*, I think is the expression. This is the friend I spoke of just now: Conrad is researching a novel at the Greenwich College.'

'My father will want to borrow the book I know. What is the title?'

'*An Outcast of the Islands*,' he said. 'It is a sequel to *Almeyer's Folly* – have you read it?'

Hester shook her head. 'No, I thought he was a man's writer.'

'Well, I hope you will read this one, it is a powerful story. We seem to have arrived; we must catch the others up.'

She had something she wanted to say before they followed the rest of the party into a pleasant, light room furnished with sofas and occasional tables. 'Van – wait. I remembered it was your birthday just before mine. I – thought of you.'

'I know. I thought of you, too,' he said. 'I pictured you in that blue dress, the colour becomes you, the last time we were alone together—'

'I gave the dress away – I'm sorry I'm not wearing it today.'

They grouped round a table, and were brought cups of steaming coffee, a jug of milk and sugar lumps. Maurice did most of the talking to begin with, giving Axel news of his nephew and showing interest in the work done for the seamen, most of whom had been down on their luck when they were fortunate enough to come here.

'Some, like me,' Axel said, 'had bad problems with alcohol. When you have that reputation and what such excess can lead to, you are signed off by the ships' companies and abandoned to your fate. There is no chance of going home to the place where you came from. I love the sea, it was my life, I was born on a boat. I was a broken man: I had no one to lean on; I had never married. I was ashamed when my nephew found me like that. A lady from the mission told him about this place. He took me from the doss house and brought me here. They will help you, she told me, but you must help yourself, give up the drinking. It has been hard, but, as you say, I can look myself in the eye once more. I cannot work, but I do what I can to help others recover, too.'

'I was also born at sea, on a dark and stormy night,' Van repeated what he had told Hester the day they met, in the hospital after his accident. 'The event was recorded in the ship's log, my mother told me. Like you, I am resigned to being a landlubber now, Axel.'

'The sea is in your soul, as it is in mine,' Axel said, but he smiled. 'We must not be sad, I have new friends, and I count you all among those now, if you permit it?'

'Of course we do,' Dora put in.

After an hour, it was time for them to leave. They gave small gifts to Axel: a tin of tobacco for his pipe, a bag of sweet oranges, a bar of milk chocolate. They assured him they would keep in touch, and Maurice promised to write to Axel's nephew with the good news that his uncle was well and content with his lot.

Van insisted: 'You must all come back to my rooms for lunch – I made provision for this; I do my own cooking. It is cold as charity outside today – my place is warm and comfortable. You can take another cab from there to catch your train, later this afternoon, eh? ' He signalled to a cruising hansom. The horses snorted, their breath curling like smoke, and the four of them climbed thankfully aboard, glad to be crowded together, out of the cold.

Hester sat by Van. She was very aware that their knees were touching, that he'd slipped his arm casually around her shoulders. 'I really intended to go to see my family after our visit,' she told him.

'I will escort you there later, if that's all right?' he returned.

They drove slowly past the Royal Naval College, which even when viewed through murky weather was an imposing sight. Van obviously felt privileged to be a member of staff in such a place. 'I imagine you all know that this was originally the Greenwich Hospital designed by Sir Christopher Wren? It has a series of buildings in quadrangles, or courts, because it was considered important that the Queen's House, in the centre, should not be overshadowed. There are some magnificent features; including the Baroque Painted Hall in King William Court.'

'What do you actually teach there?' Hester asked him.

'I am involved in the course for marine engineering. This is now the Royal Navy's staff college.'

Van's rooms were on the ground floor of a vast Georgian double-fronted house. The caretaker, who greeted all visitors in the entrance hall, lived in the basement. Hester guessed that the tenants must be professional people to afford the spacious apartments.

Van was tidier than his sisters, she thought, seeing the neat piles of text books on the desk, the lack of clutter. It wasn't a homely place though the gas fire quickly warmed the atmosphere in the living room. Hester and Dora were invited to leave their outer garments in the bedroom, and tactfully directed to the bathroom. Maurice, who was used to fending for himself since he lost his wife, helped Van in the kitchen. 'D'you mind eating in here?' Van asked the women. 'We'll call you when the meal is ready – you two have a good chat until then.'

'Well – are you two back together, Hester?' Dora asked her.

'Oh, Dora – I really can't say . . . but thank you for arranging this meeting. I'm pleased for you and Maurice though!'

'I'm a little sad I'm too old to have a family now, but Ida is a dear child and I already have fond feelings for her. Just as I do for Maurice – it's not exactly the romance I once dreamed of, but I am fortunate to have this late chance of happiness.'

'Maurice must feel the same, too. Actually, I think he looks at you in a most romantic way!'

Dora blushed. 'I'm actually glad that, well, I'm not inexperienced, I'm not nervous of that side of marriage, you know. I hope you don't think I am being too frank?'

'I'm a nurse, remember! Van would need to convince me that he hasn't any doubts, before I give up my work.'

'Lunch is served!' came the call from the kitchen.

The men had been busy with a mixed grill of kidneys, sausages, bacon and scrambled eggs.

'Better than Mrs Long's watery soup – oh, and good fresh bread too – d'you mind if I start?' Dora cried.

'May we say grace first?' Maurice reminded her, but he smiled at her childish enthusiasm for simple, but appetizing food.

Hester wondered briefly what Big Peg would have said, when she took her first sips of red wine from an elegant glass. She felt rather guilty, having been to the Temperance Home earlier, when they heard Axel's sad story.

'Everything in moderation,' Maurice observed tolerantly, 'Wine is much mentioned in the Bible, after all.'

The afternoon seemed to fly by, and then it was time for Dora and Maurice to leave. After they had seen them into the cab, Van and Hester went back inside the house.

'I should go now, I think,' Hester said. 'You don't have to come with me, you know, it could be foggy later on.'

He opened the bedroom door and followed her in. She bent over the bed to retrieve her cape. 'Don't go just yet,' he murmured, 'I have something to ask you.' His arms encircled her waist from behind, and as she straightened up, the next thing she was aware of was that he was caressing the nape of her neck with his lips. For a few moments she couldn't move, or manage to say anything.

I mustn't turn round in his embrace, she told herself. She said faintly: 'Please don't. . . .'

'Why not? I wish to ask you to marry me, Hester. Can you forgive me for taking so long to make up my mind to do so?'

She turned then, put her hands firmly on his shoulders and pushed him away. 'Forgive you . . . I can't help myself, I do. But it's not that easy for me to explain why I am going to say 'no' to marrying you, when you must be aware I want to shout 'yes!''

'Let's sit down and talk, then.' He sank down on the side of the bed and patted the space beside him. 'Nothing more, I promise.' He continued: 'I never thought I would marry, Hester. The sea – well I guess it was my first and best love, until I met you. I admit that if I had been able to continue my naval career, which I left at my mother's behest when she was at the end of her life, I wouldn't be asking you to marry me now. I'm being honest, and I'm sorry if it's hurtful. But it is important that you know that I love you, and would be honoured if you would agree to be my wife. The college preference is for tutors to be married, too.'

That final sentence was unfortunate and roused Hester to unexpected wrath. 'Is that the real reason why you are proposing?

You knew how I felt about you, Van, but you wouldn't commit yourself before. Don't you see you are being unfair to me? I love my work – why should there be one rule for men and another for women? The college may prefer to employ married men, but the hospital believes the opposite – nurses must give up their posts on marriage! I am not prepared to sacrifice my career for someone who would never have given up the sea for me! I would like you to call a cab for me now, please. My family will be wondering where I am.'

He made no attempt to detain her, to talk her round. 'If that is what you have decided, Hester, I must accept it. Let me help you into your cape, and do put on your gloves, it is even more raw outside now.'

They were both aware this could be the end of the affair.

Twenty-one

December, 1896

Edie was feeling restless. 'You look weary,' Alf said when he kissed her goodbye early in the morning as he was about to leave for work. 'Mind you rest up as much as you can. I ain't sure what time I'll be in tonight, we've got a busy day ahead – ferrying back and forth to the old Dreadnought with emergency supplies as well as patients. We'll be bringing back those well enough to go home for Christmas, too. That's only ten days away. The river could ice over if this weather continues.'

The fire was already burning brightly in the living room, but Edie preferred to sit in the easy chair by the stove in the kitchen where she could keep an eye on her breakfast porridge in the pot. She felt frustrated that Alf had risen even earlier than usual to do most of the chores. She wasn't used to all this fussing and attention, she thought. Something was pushed through the letter box and fell with a gentle plop on the mat. The early post had arrived – a solitary card by the look of it. Edie lumbered to her feet, next thing she knew, she tripped on the rag rug and lay sprawled on the kitchen floor. She lay there, feeling foolish, wondering if she could manage to pull herself up on something, maybe the table leg, when she experienced a sudden, uncontrollable sensation. 'My waters have broken . . .' she said aloud, although there was no-one to hear.

She became aware of niggling pains, first, in her lower back, then shifting gradually round to her front. She tried to look upwards at the clock, ticking noisily away on a shelf. A voice which she didn't recognize as her own, exclaimed: 'This can't be true. I must have knocked myself out for a bit. The baby isn't due for another five weeks. . . . I know what Big Peg felt like the day she fell over in the laundry – she couldn't get up, either.'

Edie attempted to roll over, hoping to scramble up on to her knees: it was impossible.

Next door, having seen Harry and Arthur off to work, Big Peg was about to leave for the coffee shop, when she noticed a scrap of paper by the door. She picked it up and read:

Please Peg, will you kindly look in on Edie before you go to work? She don't look too good to me. Thanks, Alf.

'Fred,' Peg called, 'Hurry up!'

'I thought you said I wasn't to go with you today, the roads being slippery,' he said, swinging into the kitchen on his crutches.

'Get your jacket on! We're going next door. Note from Alf sayin' Edie ain't too well. I shan't go to work if she needs me, Winnie'll understand.'

'What d'you want me for?' he asked. 'Women's talk, eh?'

'Maybe. But I got a funny feeling about this. . . . You're an old hand at babies – you seen it all before, I ain't. You can give your opinion.'

'Blimey,' he said, 'You must be worried! Come on then. gal.'

Fortunately, Alf had left the back door unlocked, but it was a shock to see Edie lying on the floor, with her wet skirts rucked up. She was clutching at her abdomen and groaning.

'How are we going to lift her up?' Peg asked Fred. She'd picked up a postcard from the front door mat, but this was no time to show it to Edie. She placed it on the table for Alf to see.

He shifted the pot off the stove. 'Porridge is burnt. Kettle's boiling, looks to be pretty full. We can't lift her, not without help, and as I recall, best not to move her – looks like the baby is well on its way.'

Peg knelt beside Edie, trying to comfort her. 'Can you get me that cushion out of the chair, for her head? We need a blanket too, she's shaking – her teeth are rattling.'

Fred had spotted a pile of newspapers in a corner. 'Try and pack 'em under her, Peg. It's a messy business. There's towels hanging on the airer, get them down, they'll come in handy. I'll find a rug – should be one in the living room, on the sofa. Then I'll go out in the street and see if anyone's about who can fetch the midwife.'

A lad was coming towards him on a bicycle. Fred recognized him, a young dock worker who was obviously late for work. The bicycle wobbled to a stop as Fred stood in the middle of the road, waving frantically.

''Ere, I got no time to chat   I'll get the sack if I don't get on.'

'Sorry. mate, but Alf's missus is in bad trouble, needs help—'

'If y'want me ter go for the midwife, that's me gran, and she's out on a job a'ready. Anyway, she ain't up to it when things go wrong.'

Fred was not surprised at the blunt admission – hardly any of the local midwives were trained, but the majority did their best for mother and baby. His Bess had ended up in hospital with the twins, and there had been a few miscarriages thereafter.

Fred fumbled in his pocket. He brought out the shilling Harry had given him as usual last Friday when he was paid. Harry meant his dad to have a beer or two down the pub now and then, but Fred usually spent it at the coffee shop these days. 'Here,' he gave the coin to the boy. 'Call at the hospital and tell 'em to send an ambulance – say it's Nurse Brown-what-was and to be as quick as they can.'

The boy sped off on his bicycle. He didn't say he'd do it, so Fred just had to trust that he would.

'Help'll be here soon,' Fred told Big Peg. She nodded – silently indicating a spreading red stain on the newspaper protruding from under Edie, whose face was now completely drained of colour.

'Not good,' Fred mouthed to Peg. 'Not *before* the baby

comes. . . . Nuthin' more happenin'?'

She shook her head this time. 'Not that I can see. Oh, Fred, just suppose—'

'Don't, Peg. Talk to her, keep her with us, that's all I know.'

Hester had recently come off night-duty. She was about to undress, go to bed for a few hours, when she became aware that someone was knocking on her door. A probationary nurse from her ward called out:

'Nurse Stainsby – are you awake? Sister sent me to tell you that the ambulance has been called to your friend Edie, and they need a nurse to go along.'

'I'm coming,' she said instantly, reaching for her cape.

Within half an hour, Edie was in the operating theatre, where the surgeon and staff were preparing for an emergency caesarean section.

Hester begged to be allowed to stay, to assist, but was gently refused.

'You can help perhaps, to contact her husband, or her mother?'

'What shall I tell them?'

'We know that the problem is *placenta praevia*, that the outlook could be dire for both mother and baby. There is some hope, as the cervix is only partially covered. We could wait for a normal birth, but with the heavy bleeding, time is of the essence. Put this in simple terms to the relatives, try not to alarm them.' Hester was ushered from the theatre by the Sister who imparted this information. 'You must pray for your friend now,' she said gently, 'and for us. This is a last resort.'

Fred and Big Peg had made their way to the hospital, and after waiting outside in the cold, were relieved to see Hester emerge.

'Come to the coffee shop with us, Winnie will see we are not disturbed. Then we can decide what's best to do,' Peg said.

The coffee warmed them up and lifted Hester's fatigue. She told them, 'The hospital will do all they can.'

'The baby – is it. . . ?' Peg ventured.

'About to be born.' Hester hesitated. 'It may . . . be too small to survive, but . . . I once looked after a baby as early as that, and he came through. You did well to call the ambulance, it was the right thing to do.'

'That was your dear pa,' Peg said, through sudden tears.

'Can we let Alf know? Pa, could you see Harry in the dock's office – he'll know how to do it.'

'The ferry will be back later and more patients will be taken on – after some come off: that's the time to catch Alf. I'll go,' Fred said.

'You'll need *me* with you,' Peg said protectively. 'Hester, are you up to going round to Edie's mum, on your own?'

'I can catch up on my sleep later,' Hester drained her cup. 'Fortunately, I have tonight off. We can't see Edie, it will be close relatives only – until things improve. We'll meet up later at the hospital. Go inside this time, eh?'

'Oh dear Gawd, 'elp us!' Mrs Brown clutched at Hester. 'My poor Edie! I can't come – young Floss is ill with a fever, and I guess it'll go through the lot of 'em. That's why I ain't been to see 'er lately.'

'You won't be allowed to see Edie anyway, I'm afraid, if Floss is suffering from something infectious,' Hester said gently. 'Would you like me to take a look at her?'

'Ain't you afraid of catchin' somethin''?''

'Nurses seem able to resist most things. I don't suppose,' Hester said, aware of the answer, 'you've called the doctor?'

'Can't even afford to join his club.'

Hester followed Mrs Brown up the rickety staircase to the bedroom Floss shared with three older sisters. She was all too aware of a fetid smell, even before the door was pushed open. The one small window was shut, but curtainless. Despite this, there was little natural light. The double bed was obviously shared by the bigger girls; Floss lay in a truckle bed, with old coats piled on top for extra warmth. There was an uncovered chamber pot beside her bed which needed emptying.

'Perhaps you could see to that,' Hester suggested, 'While I examine Floss.' I should have come prepared, she thought fleetingly, but then, I wasn't to know what was happening *here*.

She was glad that she had left her cape downstairs, but she wished she had an apron to cover her clothes.

Mrs Brown must have read her thoughts. She went to a pile of torn-up sheeting on the one chair. ' 'ave to keep changin' 'er bed. Tuck this long piece rahnd you.'

'I shall need more light: can you fetch a candle please?'

Hester knew immediately what was wrong with the patient. Floss's face was bright red with a tell-tale rash, which had already extended from the neck down to her whole body, especially prominent on the chest and abdomen, and in the creases of her arms and legs. The tell-tale scaling of the skin had begun, which meant that Floss was three to four days into the infection.

The child didn't speak, but gave sighing breaths of protest as she was examined. Hester covered her with a sheet and one worn blanket. 'She has all the symptoms of scarlet fever. Did it start with a bad throat?'

'Gawd 'elp us, it did. Them coats is to keep 'er warm.'

'She needs to cool down, she's burning up with fever. Where are the other girls?'

'At school,' Mrs Brown admitted.

'And the boys?'

'Dahn the docks, with their farver.'

'I will have to notify the hospital – they may wish to take her into the isolation ward. First, we must soak some more of the sheeting in carbolic and hang over the door. It is probably too late, but the girls should sleep elsewhere. Once the scaling of the skin becomes worse, the particles – dust – will carry infection in the air. In the hospital, patients with this condition are oiled all over, which helps.'

'Ain't got no carbolic.'

'I'll get you some,' Hester said. 'You wring a cloth out in cold water and hold to her head. I'll go to the hospital now and report this, and find out how poor Edie is. I'll be back as soon as I can.'

'The baby's come,' Peg greeted Hester. 'Fred stayed with Harry, to meet Alf off the ferry around noon.'

'What is it? The baby – and is Edie—' Hester felt near breaking point after her traumatic morning.

'Sit down, dearie. Too early to say if the little scrap'll pull through. It's a girl, that's all I know. Sister says they're doing all they can. Edie – well, it's touch and go, poor gal. Her mother not come with you?'

'She's got plenty of trouble of her own. Floss is very ill, scarlet fever, I believe. I have to report it to the office here now. She might have to be brought in to the hospital, as well.'

'I'll stay here until Alf arrives. He'll need some support, poor lad. Fred will go home later with Harry. He'll get supper for the boys, and see to Puglet, who must be wondering where we are. They've offered me a bite to eat in the nurses' dining room. What about you?'

'I'm not hungry . . . honestly. I'm usually still asleep at this time when I've been on night duty,' Hester said. 'Well, as long as you're all right, I'll be off. Tell Alf I'm thinking of him, and Edie and the baby.'

It was after one o'clock before Hester, in trepidation, knocked on the shabby front door of the Browns' cottage. She carried a rush basket of provisions, hastily bought at the nearest shop: milk, bread, eggs, margarine, soap, a scrubbing brush, and oranges. Well-wrapped was a bottle of carbolic. In her handbag were rubber gloves, a face mask and a protective apron, together with a pack of swabs.

It was some time before her knock was answered. One look at Mrs Brown and Hester knew instinctively what had happened in her absence. 'She's gone, Hester, she had some sort of a fit and then—'

Hester put her bags down, put her arms round this small woman who had been through so much in her forty-odd years. 'Floss is at rest now, do you want me to see to things for you?'

'Edie, my Edie – how is she?' Mrs Brown said instead of answering the question.

'Edie is recovering,' Hester hoped fervently this was true. 'You have a little granddaughter – that's all I can tell you.' She wouldn't say the words they had both often heard: *As one leaves, another comes into the world.*

'Yes, go to Floss now. I – can't bring meself to do it.' Mrs Brown hesitated, then added: 'I want her to wear her bridesmaid's dress, she looked so pretty in that.'

'Take the basket, the contents are for you. I'll need hot water, will you see to that?' Hester wouldn't say it now, but the house would have to be fumigated, the rest of the family quarantined. They must keep busy, despite the sadness of the occasion.

Alf sat by the bed, in the cubicle to which his wife had been taken, some time after the baby was born and swiftly removed by a waiting nurse. Edie's condition demanded that she have priority treatment.

He saw that the foot of the bed was raised, but the only part of Edie that was visible was her pale face against the white pillow. She was conscious at last, but had mercifully been oblivious during the operation due to chloroform being dripped on to a pad on the frame covering her nose and mouth. Her eyes flickered open and then shut continually. He wasn't sure if she was aware that he had been there since late afternoon.

A nurse came in, motioned him to step outside for a few moments. 'I have to give the patient another saline injection – she has lost a lot of blood.' This, which had been explained to him earlier, was an infusion into a vein. 'Blood taken from a relative by syringe, and then injected into the patient, is not a usual practice, because the mortality rate is too high,' he'd been told. It was hard for Alf to take all this in.

When he returned, the nurse handed him a soft bristle hair-brush. 'Brush her hair, just the front and sides, very gently – this massage is good after such a massive shock. I will be back in ten minutes.'

As Alf bent over Edie and with trembling hands began this task, Edie spoke for the first time. 'Is – the baby here?'

'Oh, my dear girl, she is being cared for in the nursery. She is too small for you to hold until you are stronger.'

'I'm sorry, Alf,' she murmured, 'To be so much trouble.'

'It's not your fault,' he insisted. He put the brush down. 'They asked, Edie, if we have a name for the baby – they say she should be baptised. . . .'

'Christina,' Edie whispered.

In the bleak midwinter, Alf thought. We sang that when we roasted chestnuts in the fire one Christmas. He recalled it was a poem written by Christina Rossetti. 'It's a good name,' he said now, to Edie.

Harry went next door to collect the newspaper on which Edie had lain, to burn it before Alf returned. Peg said he wouldn't want to be reminded of what had happened while he was not there. He saw the card on the table, written side upwards. It was addressed to himself – the postman had put it through the wrong door. He picked it up and read it.

Dear Harry and Arthur,

We are busy with rehearsals for pantomime, first perfor-mance on Boxing Day! We will get you tickets. We are in the group scenes as villagers. Guess what we will be singing? See you soon, we hope.

love from Polly and Laura

Harry put the card in his pocket. Polly would be upset if she knew that this card had caused Edie to trip up when she rushed to collect it. Better not mention it to Alf either, he thought.

Twenty-two

January 1897

Edie and her little Christina were not the only ones fighting for their lives: Hester was in the isolation ward having been struck down with scarlet fever. She was unaware that Edie had asked: 'Why hasn't Hester been in to see me? Did she tell my mother I am in hospital? I haven't heard from her, either. . . .' 'Hush. . . .' was all poor Alf could manage in reply.

Christmas came and went but there were no celebrations for their worried families. Arthur and Harry went to see their young ladies in the pantomime in Brixton, but were warned not to tell Polly and Granny Garter of the problems in Poplar. 'Let them enjoy their big night on stage,' Peg said. 'Hester would want that.'

Christina had survived her first two weeks of life, and was now able to take her nourishment from a wet nurse – a mother with a baby of her own. This gentle woman had endless patience with the baby, who at first seemed too sleepy to suckle. Those concerned with Edie's welfare had deemed that it would be stressful for Edie to attempt to feed the baby herself, so her tender breasts were bound tightly for some days, which added to her discomfort.

The hospital hoped that in a year or two they would have one of the new incubators, now being tried out in France, where they had been invented. In the meantime, they followed their usual practice of keeping premature babies warm in a small nursery where a well-guarded fire burned day and night. The babies were cleansed with olive oil and wrapped round with cotton wool instead of clothes. Like Hester with little Samuel when she was on the children's ward, each infant had its own nurse to care for, and to monitor it.

Christina was now over four pounds in weight, and would, it was hoped, soon be reunited with her mother for a short period each day.

Edie's progress was slower and her condition still gave cause for concern. She had no appetite for food, but the nurse who attended her every need, painstakingly spooned calves-foot jelly and beef broth into her mouth. It was painful for her to sit up, with the padding round her body, and the wound still throbbed. The weakness, she was aware from her training, was because she had lost so much blood. Rest was essential. The doctor had told her, in Alf's presence, that there might not be any more babies for them after Christina.

Did I really have a baby? She tried to suppress her fears. If I did, why can't I see her? Is she . . . normal? These were questions she could not bring herself to ask.

Edie was woken from one of her frequent cat-naps, when the nurse's voice said in her ear: 'Edie, you have a visitor – someone you will be really pleased to see.'

She was propped up with a pillow behind her, and a tiny, warm bundle was placed carefully in her arms. The nurse loosened the shawl round the baby's head. 'See, Edie, she takes after her father, with this mop of bright hair. What d'you think of your daughter?'

Edie asked the question at last: 'Is she all right?'

'Ten tiny fingers and ten tiny toes, she's all right, my dear. When she opens her eyes, you'll see they are blue. Her complexion is very red, but that will improve, about the time she should have been born.'

'When I asked Alf what she looked like, he said a bit like a boiled shrimp!' Edie said. She even managed a little giggle at the thought.

'He's a man, my dear,' Nurse smiled. 'He's longing to hold her,

I know, but we said you must be first.'

'When do you think we can take her home?'

'That depends more on your progress, than Christina's. So don't make a face when I bring you more delicious broth today, eh? Well, time's up, I'm afraid. Back to the nursery, Christina.'

'You are looking much happier today,' Alf told her. He called in nearly every evening to see her, before going home to his supper, which Big Peg insisted he had with 'our boys'.

'I cuddled our baby,' she said proudly. 'Alf – why hasn't Hester been to see me? I knew it would be more difficult for my mother to come, but Hester is on the spot here, after all.'

'I wanted to tell you – but I couldn't, 'til you turned the corner. No easy way to do it, Edie. Your mother has the children all at home, in case – in case they take the scarlet fever – little Floss was very ill.' He broke off, wiped his eyes and then continued unsteadily, 'Sadly, she passed away . . . it was her funeral yesterday. She . . . had a wonderful send-off, the neighbours collected enough money to pay for it. Your mum is being very brave, and your dad has made an oath not to touch a drop of drink again.'

Edie was sobbing silently. He wiped the tears as they welled from her eyes. He said: 'Edie, our baby will be a comfort to your family.'

'Hester?' she managed. 'What about Hester?'

'Hester caught the fever when she went to tell your mother what had happened to you. She helped them, and that was her reward. She can't come near you or the baby until she is well again. She was with you in the ambulance when you came to the hospital, Edie, before she visited your old home. She wouldn't want you to worry about her.'

'Has anyone told Mr Van der Linde?' she asked.

'Why should they? I heard Hester decided agin them bein' together. '

'Oh, Alf, I *know* she really loved him.'

'Well, he can't come near her now she's in isolation, can he? But I'll ask Arthur if he's said anything to him – he's not far away at Greenwich.'

'Thanks Alf, I hate to think of Hester pining away.' Her bottom lip trembled. 'Will you write to Mum – I know you can't go round there, because of me and the baby, but I want you to say I love her and I'll pray for them all, and dear Floss. Tell Mum, Christina will have Florence as her second name.'

'I will,' he said. 'You sound like your old self, Edie – determined. That's what I love so much about you.'

Hester, hallucinating with fever and pain in her joints, thought she was having a long nightmare. She was aware of nurses rustling past, of being lifted to have the sweat-soaked sheets removed and replaced with fresh, cool linen, of calling out but no-one seeming to hear her. Often the bed shook with her rigors, and she also endured incontinence, for she appeared to have no control over her bodily functions. She felt gentle fingers rubbing pungent eucalyptus oil into the sore, flaking places, and once she had been half aware that someone was cutting off her long hair. The short crop which remained, made it easier for the nurse to oil her scalp to hopefully prevent hair loss when the hair follicles inevitably became choked by the scaling of her skin. The peeling of her skin was worst on her extremities, another reason for the frequent changing of the bedclothes. Her ears were syringed with warm boracic lotion regularly and her tonsils inspected for signs of inflammation daily. There was still the possibility of complications from the illness, like Bright's Disease of the kidneys, long-term damage to the heart and rheumatism. She would need a period of convalescence before – if – she could return to nursing. . . .

In a lucid period, when she was being given a blanket bath, she asked: 'When can I have a proper bath?'

'Soon,' the nurse, an old friend from her probationary days, told her. 'When the scaling decreases. You will feel much easier then.'

'Has – anyone asked after me?'

'Indeed they have. One or other of your family calls in at the hospital every day. There is a bundle of letters for you, when you feel like reading again. Oh, and yesterday, a box of hot-house red roses was delivered. You know the rules – no flowers allowed on the ward, but they brighten up Reception.'

'Who sent those?'

'The card just said: *From an old friend*. I reckon you have a secret admirer, Hester!' The nurse patted her dry with a soft towel 'There, you'll do. Don't you want the good news about Edie now?'

'Of course I do! I was afraid to ask. . . .'

'She's progressing, slowly, of course, and it will be some weeks before she can go home. The baby is thriving, thanks to the wet nurse. She was baptized soon after she was born, her name is Christina. One of the nurses stood proxy for you as Godmother. Christina sees her mother every day, now.' The nurse put a cool hand on Hester's brow. 'No more talking, it's almost time for breakfast.' She hurried off to report the encouraging news to Sister that Hester had communicated properly for the first time in weeks.

In February, Alf wheeled his wife in a hospital chair along the corridors to the nursery to collect their precious bundle. Christina was dressed in the warm woollen jacket and leggings presented to her by the staff, with a hand knitted shawl made by Big Peg, ready to be wrapped around her before her parents took her home in the ambulance, for it was much too risky to walk out with such a small baby in inclement weather.

Edie was still very frail, and her clothes, like the baby's, swamped her thin frame. However, she was happy and excited to be going home at last. After thanking the nurses who'd been so devoted to their care, Alf lifted Edie into the ambulance. Then he took the baby from Matron's arms and handed her to her mother.

'Come back and see us soon!' was the cry, as the horses moved off and the wheels turned.

Upstairs, from a convalescent room window, Hester watched their departure wistfully. Soon, she hoped, it would be her turn.

'Nurse Stainsby, you have a visitor – ten minutes only,

remember.' Sister came up behind her, and put an arm round her shoulders. 'The rest of the patients are resting in the ward, so go into the day room, you will be undisturbed there.'

Pa or Big Peg, she thought, pleased – maybe even Polly, they've told her about my illness rather late in the day – she said in her letter that she'd come as soon as she could.

There was I, showing off my drawers on stage as usual, you should have heard the whistles! And there you were, all scarlet with the fever! Why wasn't I told? I love you, too!

She opened the, door and saw immediately who it was. 'Van. . . .' she said faintly. They stood apart, facing one another.

'Is it permitted to give you a hug?' he asked. 'Did you receive the roses?'

She moved towards him, conscious of her ruffled short hair, her pallor, now the rash had gone. She tightened the tie belt of her dressing gown. 'I'm not infectious any more,' she said. 'As for the roses, I was told how beautiful they were, and I guessed they were from you.'

'Are we friends again?'

'Of course we are,' she said. 'And yes, I'd like a hug. I've missed you.'

He drew her close, kissed the top of her head. 'I was devastated, Hester, when I heard how ill you were. It was so stupid, the way we parted the last time we met. I thought I'd never see you again.'

'I haven't changed my mind, you know, I can't give up my nursing just yet – I'm so sorry, Van.'

'I'll wait until you're ready to marry me – we'll have as long a courtship as you want, a proper one, this time.'

'Until you've got a long, grey beard?' she attempted a joke.

'I admit that, if we are to eventually have a family, I'd rather be this side of fifty!'

'Oh, I didn't mean I intended to make you wait *that* long...'

'No wedding discussions today, I promise, but I intend to see you whenever I can while you are at home,' he said firmly. 'My sisters send their best wishes: Dora was married last month to Maurice, by the way. She's an excellent example of how married bliss can change someone. . . .'

A discreet knock on the door made them jump. 'Time's up!'

'Give me a proper kiss,' Hester said, 'I'll be at home in the middle of next week, I hope.' She'd need to sit down, she thought, after he'd gone, for she felt all weak at the knees. Maybe it was because she was still recovering her strength, but actually it was a good feeling.

'I feel like a bride again,' Edie said artlessly, as her husband carried her effortlessly up the stairs to bed.

'I promised Sister I'd see that you rested up after your busy day,' he said, helping her take off the dressing gown and slippers, in which she'd travelled. Then he settled her in the big feather bed and she gave a blissful sigh: 'Oh it's so good to be in me own bed again!'

'Look, a nice fire in the grate. Have to keep you and the little 'un warm and cosy, eh? I'll bring the baby up when the wet nurse has finished feeding and changing her.'

'We're so lucky,' Edie said, 'that she agreed to carry on the job, here – are you sure we can afford five shillings a week?'

'Of course we can. Violet's pleased to help us because it means she can have her own baby with her all the time. I'll bring you up your supper later. Did you see the crib? Big Peg asked Granny Garter to make all the trimmings – don't it look splendid? Your mum will be round in a day or two, she's bearing up well, but she's missed you.'

'Give me a proper kiss,' she said, 'but Alf – we won't be able to, you know, for a while yet. . . .'

'I understand. All I care about, is how I can make up to you, all you've been through,' he said, before he kissed her, in a thoroughly satisfactory way.

Twenty-three

'Going out again – you need an early night now and then, my girl,' scolded Granny Garter. 'You've got a busy time ahead.'

'Don't you remember what it was like, being taken out by a young man?' Polly sauced her.

'Safety in numbers. Has Harry given up on young Laura?'

'Harry, Granny, is going to night school, to better himself. Laura's only sixteen – she's the one what needs a chaperone, not me. Me and Arthur, well, we're older.'

'Not more sensible! I oughter tell you a few facts—'

'Oh, Granny, I know 'em all! Don't worry about me, I ain't about to succumb to Arthur – not yet anyway.'

'I hope you're just teasing me, Polly.'

''Course I am, you silly old goose!' Polly seized her granny round the waist, and waltzed her around the bedroom her grandmother shared with Mira. She was sitting at her desk by the window with her back to them, but Polly could sense her disapproval. She knew that Mira felt she had let her down. It isn't fair, she thought, I'm young, and I love what I'm doing, appearing thrice weekly at the music hall. What will they say when I tell 'em I'm going to take up the offer to go touring on me own, as Laura's mum says she's too young for that?

'Not a pie and mash night,' Arthur said, when they walked arm in arm along the high street, pausing to look in the shop windows at all the displays – Bon Marché was a particular favourite. 'It's my birthday on Saturday, as I hope you are aware, and because you'll be on stage that night, it'll be a slap-up meal tonight. Ever been in a hotel?'

She shook her head. 'No – I'd have dressed up, if you told me. I wondered why you was wearing your best togs.'

'You always look beautiful, you're the smartest girl I know.'

'Oh, how many *do* you know?' she quizzed him.

'None of 'em count, except you.'

The hotel was not in the main thoroughfare, but along a side street with large houses very similar to the one in which Polly boarded with Lula. She studied the sign outside: HOTEL ELECTRA. 'Oh, this must be owned by a Greek family,' she decided.

Arthur enlightened her with a grin: 'Built around the same time as Electric Light Avenue, I reckon! Right,' he opened the main door with a flourish. 'After you, my lady.'

They trod carefully along the Turkish carpet and were ushered into the main dining room, which had only a few occupants at discreet little tables set between pillars, with red plush banquette seats, which could be curtained off, if privacy was required.

The waiter took their coats, Arthur's hat and umbrella, but Polly tucked her bag into a corner of the seat to keep an eye on it. She wore a cinnamon brown velvet skirt, tightly banded round the waist, and a coffee coloured satin blouse, with exaggerated puff sleeves, which accentuated her high, full bosom. Her hair hung in beguiling, hastily tonged ringlets. Her small hat, which matched her skirt, and the coat she'd discarded, sat at a rakish angle on top of her head.

Arthur gazed at her appreciatively. 'If you don't call what you're wearing tonight, dressing up – you can't have looked in the mirror!'

'I certainly did that,' she returned. 'I'm just like Granny Garter, I love fine clothes.' She noticed a gilt mirror on the wall and smiled at herself approvingly. The lights in the room had rose pink shades, which cast a flattering glow on everything – the fine damask table cloth, the sparkling glasses, the silver cutlery.

They studied the menu. 'What can you afford?' Polly asked,

frank as always.

'As I said, this is my birthday treat – My parents sent me a welcome cheque and what better way to spend it, than on a lovely girl like you?'

As they decided on the food, there was the sound of music in the background. 'A fiddler!' Polly exclaimed, pleased.

'He might prefer to be called a violinist – he will be serenading us over our meal, I hope you don't mind? I asked for him to play for us as this is a celebration. In more ways than one, I hope.'

'What do you mean?' she demanded, excited.

'You'll find out later,' he said.

They started the feast with oysters. 'I know what they say about these!' Polly teased. 'And I know how to eat 'em – Bobby down the market gave me one once and told me to tip my head back and swallow it quick – it wasn't as easy as he said, but I managed it. It didn't have the effect on me he hoped for – he wasn't married then, you know – but I was never interested in him.'

'I hope you feel differently about me,' Arthur said.

The roast duckling which followed, with braised mixed vegetables was superb. The waiter refilled their wine glasses, and the violinist, who wore a scarlet cummerbund and a matching cravat with his dinner jacket, stood a few feet from their table and played gipsy music. 'I said he was a fiddler!' Polly said rather too loudly. The wine was going to her head.

They could just about manage the ice-cream and whole peach in raspberry sauce, and when they had drunk the last of their wine, Arthur looked at his fob watch and announced: 'Now for another surprise.'

'It's after nine, and I have to be in by ten,' Polly gave a little hiccup. 'Pardon me!'

'Nonsense, you must stand up for yourself. You're nineteen years old now, and a more or less independent young woman. Or you will be, from next week, when you go on your travels.'

'Well, put a gal out of her misery, and tell her what you've got planned.'

'We are retiring to a small private room to enjoy our coffee,' he said.

'And what else d'you have in mind?'

'That depends on you entirely,' he told her. 'Look, the manager is signalling to us, to follow him, through that door.'

They went up a staircase, and Polly whispered to Arthur, 'Not to a bedroom, I hope. . . .' The first door they came to led into a small sitting room with a long couch, drawn up invitingly to a roaring fire. Awaiting them was a coffee jug, cups, cream and sugar bowls on a small table.

'I will come back in an hour, Sir, with your coats, as you requested,' the manager said, before disappearing smartly.

They drank their coffee, and each wondered who would make the first move. Arthur took her empty cup, and moved the table to one side.

'I shan't be offended if you don't want me to . . . make love to you, Polly, and despite what you may have heard, I don't make a habit of this. In fact, I've done my share of flirting, but never wanted to fully commit myself. I love you, Polly, and I want us to be always together, but I don't believe either of us want to marry just yet – we both have our ambitions regarding our careers. I know better than to get you pregnant, please believe that. How d'you feel about me? That's more important.'

'I love you Arthur, and we'd better get on with it, because we've been up here for quarter of an hour already,' she said. 'The oysters must have worked by this time!' She pulled off her boots, lay back on the cushions and closed her eyes.

Granny Garter had a fair idea of what her beloved Polly might be getting up to. I can't say anything, she thought, because my dear old Claude had his wicked way with me when I was only seventeen and Bess was the result. . . . I could never resist snuggling up to him in bed and inviting him to make love to me – I never wanted more children, but I soon learned a trick or two to get round that . . . I was a passionate young woman in those days, headstrong like Polly – ambitious like her, too. Maybe she's a touch snobbish like me, too, fancying an upper class type. Not that Claude was that, more quick-witted and good at making – though unfortunately also spending – money. Hester, now, she's much more prim and proper. I don't know about young Harry, but it's just as well, Laura's mother has demanded we watch out for her daughter's moral safety – *she* can talk, the trollop. . . .

Polly wound her arms round Arthur's neck, and demanded one last kiss. He fumbled with her buttons: 'Just in case we're disturbed. Oh, Poll, this is the most wonderful evening of my life, so far. Problem is, we won't be able to stop, now we've started, will we?'

'Who wants to?' she said softly, before their lips met.

Later, they walked home in a happy daze. 'I'll be waiting at the stage door on your last night here,' he told her. 'This will be our secret, won't it?'

'I promise,' she said. They paused at the Academy gate. 'Goodnight, darlin',' she said, 'I love you, never forget that.'

'And I love you, too,' he said.

Granny Garter popped her head round the door as she heard Polly tiptoeing up the stairs to bed. 'Had a good time, dear?' she asked.

'Yes, thank you, Granny.'

'Your hair's come out of curl. . . .'

'Not surprised. . . .'

'What did you have to eat?'

'I'm tired Granny. I'll tell you in the morning. . . .'

She looks all right, Granny thought, a bit flushed, I hope she ain't been drinking. . . .

Unexpectedly Polly added: 'I'm a woman now, Granny. You must know that. Goodnight.'

Mira was sitting at her end of the room, with a towel draped over her head, breathing in the vapour from a bowl of Friar's balsam, to 'clear her passages'. This was a nightly ritual, for she seemed to have a constant battle with catarrhal head colds and her voice was her biggest asset. Eventually, she emerged from her cocoon, red-faced from the heat, and called out to Granny Garter: 'Goodnight, Vicky,' before she climbed into her own bed. She tied the strings of her night cap firmly under her chin to prevent snoring, then settled down to silently say her prayers.

Vicky did not answer. Her eyes were closed, but she was not asleep. Claude, she thought, I still miss him. She stretched out a hand as if she thought she might contact a warm, breathing body beside her, but the space beside was empty, and the sheet was cold and clammy. Sighing, she placed her feet on to the stone hot water bottle for comfort.

Downstairs, a light clicked on in the practice room. Emmy lifted the lid of the piano. Lula had been in a bad mood all day, railing at her, saying that the debts were piling up, and that the Academy would be forced to close. What would happen to all the misfits here, then? Her fingers struck the keys, discordantly at first, then the music flowed, loud and majestically, resounding all round the house.

No-one came to remonstrate with the frustrated pianist – she might not hear the music she made, but it echoed in her mind.

Upstairs, Lula opened her silver cigarette case. The tumbler of whiskey brought to her by the devoted Carlos earlier had not yet had the effect she desired: sleep, oblivion.

Polly slept though the cacophony in the room she shared with Laura and two new girls. The latter pulled the covers over their heads – no doubt thinking, what sort of madhouse is this? Little Laura, of course, had heard it all before. Her face was tearstained because she was desolate that Polly was soon to leave her. A shaft of moonlight through the gap in the curtains, haloed her friend's head on the pillow. Polly's face was both beautiful and innocent.

Twenty-four

March, 1897

'Spend the afternoon with Edie,' Big Peg advised Hester. 'You'll be back at work before you know it, so make the most of your time off.'

'You make it sound as if I've been having a holiday, not convalescing – though I must say I've enjoyed being in the bosom of my family again,' Hester said. 'Which is just where Christina is at this moment, I reckon!'

She was right. Edie was comfortably seated in her nursing chair, the baby tucked securely inside the bodice of her blouse, with just her tiny face peeping out and that blaze of silky red hair on the crown of her head. The warmth of a mother's body, the close contact, was still considered the best way to nurture premature babies. The only drawback was their slipperiness due to oiling, rather than washing. 'All my blouses have grease spots,' Edie said wryly, 'Alf says I smell like a fried breakfast, not of carbolic, as I did during my hospital days.'

Hester bent over to give them both a kiss. 'She's looking stronger every time I see her, and so are you.'

'She is able to move much more freely now her binder has been removed. She had that on for six weeks! Though she has a nice flat navel as a result.'

'Alf is bearing up well it seems.'

'We don't see enough of him. He works extra hours when he

can, to pay for the wet nurse.' The corners of Edie's mouth turned down. She obviously wasn't happy that Alf had so little time at home.

'And how's *your* poor old tum? Is the wound less tender?'

Edie winced. 'It's healing, but still livid: I haven't let Alf see it yet.'

'Well, you should, I think. He knows how you suffered, and he did, too, because he thought he might lose you both.'

'We'll have a cup of tea when Violet comes to feed the baby, eh?' Edie changed the subject. 'When are you returning to the wards?'

'Next Monday. Light duties at first, but not on my old ward: another nurse took my place there, of course.'

'Have you seen Van lately?'

'We keep in touch by letter.' Hester paused, then confided: 'I've just written to ask him to come to tea on Sunday.'

'I don't suppose you'll get much time on your own. . . .'

'Perhaps it's just as well,' Hester said.

Harry borrowed the Joseph Conrad novel from Hester, on the recommendation of his pa. 'He's a chap what can make you smell the sea, Harry – it ain't all plain sailing.'

'I know that, Pa. But I aim to be a master mariner one day. I ain't in a rush like I was. Me studies come first.'

'Oh?' Fred's eyes had a roguish twinkle. 'Has your little dancer anything to do with it, as well?'

'I ain't seen her lately, as you know. She went with Arthur to the station to see Polly off for her first week on tour.'

'I trust Polly will be orl right on her own.'

'She can look after herself, she always could, Pa. Me – I'm the cautious one.'

'Well, mind you don't miss the boat!' Fred guffawed. Puglet sneezed in protest and turned round on his lap. Fred exclaimed: 'Watch out, old feller! You've torn me newspaper. I was just reading the h'article about gold bein' found in the Klondyke. . . . Canada, that sounds the place to go, don't it?

'Harry, we'd better practice a few new tunes, you and me, the Penny Whistlers'll be in demand during the Jubilee Celebrations in June! We'll make a bob or two, if not a golden guinea.'

'If I had a guinea, I know what I'd do with it,' Harry said wistfully. He thought, I might not be able to join Pa at the whistling, 'cos if I get a chance to sail away, I know I'll take it. . . .

Hester applied a little olive oil too, in her case, to her scalp to deal with the dry, scaly patches, and to add a shine to her bobbed hair, which had grown a couple of inches since her illness. Should she wear the new dress Granny Garter had made her, she wondered? She guessed that Peg had paid for this, knowing that Granny's time as wardrobe mistress for her friend Lula, was running out. She'd recognized the blue velvet: revamped from Granny's Sunday best of years ago, which she'd worn with a string of pearls. Oh well, I've got the silver chain and locket Ma wore on her wedding day, she thought.

'I reckon Granny'll be coming back here to live,' Peg said.

'Just as well, I'm back at work from tomorrow,' Hester said. 'Though I think poor Harry was looking forward to having his room back – he's too big for the box room now.'

'Well, we can't give Arthur notice – he's one of the family now.'

'What about Polly? It's her last week at Birmingham. Where will she go between engagements?'

'The Brixton house will be kept going with lodgers, Granny reckons. Mira will need to find a job, when the students leave. Poor woman's been under her aunt's thumb for far too long. It could be the making of her.'

'Edie and Alf have got a spare room.'

'That might suit Polly,' Peg said, brightening up.

'I was thinking of Granny Garter.'

'Now, you know she can't stand babies, Hester. But if she comes here I shall expect more of her than when she was here before. Did I hear a knock on the door? What time d'you expect Mr Van der Linde?' Peg took off her apron and threw it at Fred.

She missed, and it enveloped poor Puglet. 'You'd better go see if it's him, Hester.'

Van presented Hester with a bunch of snowdrops. 'I asked the cab driver to stop when I spotted a flower seller on a street corner. It's good to see you looking so well, Hester. Aren't you going to ask me in?'

'Oh dear – yes, of course! You look in good health too.' She led the way down to the basement kitchen. 'I must put these lovely flowers in water. Then we'll make a pot of tea and take it upstairs – you're early, you know, and caught us all on the hop—'

'Stop babbling,' he said, smiling, 'I called a cab instead of coming by bus, as I couldn't wait any longer to see you. Forget the kettle for five minutes and let me show you how much I've missed you. . . . I do like your blue dress – is it new?'

'Granny made it for me – she said I'd charm you in it!'

'She was right, you certainly do that. How long will it take you to grow your hair I wonder?'

'About a year, I should think. Why?'

'Well, that seems to be about the right length of time.'

'What for?'

'Before we get married, my darling.'

'Oh, *here* you are,' Big Peg appeared in the doorway, beaming to see them in a close embrace: 'Shall I leave you to it?'

'Please do.' Van kept his arm firmly round Hester's slim waist.

'We were about to make the tea,' Hester, blushing, told Peg.

'There's no hurry,' Peg said. 'You've got better things to do!'

Hester, to her surprise and delight, was reunited with a young friend on the Convalescent Ward. She didn't recognize the three-year old, who had been a tiny infant in her care when she became a fully trained nurse and was on the Children's Ward, for then he had been dark-haired as the new-born often are. Now, he had pale blond hair, cropped short, for Samuel, too, had been very ill with scarlet fever. Thanks to the nourishing food and care he'd received at the Coram, he appeared to have a good chance of recovering well. He was small for his age, but with an engaging personality.

Her role in this ward was as companion to eight children, to supervise their play and, with the older ones, reading and writing for a couple of hours each morning. There were still temperatures to take, bathing and meals to serve up, but five of these children were almost ready to return home, which was the most satisfying outcome of their time in hospital. The rest were impaired in health to varying degrees by the illness they had suffered. Samuel, Hester was aware, had a heart murmur. This could delay his departure.

Sometimes, Hester glimpsed an anxious parent looking through the glass panels in the doors, but they would put a finger to their lips and shake their heads, for they were not yet allowed contact with their offspring. She wished that Floss had been as fortunate; she regretted that she had been unable to do more for that poor child and her mother.

All the children rested on their beds after their midday meal. The curtains were drawn, and books were put aside. Hester moved quietly up and down the length of the ward from time to time, filling a tumbler with water when requested, or taking a child to the WC.

Samuel was usually awake when she paused by his cot bed. He made up little stories which he murmured aloud: he was an imaginative and intelligent child. Sometimes Hester caught a word or two – she smiled to herself, for he didn't talk of elves and fairies, but about exotic animals, which Hester told him could be seen in the Regents Park Zoo. This was an attraction he'd never visited, nor had she, but the photographs taken there of zebras, monkeys and elephants in the board books they looked at together, obviously impressed him.

'What's it called?' he asked her, then repeated the name of the animal after her. 'Why has it got a funny nose – a long tail – all them stripes?'

'The elephant giving rides to children was called Jumbo,' she said.

'*Jumbo*! That's a funny name. I like it.'

She wouldn't tell him that poor Jumbo had met an ignominious end in a collision with a locomotive. . . .

One morning when she went on duty, she discovered that Samuel was not in his bed. Sister explained that the small boy had been taken ill in the night with pains in his limbs. 'The doctor on duty was called. Samuel is under observation in the side ward. Doctor suspects this is rheumatism, the aftermath of scarlet fever. Hopefully, it is only a setback.'

Hester felt suddenly faint, and was forced to sit down on the chair by the empty bed. Sister called for a glass of water. She looked sympathetically at Hester. 'I know he is a favourite with you, because of your past connection with him—'

'I should have seen something was wrong!'

'My dear, none of us expected this. He is uncomplaining, but he may have been in some discomfort. These things happen, you know. Samuel is at this moment receiving treatment; the doctor suggested cold packing.'

Hester was well aware of the procedure for this. The patient was divested of any clothing, the mattress was protected by a mackintosh sheet, and he was placed carefully on a couple of blankets. A doubled-up wet sheet would be placed beneath him, and another sheet placed over him, then the blankets would be tightly folded over him. This cold packing would be in place for up to fifty minutes.

'I could have done that for him!' Hester exclaimed. She thought – Oh he *must* pull through!

'He is in good hands,' Sister mildly rebuked her. 'A word of advice, Nurse. I will repeat something you were told when you first became a probationer here. A nurse must be dedicated to the care of patients but she should not become too attached to them. You are aware of why this must be, of course. . . .'

'Yes, Sister, I am.'

'Now, if you are feeling better, your other patients need you.'

Hester was off-duty from Saturday afternoon until Sunday

evening. Van was waiting with a cab to take her to Greenwich to spend the rest of the day with him. She had hurriedly changed into the blue velvet dress because she knew he liked it. 'Soft to the touch,' he'd said daringly, when he'd embraced her the first time she wore it.

'You look solemn today, what's troubling you?' he asked.

'Samuel, the little boy I mentioned, is not too well. He's suffering from a bout of rheumatism. He's confined to bed again – just when he seemed to be so much better. I didn't like leaving him. . . .'

He took her gloved hand in his, squeezed it gently. 'He'll be well looked after. You sound more like his mother, than his nurse.'

She pulled her hand from his clasp. 'He's an orphan, his mother died when he was born. I can't help how I feel!'

'Of course, you can't,' he said soothingly. 'I'm glad to see that you have a strong maternal instinct – which I hope means you will be as anxious as me to start a family in due course.'

Her indignation evaporated immediately. 'You know I am. It's just that, well, I wish Samuel was *my* little boy. Will you promise me something?'

'If I can,' he smiled.

'When he's out of hospital, could we ask permission to take him out now and then? He'd love to go to the zoo, and so would I.'

'That sounds like a very good idea,' he said.

Later, they sat on the fireside rug and Van toasted muffins over the glowing coals in the grate. Hester spread the muffins thickly with butter, then they tucked napkins round their necks and enjoyed the treat, followed by cups of tea, from the pot Van placed on the trivet.

'Just like a picnic indoors!' Hester was thoroughly relaxed now.

Later, Van drew the curtains to shut out the wintry scene. 'It's officially spring, but not many signs of it yet.'

'My hair is a whole inch longer – that's a good sign, isn't it?'

'This chair will take two of us – come and sit with me and let me run my fingers through your locks,' he said softly.

'You know what that could lead to.'

'I know. I promise not to get too carried away.'

Some time elapsed before she reluctantly disengaged herself from his embrace. 'I was about to say – when you distracted me! – how do you feel about arranging the wedding after the Blackwall Tunnel opening in May?'

'What made you change your mind?'

'I don't know.' she said softly. But she did. She thought, it's how I felt when I saw little Christina snuggled between Edie's breasts; it's loving Samuel and wishing he was mine. It's knowing that Van is the right man for me, and the joy we will experience if we can have a family of our own. . . .

'Could you stay overnight?' he asked tentatively.

'I'd like to, but I *can't*,' she whispered. 'I know you will understand – I want the *first time* to be on our wedding night.'

Twenty-five

That same evening was Polly's swansong on stage in Birmingham. She had all the patter now to link the songs. Mira's coaching had, after all, been invaluable – she looked up, and sang to the gallery loud and clear. She had the toffs in the stalls rising from their seats with a roar of approval when she cartwheeled across the stage and showed off her trademark garter. 'Polly Garter, mistress of mischief and mirth,' the chairman with his pince-nez and oiled back hair, announced.

Polly wasn't yet aware that Arthur had travelled up to see her last appearance there, and to take her home, the following day, Sunday.

After the saucy songs, then a quick change of costume in the wings, Polly appeared in a crinoline ballgown, clutching a large ostrich feather fan, to render the most popular song of the day, *After the Ball was Over*, a tearjerker if ever there was one. The entire audience sang the chorus with her:

After the ball was over, after the break of morn –
After the dancers' leaving, after the stars are gone,
Many a heart is aching, if you could read them all –
Many the hopes that have vanished after the ball.

Polly waved the fan in acknowledgement of the cheers which greeted her bow. However, she was not quite finished yet, a stage hand handed her a penny whistle. As her pa had taught her, she raised it to her lips, and repeated the tune of the chorus. The audience erupted once again. One final cartwheel and the curtain came down.

'Polly, you're a star!' Arthur cried, when he burst into her dressing room without knocking.

'I knew you would come!' she said, flinging her arms round him.

'You've smothered me in cold cream and greasepaint,' he said.

'D'you mind?'

'Not at all – but we'll both need to clean our faces before we ask your landlady if she can find me a bed for the night.'

'If she can't oblige, you can share mine.'

'Polly – you're shameless,' he said.

'I know, but I'm honest, I say what I think. Before we go back to my digs, we'll have to celebrate with my friends here – they plan to take me out. You can come along, eh?'

'So this is to be my role in life – follow my leader!'

'D'you mind?' she demanded once again.

'I don't believe I do,' he said, feeling bemused.

The ball was far from over, as Arthur shortly discovered when he tagged along behind the motley crew of dancers, comic singers, a family balancing act, a pair of jugglers and a lone ventriloquist with his dummy in its bag, which 'piped up' from time to time. They jostled one and another to walk beside the star attraction, Polly Garter.

They piled into the nearest hostelry, with its beer-stained tables and a jovial bartender, who filled a row of tankards as he saw them come in. Before Polly could take one, Arthur managed to attract the bartender's attention and ordered a carafe of wine and two glasses.

'Find us a table for two,' he hissed in Polly's ear. She said loudly, 'Oh, we mustn't disappoint the girls and boys – they want me to entertain them here, this last time, as I am booked solid for the London halls when I get back to Brixton.'

'You're going to *sing*?'

'Of course I am!' she declared.

A damp cloth was flicked across a long table, and more chairs were brought over to accommodate the crowd.

The ventriloquist had a further talent – he could play the piano. He placed his beer on top of the instrument, cracked his knuckles and settled to his task.

There was a rhythmical thump of fists on the table – 'Up you go, Polly!' they cried. She was hoisted up by the jugglers and set down in the centre of the table.

'What d'yer want?' she asked in fair imitation of Marie Lloyd.

'*After the Ball!*' they shouted.

Polly wasn't in a crinoline dress now, but she lifted her skirts to display her neat ankles and sang her heart out. As she swayed, the beer swilled, and Arthur caught some coarse comments from the regulars propping up the bar.

When she finished singing, she held out her hand to Arthur to help her down. 'Drink your wine,' he said hoarsely, 'Then we'll leave. . . .'

'But they'll want an encore—' she protested.

'They can want all they like. I came a long way to see you, and this isn't what I had in mind. If you won't come, I shall leave by myself, and you won't see me again.'

'Arthur! You don't mean it, do you?'

'Yes I do. I reckon you think I'm jealous – well I am. I was proud of you on stage, but not here, among this boozy lot. What would your pa say, or Harry and Hester and Big Peg? Granny Garter would have a fit, fond though she is of you.'

Polly was actually smiling. 'Well, as you can see, my young man wants me all to himself! I'll say cheer-ho then, 'til we meet again, eh?'

'The only bed I can offer,' said the large landlady, suspiciously sniffing to ascertain if they had been drinking, 'is the sofa in Miss Garter's little sitting room.'

'That will suit me, thank you,' Arthur said gratefully. 'Is there any chance, I wonder of a sandwich – I haven't eaten since lunch time.'

'I've got a cold sausage if you'd like that, with bread and butter.'

'You must put that on my bill.'

The landlady snorted. 'That's my intention. I'll be up in a while.'

'Tea for two?' his charm was irresistible.

'That lot'll cost you a bob,' she said promptly, then bustled away to the kitchen.

'The sofa's not long enough, your feet'll hang over the end,' Polly giggled, when they were upstairs.

'You don't imagine I'm going to sleep on that, d'you?'

She giggled again. 'I've only got a single bed.'

'That'll do – we're two single people now, but I aim to change that shortly. When my contract finishes with the tunnel, what d'you say I become your manager – you need someone to keep the hordes at bay.'

'Are you actually asking me to *marry* you? I thought you said, it wasn't on the cards.'

'Well, after tonight, it definitely is. Where's that sausage sandwich, I'm starving!'

They sat opposite each other in the carriage, because they'd both wanted the window seat. Arthur smiled Polly. 'Compromise,' he observed, 'I can see what our life together will be like.'

'Changed your mind?' she retorted, not bothered whether the two men earnestly perusing their newspapers at the other end of the carriage were listening or not.

'After our reunion last night? Certainly not.'

'I haven't met your parents yet, they might not like me.'

'I'm sure they will. You could say they are liberal minded.'

'What if I joined them suffragettes? I believe women should be equal to men.'

'So do I. Most of 'em are, anyway,' he said wryly, 'even if they haven't got a vote.'

'Are you goin' to ask me pa's permission?'

'Naturally. Though it seems to me you usually get what you want. You've been an independent young lady for some time, now.'

They had left the great city and the tall smoking chimneys behind and were now travelling past row upon row of railway houses, with long, narrow gardens. Soon they would be looking out on fields, ploughed into furrows – a rural scene.

Polly had been silent for some time, turning the pages of a magazine. She leaned over, tapped his knee. 'Don't go to sleep!'

'I was just thinking,' he said. 'You'll find things have changed when you get back to Lula's. She has had to give up the business. You knew that might happen, eh? Well, you'll be a lodger there now, like I am at your pa's house.'

'Why didn't anyone write and tell me?' she demanded.

'They thought it best to let you enjoy your success on tour.'

'Laura – where is she?'

'All the students have departed, Laura included. She's gone home to her mother. Harry's not allowed to call on her there.'

'Poor Laura – and poor Harry!'

'He says he's going to join the Merchant Navy – continue his studies by post. I hope he stays around long enough to be our Best Man, though Granny Garter's already decided to move into his room.'

'When do you plan to tie me down?'

'Don't put it like that! Soon as we can arrange it.'

'Where'll we live?'

'I imagine my parents will help us out in that respect.'

'And I'll soon be able to keep you in the style to which you are accustomed!' she reminded him.

Arthur had no answer to that.

Twenty-six

April, 1897

'A wedding!' Fred exclaimed. Prodded by Big Peg, he added quickly: 'Good news, of course, just unexpected.'

They were having a family get-together to celebrate Granny Garter's return to the fold – some of them didn't exactly view it like that, but Granny was holding court and boasting about the flood of orders she'd already received from old customers, eager to look their best on the occasion of the old Queen's Diamond Jubilee procession, when they intended to swell the loyal crowds.

Harry was leaving the next day to join the crew of a coaster about to leave the dock, so this was an opportunity for them to wish him well, too. Polly had arrived earlier with Arthur in tow and Van met and escorted Hester from the hospital. Peg had made a celebration cake, so Puglet sneaked under the table; he disapproved of all the upheaval and talking, but was mollified by the crumbs.

Polly's announcement took them all by surprise. After the initial stunned silence, the congratulations began. Van squeezed Hester's hand. 'It's not fair,' she whispered, 'Just when we were about to tell them about *our* plans. . . .'

Polly cried, 'Oh, I just knew you'd be pleased for us! It'll be a quiet wedding, because Arthur says we don't want all my stage admirers filling up the church!'

'Have you picked a date?' Hester tried to sound casual.

'Well, we wanted it to be before Harry went off to be a mariner, but he's beat us to it – so now we've to find another best man.'

'Van? How about you?' Arthur cut in.

He managed a smile. 'You've upstaged Hester and me! We were about to announce our own wedding plans for the end of June.'

'That's the time *we* had in mind,' Polly said. 'But I reckon we should let Hester be a bride first, because she's getting on a bit.'

'Thank you for that,' Hester said drily.

Van said quickly: 'Surely it's me who is "getting on a bit", as Polly says, not Hester. Arthur, despite me being second choice for you, I'll be delighted to be your best man, if you'll be mine. We were thinking of Saturday, twenty-sixth June, by the way.'

'Well then, we'll settle for a fortnight later, early on in the morning, for Polly will likely have two performances that day.'

'No honeymoon?' Granny Garter said archly.

Polly had the answer. 'The show must go on!'

Arthur said gallantly, 'Every day will be a honeymoon with Polly.'

'Two more celebration cakes,' sighed Big Peg. 'They take so long to make, and get eat too quick.'

'Two bridal outfits . . .' exulted Granny Garter.

'You'll have to keep my share of wedding cake, if I'm away on a trip,' said Harry.

'Bearing exotic gifts from afar, I hope,' Polly grinned.

'Blimey, Sis, I'm only going up the Thames to far flung places like Norfolk for hay, and Ipswich for grain – but it's a start, ain't it? I'll find out if I can get me sea legs before I go to Australia!'

Hester stood up. 'If you don't mind, Van, I would like to pop next door to give the good news to Edie and Alf.'

'Of course I don't. I ought to discuss a few things with Fred.'

'Give me a hug first, dearie,' Big Peg requested. When Hester obliged, she murmured, 'I feel like the mother of the bride – brides! – even though I ain't.'

Edie was delighted to see her, and excited by her friend's news.

'It's a pity Christina's too small to be a bridesmaid.' The baby was now propped up in a Moses basket, watching them and gurgling.

'Oh, when did she learn to do that?' Hester marvelled.

'That's not all she can do: she cries and lets you know when she's hungry now! Violet says that's a very good sign. She sounded like a mewling kitten before.'

'Where's Alf?'

'In the wash house, seeing to the napkins. He only got back from the ferry a couple of hours ago, but insists he does the washing, until I'm stronger. How lucky I am, eh?' However she sounded wistful, trying to convince herself.

'Yes, you are! I can't imagine Van doing such chores.'

'Alf's the perfect husband and father,' Edie said proudly.

Hester found Alf at his task, poking the washing in the steaming copper, with the stick. 'Alf, still at it, I see. I wanted you to share in my good news – Van and I are getting married, just after the Grand Opening of the Tunnel! I haven't told them yet at the hospital, so you won't say anything to anyone there, will you? I hope you're pleased for us?'

He mopped his damp brow and gazed at her thoughtfully.

'Well, aren't you going to congratulate me, Alf ? Why are you looking so solemn?'

'I *am* pleased to hear the news,' he said. 'I had hopes once, of course, that you and me – but it was more on my side than yours, I know that. But marriage ain't a feather bed, though that helps . . . Edie and me, we never have time to ourselves, to really get used to one and t'other. It was three of us, from the start – we was parents before we knew it.'

'Oh, Alf, you wouldn't be without your lovely baby, would you?'

'O' course not. But now, Edie says we must wait, like, in case we fall with another too soon. We don't come together in our feather bed,' he stated baldly. 'We've only been married nine months. . . . It's not our first anniversary until July.'

'She might have been thinking that too. Things *will* get better,'

Hester said, trying to sound confident. 'She isn't over Christina's birth yet. Be patient.'

The next thing she knew, Alf was hugging her to him. 'Sometimes, you know, Hester, I wish it *had* been you.' He attempted to kiss her lips. He's been drinking she thought: this was not like Alf at all. She knew that half a pint of beer had been his limit on a Friday night in his single days.

Shocked, she pushed him forcefully away. 'No, Alf, you mustn't wish you'd married me! Be gentle with Edie, and tell her just how much you love and need her, because you *do*. She had a rough old drunk for a father, and then she found you, the love of her life. Don't let her down, don't tell her what you said to me. She needs your company *now*, leave the wash to soak. There are – surely – other ways you can express your love, and the rest will follow.' She hoped fervently she was right, thinking, what do I know about married life? I'm worried I won't be able to respond in that respect myself . . . perhaps Van feels the same.

'Forgive me, Hester,' he muttered hoarsely.

Then she hurried back next door, knowing that she would have to keep this encounter to herself.

Both couples left soon afterwards. Hester wanted an early night in her hospital room, for she was not back to her full strength, and she was on duty tomorrow. Arthur had arranged to take Polly to meet his parents on Sunday and to have lunch with them. Fortunately, Polly had no qualms, but he certainly felt nervous. What would they think of him marrying a music hall artiste, and changing his occupation so radically?

Polly was quite blasé about rail journeys now, having made several by herself. She smiled to herself, *Oh Mr Porter*, was obviously based on fact. You merely have to look helpless, and not only porters rush to your assistance, she thought complacently. Though perhaps this was what worried Arthur, eh?

The Hon. Giles Winwood and his wife Patricia had a country house in West Sussex. A gleaming Packard motor car with a uniformed chauffeur was awaiting their arrival at Worthing, for the Winwoods lived a few miles distant from the sea. Polly concealed her disappointment, for she'd been hoping to promenade along the front and perhaps dip her toes in the water.

'Tie your scarf over your hat,' advised Arthur, 'it's breezy today and the lanes are dusty.'

'I've been in a motor before,' she retorted. She wouldn't admit that it had been one of the new omnibuses, which she'd boarded in some trepidation.

They sat in the back seats, which were covered in sumptuous leather. They moved off smoothly enough, with much squeezing of the horn by the driver, to warn lesser vehicles to move out of their way.

They swept up a long, winding drive, bordered on both sides by masses of golden daffodils. The house was double-fronted, with ivy-covered walls and latticed windows. The door opened and Mrs Winwood came rushing out to greet them. Her hair was as blonde as Polly's, but in her case enhanced artificially. However, she was still an attractive woman, with a fresh complexion, and not yet out of her forties.

'I've heard so much about you Polly!' she cried. 'Come inside, and meet the family!'

'I thought you were an only child,' Polly said to Arthur, as they entered the hall.

'I am. Mother's family is her dogs – you'll see! I hope you like Pekinese?'

'I've never met one. Mostly old scruffy dogs our way but Puglet, of course, is in a class of his own.'

Invited to sit down on the sofa, Polly gingerly moved a Peke or two to make room, when one promptly jumped on her lap.

'Chu-chu approves of you!' Mrs Winwood beamed. 'We've just got time for a sherry before lunch.'

The Hon. Giles put in a brief appearance, explaining that he must change before he joined them. He wore a formal dark suit and waistcoat, and Polly glimpsed a gold Albert chain, linked to his pocket watch. He also had a monocle, which Polly had only seen before on rather dubious comic performers with bulbous red noses, on stage.

'Giles got talking to the rector after the morning service, as usual,' his wife said. 'I reminded him you were coming, but he's so forgetful since he retired – lives life at a snail's pace. Now tell me all about yourself, Polly – we know so little, and here you are, about to marry our son!'

Polly for once was lost for words; she mouthed 'Help!' to Arthur.

'Mother,' he said smoothly, 'You two have a lot in common. Mother was an actress too, when Father met her, Polly. He was a stage door Johnnie. She was appearing in a show in the West End.'

'Don't be a snob, Arthur, why don't you say I was in the chorus, and renowned for my high kicks,' his mother said.

'So am I,' Polly told her, 'my cartwheels are the talk of the town!'

'Good for you. We obviously do have much in common. Why don't you call me Patsy? All my friends do. Most of them date back to my childhood in Bow. Oh, is that the gong? Hinds, the chauffeur promised me he'd strike it at one o'clock precisely. You may escort us both to the dining room, Arthur, if you will. *Where* has your father got to?'

'I knew you two would like each other!' Arthur said happily.

Arthur had noted the lack of servants, apart from Hinds, who obviously nowadays doubled-up as the gardener, for they could see him out of uniform, through the French windows, pushing a lawn mower over long grass. 'Where are they all, Mother?' he inquired, pulling out the dining room chairs. He waited until they were seated, before he sat down opposite Polly at the table, which was laid with silver cutlery, finger bowls, and gleaming glasses, but not much food.

'Oh, dear, you might as well know now, as later. Your father, as I said, is not as astute as he was. He invested unwisely on the stock exchange. We're broke, dear boy, no other way to put it. We have tried to economize, but now we must sell the house, the car, and move into the lodge. Don't worry, we shall have a very modest income, and must learn to live within our means – easier for me, recalling hard times when I was a child, but hard for him. . . .

'Now Polly, would you like a piece of this chicken and ham pie? Baked by the rector's wife, in your honour – she was a cook before she married. The salad is fresh from the glasshouse: I made the dressing myself. Arthur, top up the sherry glasses, please. Good, here comes your father.'

Nothing more was mentioned over the meal, which was rounded off by a delicious syllabub of whipped cream and wine, about the Winwoods' straightened circumstances. After lunch, Patsy and Polly cleared the table and took the crocks to the kitchen. The sink was already full of washing up waiting to be done, but Patsy insisted: 'I have a woman coming in tomorrow to see to all this – shall we go for a walk in the grounds, with the doggies, while the men talk and smoke?' She took down a basket from a hook, while the Pekes lined up in anticipation by the back door, eager to chase Hinds off the grass. 'We must pick some of the daffs for you to take home with you.'

That evening in the train going back to London, Polly leaned her head on Arthur's shoulder. He was very quiet, she thought, wondering what his father had said to him. There had been no further talk of the wedding, by unspoken consent.

'I think they like me,' she ventured.

'Yes, I'm sure they do. What did you think of them?'

'I think your mother is the stronger one,' she said candidly. 'She will take the lead in their new life.'

'They won't, I expect you've realized, be able to help us after we are married,' he said.

'It doesn't matter. You can always move in with me at Lula's, or I will move in with you – I'm sure Pa and Peg wouldn't object. Mind you, Brixton would be better than Poplar for it's just a tupp'ny bus ride from all the London theatres!'

'I'll have to find another job. No more handouts from Father.'

'You can still be my manager as well! We'll manage.'

'You're a chip off the old block,' he said affectionately, 'ever optimistic. Well, it really will be a quiet wedding after all, but I can hardly wait.'

'Nor can I,' she said.

Twenty-Seven

Spring 1897

Hester decided to give the required month's notice to Matron right away, for she worried that she would not be up to more strenuous duties if she were transferred to a regular, busy ward. Van's sisters had also invited her for 'some good country air and relaxation' in Surrey for a week, before she joined Van at the Grand Opening of the Blackwall Tunnel in May, and shortly after that, of course there was their wedding.

'We shall be extremely sorry to lose you,' Matron said. 'You have proved to be a most reliable and dedicated nurse. However, you are, I am aware, not fully fit after your illness, so I think you have made a wise decision. In any case, your impending marriage is a cause for congratulation. You have served the hospital and your patients well, and will be missed by us all.'

'I shall miss all of you, too,' Hester said. 'This has been the most rewarding seven years of my life. Thank you for giving me the chance to prove myself.'

She shed a few tears when she told Van what Matron had said.

'You need a treat now,' he told her. 'On your next afternoon off, if I can rearrange my lectures at the College, why don't we take Samuel to the zoo? The Coram have approved us, so we only have to ask.'

'We'd have to push him in an invalid carriage – he still has pain in his legs if he walks far. It might help us along too!' she joked.

'We could take a picnic, he'd like that, wouldn't he?'

'Oh, Van, you always know how to make me smile, when I'm down!' she said.

'Samuel and I,' Van said thoughtfully 'are linked. We were both nursed by you, and we both adore you. Maybe—' he broke off.

'Maybe, what?' she asked.

'Just an idea I am mulling over. Let's get married first!' was all he would say.

Regents Park Zoo contained an amazing collection of animals belonging to the Zoological Society. The parkland surrounding it, with leafy paths close to the aviaries, had an added attraction: the Elephant Walk. Excited youngsters and even some adults, eagerly awaited their turn to ride aloft on these great, serene animals.

'*Jumbos*!' Samuel cried out in great excitement. Hester looked at Van, who was taking his turn at steering the wheelchair.

'Yes, Jumbos,' he repeated. 'Would you like to sit in one of those seats – they're called howdahs – and see the world from that height?'

Samuel nodded. 'Can I?'

'Of course you can.'

'Will you come with me, Nurse Hester?'

'If you promise to hold my hand!' she said.

Hester was the one who felt nervous; Samuel obviously had a good head for heights, she thought ruefully. She held on tight as they swayed from side to side with each ponderous step.

When the elephants returned to the waiting families, Samuel was lifted carefully down and placed in Van's outstretched arms. Van, hoisting him to his shoulder, walked him round to touch the elephant's trunk. 'Jumbo is very nice,' Samuel said. 'I like him. Do you like him, Mr Van?'

'I certainly do,' Van agreed. He put the child down: he needed his stick to support his own weak leg after all the unaccustomed exercise, and there was still a lot of walking ahead of them.

Hester, safely on the ground herself by now, watched them chatting, as she held on to the wheelchair handle. She had a lovely warm feeling inside. He likes Van too, she thought, and the feeling is obviously mutual. Van isn't rather old to be a father as he believes, he's natural and relaxed with little Samuel.

The zoo opened in the mornings at nine o'clock and closed at sunset. Hester, Van and Samuel had arrived there just before one and eaten their picnic before moving on to see the animals. Even for half a day, the experience was well worth the shilling admission for adults, with half-price for children.

Following their ride, they inspected the elephants' living quarters, which included a bathing pool. 'You are more likely to see them enjoying playing in the water in hot weather,' the keeper informed the crowd. 'They suck up water with their trunks, and hose themselves down.'

It was typical April weather – sunshine, and a few showers. They had an umbrella apiece, so didn't need to seek shelter. Feeding time saw them moving on to watch the pelicans grabbing and gulping down fish, then the otters, who ducked and dived for their share, emptied from a bucket into the pool.

It was time to visit the monkeys and apes – Samuel couldn't stop giggling as a long furry arm shot through the bars of the monkey cage, startling them all, and pulled a feather from a woman's hat, as she leaned over the barrier.

There were lions and tigers, some pacing endlessly, some gnawing fiercely on great meaty bones. The new lion house was kept warm and well ventilated, they were informed. The cages were much more roomy than the original ones, and there was a hefty safety barrier between them and the visitors – nothing was permitted to be thrust through the bars of the cages.

Samuel preferred the polar bears and grizzlies, though these were also labelled as DANGEROUS ANIMALS. Animals to wonder at were the tall giraffes, with their haughty expressions, huge rhinos, snoring alarmingly as they snoozed on piles of hay, and a hippo, with ugly warts on its hind feet.

'I wouldn't like to ride on him,' observed Samuel.

He and Hester were not so keen on the reptile house, but went round this uncomplainingly because Van was interested.

It was getting on for tea time, Samuel was due back at the orphanage by five. They hurried to the exit, at the first rumble of thunder, umbrellas raised.

They handed Samuel over to his house mother with five minutes to spare. 'Did you have a good time? What did you see?' she asked the little boy. He was out of the wheel chair now. He made them all laugh when he said, 'I saw monkeys there with *blue* bottoms!'

Hester and Van took a cab to his apartment. They were both tired from so much walking, but agreed that it had been well worth it.

'An evening by the fire, I reckon,' Van suggested. Hester stretched up to give him a long and lingering kiss on the lips. Her arms went round his neck; his arms clasped her waist tightly. 'You never cease to surprise me,' he murmured, even as they overbalanced, falling backwards onto the long sofa behind, dissolving into breathless laughter, as they lay there, still entwined.

'You're not too old at all,' Hester said dreamily.

'Too old for what?' he asked, as if he didn't know. He would respect her wishes, to go so far, but not all the way. . . .

'Why don't you have a double wedding?' Big Peg asked Polly, when she came over to see her parents, Granny Garter and Arthur, of course, on Sunday.

'I suppose we thought that Hester and Van would prefer separate occasions. Now, I realize it's a lot for you and Pa to arrange, and it will be more expensive to have two weddings. What do you think, Arthur?'

'I don't mind at all. They say they want a quiet wedding, too, and we haven't made any arrangements yet.'

'Get together soon, then,' suggested Fred.

Granny Garter was not so keen on the idea. 'You'll want matching gowns, I suppose – but I've already started on Hester's frock. It was meant to be a surprise for the rest of you, 'specially

Van, but he's insisted on paying for it.' She fixed her gimlet gaze on Arthur.

Flushing, Arthur said, 'Van, being older, is better off than me. I'll need to get a new job after the wedding.'

'I should have thought your parents—' Granny insisted.

'I suppose you'd better know – no easy way to say it – my parents are on their uppers; Father lost nearly everything on the stock exchange. I proposed to Polly before it happened, as I expected a generous settlement on our marriage—'

'I told him it didn't matter, we'd go ahead anyway,' Polly put in. She glared at Granny Garter. '*I'll* pay for my dress and all the trimmin's, Granny, you needn't worry.'

'Don't speak to me like that. It'll be my wedding present to you!'

'Thank you,' Arthur said quickly. 'Much appreciated I'm sure.'

'Have you thought yet where you might live after the wedding?' Big Peg asked tentatively. She and Fred had already discussed this and come to the conclusion that it wouldn't really be suitable for the young couple to share Arthur's room, especially as it was next door to Granny Garter's bedroom.

'She'd have a glass to the wall, listening in, no doubt,' Peg said to Fred, 'and criticizing their every move. Also, Polly's a late bird at nights, due to bein' on stage, and you've always been a worrier Fred, wondering if young Harry's been lured into a gambling den, which never was likely.'

'I like to know all are tucked up by ten o'clock,' Fred insisted.

Now, Polly had an answer pat. 'We might ask Lula if she's got a couple of rooms to rent – if not, we'll prob'ly look for a flat in Brixton – it's handy for getting to the West End, as you know.'

'That sounds right.' Peg tried not to show her relief.

'Well, if you don't mind, we'll go up to Arthur's room so we can discuss other plans in private.' Polly nudged Arthur, he rose and said politely, 'Please excuse us.'

'I suppose it's difficult for them to find a place to be on their own,' Big Peg said, after they'd gone upstairs.

'I can guess what for,' Granny Garter said grimly. She stabbed some pins in a pin cushion, to emphasise her point.

'Surely not. . . .' Peg was shocked by Granny's spitefulness. She must be jealous, she thought.

Polly didn't waste any time: Arthur locked the door, and when he turned round, she was already on the bed, inviting him to join her.

'They say what you've never had, you don't miss,' she whispered.

'Whoever *they* are, they're right,' he sighed. 'I feel guilty, though. . . .'

'I s'pose I do, too. Well, we won't have to worry about it soon.'

Big Peg was worried about Fred. He appeared to have lost weight recently, but he insisted there was nothing wrong. 'Got no pain apart from the usual twinges, and I'm used to that, old dear.'

'I want you to be fit to take them gals down the aisle.'

'Why shouldn't I be?' he replied.

He was already in bed, watching her brush out her hair, as he always did each night.

'Winnie said you drink a lot more coffee with the customers, nowadays.'

'I put a contribution in the pot, don't I?'

'I know, but you never used to have a thirst like that.'

'You'll be saying next, I got the old sugar diabetes.'

'Oh Fred, I never thought of that – but it seems *you* have,' she challenged him.

'Best not to know. Nuthin' can be done about that. My own pa had it. He suffered terrible boils on his neck, as I recall.'

'He passed away quite young, I know.'

'Well, it'll keep 'til after the weddings, Peg – I don't want to find out before then, so don't say no more about it,' Fred said firmly.

He was asleep within a few minutes, cradled in her arms, while she lay awake for what seemed like hours, tormented by her thoughts. How will I carry on, if I lose my dear Fred? I've been through that agony already with Thomas. I had to carry on and be cheerful, but I was young then. Fred and me, we believed we would go on together into old age. The house will empty of young people shortly; we have to accept that. I will miss them because they have become to me the family I always longed for. I shouldn't have to face being alone again.

In the morning they were shocked to discover that Puglet had passed away quietly some time during the night. Peg stroked him as he lay curled as if asleep in his box. He was wearing his Whistlers weskit, which had kept him warm all winter at nights, and somehow that seemed fitting. Peg shed tears for the little dog who had been instrumental in bringing her and Fred together.

She turned to comfort Fred and saw that he was crying too, which she knew he never had when he lost his leg.

Twenty-eight

First week in May, 1897

Hester was aware of a subtle change in Van's elder sister's attitude towards her. Van had returned to London, to the college after escorting her to Surbiton where he'd stayed over the weekend with the family. Lucy was able to spend time with Hester, while Dora taught alongside her husband. They got to know each other better and Hester felt that she was now on an equal footing with Lucy, as her sister-in-law to be.

In the early evening after school was out, the sisters, Hester, Maurice and Ida, his rather precocious child, would sit out in the garden and enjoy a welcome cup of tea. Ida didn't stay still for long, however, but roamed about bouncing a ball on a long piece of elastic. Hester was reminded of her own sister, when Ida tucked her skirts up in her bloomers, and when she thought none of the others was looking, turned a cartwheel or two, followed by several somersaults, forwards and backwards. Maurice caught a glimpse of this, and when he saw Hester smiling, he winked, which startled her, for it seemed not quite the thing for a missionary, retired or otherwise, to do.

'Children like to let off steam,' he observed.

'You make her sound like a kettle – or a train!' Hester said.

'What *are* you talking about?' Lucy followed their gaze and saw Ida attempting to walk on her hands. 'Ida!' she called, 'Go and change out of your school clothes, *immediately*!'

'You're her honorary aunt,' Dora reminded her. 'You must stop being her headmistress, when she's not in school.'

'Come, Hester, let's go for a stroll before dinner, eh? Let the parents discipline their child, if they are so inclined.'

Hester rose rather reluctantly, and she and Lucy walked along the path to the glasshouse, to inspect what was growing and in a month or two, might be edible. Once they were out of earshot, she thought, Lucy would no doubt have something to add to her previous comments to her sister. She was right.

'In my opinion, Hester, I think Dora is too ready to let Ida do what she likes. Maurice appears to encourage this.'

'Surely, it's a good thing that Ida has accepted her stepmother?'

'Like me, you have no children of your own – I am surprised at your attitude, Hester.'

'Van – Nicholas and I hope to have a family as soon as we can, after we are married.'

'You surprise me. He is not a junior master at the college, who would be expected to have small children – he has a senior position to keep up. He is marrying, in you, a professional woman, of which I heartily approve. Surely you could help him further his career by supporting him in that.'

'I would, of course!' Hester flared, 'But I will be twenty-five later this year, and I am ready to settle down and be a wife and mother. I'm sorry if that sounds hurtful, when you did not have the same chance.'

'I never wanted it! Especially after Dora's unfortunate experience, which I presume you know about?'

'Yes, I do. I don't condemn her for it, for she was very young at the time. She must have been sad to part with her baby.'

'She is making up for it now, by indulging that child!'

Hester's indignation evaporated. She said quietly: 'Let's not quarrel, Lucy. We must agree to differ. I am pleased we are becoming good friends – you have been a wise and kind sister to Van, and he appreciates that, you know.'

'You're right – I apologize. Nicholas is a very lucky man to have found such an admirable partner in life.'

'You were right, too, to persuade me to spend this week in the country, when I felt I should be busy with wedding plans. I'm full of energy now, thanks to you,' Hester said gratefully.

Van appeared again the following weekend to take her home. He didn't like to think of her travelling by herself. She was glad to see him but she felt a little piqued that he was sometimes over-protective. After all, she had been a free spirit for some years now.

When he fussed about helping her aboard the train, she thought, I assisted him, when we travelled here that first time. She didn't say that, because the family were gathered on the platform, waving them goodbye, and calling out: 'See you at the wedding!' to the interest of passengers already seated in their carriage.

Aware that their fellow travellers were listening in, Hester wasn't too pleased when Van remarked: 'One week to go before the big event – and two weeks, before we tie the knot. Will we be ready in time?'

They will be wondering, she thought, what event could possibly be bigger than a wedding!

The Blackwall Tunnel was officially opened by the corpulent Edward, Prince of Wales on Saturday, 22 May. There were still workmen about, and his first duty was to close the barrier, rather than open it. There were rousing cheers from the crowd along the route and the genial Prince waved a gloved hand from the royal carriage. Those in the know imparted the information that the tunnel was 4,410 feet long, that six hundred dwellings had been demolished to accommodate the long entrance tunnel before the section under the river, including the house reputed to be where Sir Walter Raleigh lived and smoked a pipe of tobacco – which was promptly doused with water by an alarmed servant. The tunnel they said, had several sharp bends, to prevent horses bolting once they saw daylight at the far end – motors of course, being a novelty still, were not taken into consideration. Though rumour had it that the bends avoided tunnelling through a Black Death burial site. Higher vehicles must keep to the left hand side, to avoid damaging the tunnel's inner lining. The fact that seven lives had been lost during its construction was not much mentioned.

Hester and Van, Polly and Arthur had an excellent view of all the dignitaries who were present. The Prince was very much a man of the people, and popular with the crowd. Arthur had good news to impart, he had been offered a new contract with the engineers to start shortly.

'We're all settling down,' Van observed.

Polly wisely kept to herself the thought that in a couple of years she and Arthur were hoping to go to America. Vaudeville was the big attraction. . . .

'We could have brought Samuel with us today,' Hester told Van.

He was leaning heavily on his stick. 'Too much standing about – he would have tired like me – you would have had to carry him. He'll need a wheelchair if we decide to fetch him to watch the Jubilee in a month's time. You can tell him all about this when we see him next.'

'I know he is well looked after where he is, but he deserves a real home of his own.'

He appeared to ignore that remark, exclaiming: 'The Prince is coming along the line now, shaking hands, I wonder if *we* will be lucky!'

Granny Garter was still busy with her dress-making, but she found time to run up a tiny dress from a piece of muslin left over from the bridesmaids' frocks worn at Edie and Alf's wedding. 'For Christina,' she said, when Big Peg admired it. 'I enjoy hand-sewing now and then.'

'We must be the only folk indoors today,' Peg thought. 'I thought it was too much to expect Fred to manage on his crutches in a big crowd. Well, it'll be over, I reckon – and the Prince'll be gone.'

'Where is Fred?'

'Havin' a rest, before they all come back here for tea.'

'Not like him,' Granny stated. 'But gives me a chance to ask you if you've decided what to do with Arthur's room?'

'Let it again, I s'pose. Why?'

'Well, it used ter be my room, didn't it? I would like it back – I can pay you what Arthur does. I'm better off these days, due to all me work.'

'What about the room you use now?'

'Ah, I got plans for that, too. If I carry on paying my board and lodging, I want that to be my work room. Clients can come to me, then, and I can do fittin's in there – I wouldn't need to clutter up the livin' room, like I do now, eh?' She played her trump card. 'You and Fred can have it to yourselves.'

'The only thing is, what about Harry, he'll be home now and then.'

'*He* can sling an 'ammock anywhere,' Granny said firmly. 'And there's still the box room, ain't there?'

The weather remained variable, but the two brides, Fred and Big Peg were taken to St Matthias in a smart, hired carriage drawn by two matching chestnut horses with manes and tails plaited with ribbon. Peg, as matron-of-honour, followed the brides and their father down the aisle, where a chair was provided for Fred; although it was a shared ceremony, the wedding vows were due to be taken separately, which meant a lengthy time for him to be standing.

The carriage had been ordered and paid for by Van, who'd stayed the night with Arthur. He also arranged for a cab to arrive earlier than the bridal carriage, to take the pair of them to church, then return to The Rise for Granny Garter, Edie, Alf and baby.

Hester wore a blue silk dress, in the more relaxed style now popular, with a skirt just skimming her ankles. Because both girls

possessed slim waists, though Polly was more curvaceous, they
had been able to dispense with a corset, for which they would be
grateful, on a day which promised to be hot later on. The loose,
floating sleeves, which fell to the elbow, would also help in that
respect.

'The old Queen favours sleeves like these,' Granny said.

'If I didn't like them meself, it would put me off.' Polly was as
tactless as her grandmother.

Hester's hair, now shoulder length, had been trimmed neatly
by Granny Garter with her sharp scissors, and the fringe suited
her. She hadn't wanted a hat or veil, but Granny had insisted on a
band of tiny artificial rosebuds around her head. Her only jewel-
lery was her mother's simple silver cross and chain, presented to
her earlier by her father. Big Peg had fashioned the posies both
their girls would carry.

Polly wore the same colour, but with a fuller skirt and lower
neckline. Her gift from her father was a little brooch, a silver bird
with a pearl drop in its beak. Both girls had a well-hidden garter
made by Granny, but in Polly's case, Hester suspected, it might
be displayed before she and Arthur departed for the afternoon
matinee at the Empress. Polly had washed her hair in an infusion
of camomile flowers, to enhance the colour, and Granny had
curled it with tongs that morning. Polly's preparations had taken
twice as long as Hester's.

Both grooms were splendidly attired in morning suits, and Fred
had done his best with a modest outlay. Peg had a new costume,
and Hester had persuaded her to allow her to plait Peg's lovely
long hair into a regal coronet. 'You carry that off well, like
Princess Mary of Wales!'

Among the guests, little Christina attracted the most admiration. Edie and Alf were very proud to show her off, with her now
plump limbs, and pretty dress.

The service went off smoothly, rings and vows were exchanged,
the rector pronounced 'You are now man and wife' twice, and
before they knew it they were all blinking in the sunshine outside

the church, with old friends clustering round to congratulate the happy couples.

A hand touched Big Peg's arm as she was busy settling Fred on a bench in the church porch. She straightened up. 'Harry, you made it after all!'

Harry, still in his sea-faring clothes, with the beginnings of a beard on his face, grinned happily. 'We came in late, but slipped into the back seats so as not to disturb the congregation.'

Peg saw then, that he was not alone. Laura, pale-faced and red-eyed, clung to his side. 'I've run away from home,' she said, 'I couldn't stand it any more – Mother wanted me to be a society hostess like her – she said I could earn more than if I was on the stage – but I wrote to Harry, and heard he hoped to be back early today, and I got out of the house, before she woke up this morning, and he came to pick me up. Can you put me up for a while?'

'My darlin',' Peg drew her close and hugged her. 'O' course we can. It's time to leave for the coffee shop now, they're lending us a room for the reception. Come along o' us.'

Others were trying to attract her attention. Peg turned to greet Lucy, Dora, Maurice and Ida. 'We're all going to walk together to the coffee shop,' she said. 'Follow me! Just let me collect Fred. I'll introduce everyone later.'

Twenty-nine

Winnie had been busy, while they were at the church. Earlier, she had cooked a whole salmon, generously provided at half-price by Bobby and Lin the fishmongers. She garnished it now with sliced cucumber and parsley. It would be served with more cucumber and Hollandaise sauce. This had been more difficult than presenting the salmon, in her opinion. Peg had contributed the extravagant ingredients for the sauce. Winnie studied the recipe carefully, muttering aloud the amounts, as she used them. As the recipe required, she made the sauce in a double saucepan, being vigilant that it didn't boil, and curdle the eggs.

Winnie mopped her forehead and changed her apron for a serving one. Customers were arriving for their morning coffee, and looking at the door she had just closed to the other room which bore a large sign: PRIVATE FUNCTION. She sat down herself at one of the tables near the shop door and awaited the arrival of the wedding party. One of her assistants brought her a steaming cup of coffee. Hot as it was, she gulped it down gratefully, then had to dab at her head again.

The tables had been pushed together and covered with a white sheet. The salmon was sliced ceremoniously on to plates; crusty bread and butter was handed round, then the salad bowl, and then the sauce was poured. There were jugs of lemonade and plain water, with ice added. Coffee would be served later with the splendid cake, for Peg had been able to bake one larger one instead of two, which had made her task easier.

It was midday, and although it was early for lunch, everyone present seemed to have a good appetite, apart from Laura, who was looking more cheerful, but obviously wondering if her mother had found her note yet. It read: DEAR MOTHER, GONE AWAY. DON'T TRY TO FIND ME. ALL THE BEST, LAURA.

Hester held Van's hand under the cover of the overhanging cloth. 'You look beautiful, so bridal,' he said softly. 'I didn't get a chance to tell you earlier.'

'I'm so happy,' she whispered in return.

'So am I – and look at Polly and Arthur – you can tell they feel the same way.'

'A pity your parents couldn't be with us,' Polly said to Arthur. She twisted her brand new wedding ring round her finger. 'I wonder if any one will notice it when I'm on stage?'

'I hope they do, then they'll know it's "hands off".'

'Where are we staying tonight?'

'It's a secret. I've booked a late dinner for us.'

'We'll have to begin flat-hunting in earnest tomorrow—'

'I thought we'd have a quiet day with all our meals in our room, we'll actually be there until Wednesday. My mother sent me a cheque to cover the cost until then – she has an account of her own.'

'Oh does she! That's a good idea, *I'll* have one too!' Polly had realized, rather late in the day, that Arthur was impulsive with money like his father. She would need to control the purse strings.

Fred was getting up to make his speech. 'As Polly and Arthur must leave us shortly, I want to thank you all for bein' with us, on this very special day. A toast to Polly and Arthur, everyone!'

He sat down, and Peg rose to propose the following toast: 'I know you will all join us in raisin' your glasses to Hester and Van!'

It may have been lemonade they were drinking, being in a temperance house, but those present followed the toasts with a cheer.

There were others to thank, including Peg and Fred, Granny Garter, Bobby and Lin and Winnie, who rang a hand bell to summon the helpers to bring the coffee, and a warmed bottle of milk for Christina.

'I'm glad I got back in time for the cake,' Harry said, 'because I don't reckon there would have been any left over.'

Laura gave a hiccupping sob. 'I wish it had been us that got married today, Harry. But my mother would never give me her permission.'

'We can always elope,' he said, but he sounded rather doubtful.

Polly and Arthur departed before one o'clock but Hester and Van stayed on until the party ended an hour later.

Hester had no idea where her new husband was taking her – they were having a brief honeymoon after returning to the apartment in Greenwich to collect their packed bags, she did know that. Van had booked a cab to take them to both destinations. Their first ride through the Blackwall Tunnel, she thought, feeling rather nervous about that.

'Is it far?' she asked him, yawning. 'I didn't get much sleep last night, it's a long time since Polly and I shared a room, and I'd forgotten how she could chatter in the small hours.'

'We'll have a snooze until dinner time,' he replied. 'I'm tired, too. Arthur snores – I pity poor Polly when she finds that out.'

'I expect she knows that already.'

'I shouldn't be surprised, I suppose.'

They were staying at a plush hotel, she shortly discovered, in a quiet London square. Their room was at the end of a corridor, and there was a bathroom next door for their exclusive use.

'This is perfect!' she exclaimed, taking off her shoes, then her wedding dress before stretching out on the bed on top of the coverlet. He followed suit, after divesting himself of his jacket. He was still wearing his waistcoat, and glanced at his pocket watch. 'Dinner at seven . . . we've plenty of time.'

'What for?' she asked demurely.

'Didn't you mention a nap?'

'That was you. Can't you think of anything more exciting?'

'I certainly can,' he said, looking speculatively at her petticoat.

'You've got that twinkle in your sailor-blue eyes.'

'How d'you know? Your eyes are closed.'

'That's so you can't tell what I'm thinking.'

'Yes, I can. You're thinking, why doesn't he stop talking. . . . '

'I can't hide anything from you,' she murmured fondly.

'That's what I hoped you say. . . .'

Polly was about to go on stage. She wasn't tired at all, she was determined to give a good performance, with her new husband in the front row of the stalls. She went through her act, singing, dancing and banter with the audience, then she sang an old favourite, the one which had entranced Arthur the first time he saw her down the market – *I Dreamt I Dwelt in Marble Halls*. When the audience called for more, she took up her penny whistle and played the tune on that. She was still wearing her silk wedding dress and it shimmered in the spotlight, which also illuminated her golden curls. However there was no cartwheel tonight.

She said to Arthur much later, in the same hotel where they had first consummated their passion, 'I wanted you to be the only one to see my new garter.'

Edie had recently been given some good advice from Granny Garter, when she called to give Christina her dress. 'You don't look so happy as you did, Edie. What's up?'

She was the last person that Edie thought she could confide in, but somehow it all poured out. How she was afraid of Alf making love to her because she had been so ill when she had the baby. 'I push him away and I know I hurt him, Granny, when I want to show him how much I care for him.'

'You must prove that you do,' Granny said firmly. 'I can tell you a wrinkle or two which worked for me and my Claude. I'm surprised you don't know, bein' a nurse. He had no idea and I didn't tell him. You don't want Alf to look elsewhere, d'you?'

'Of course I don't! And when I get over – having her – I want another little one to go with our Christina, same as Alf does.'

Edie made up her mind to follow Granny's advice that night.

When Christina was settled in her crib, and the light was dimmed, Alf gave Edie the usual brotherly peck on her cheek. 'Goodnight, my dear. Our friends had a grand day, didn't they?'

'Oh, they did,' she moved closer and to his surprise, slipped her arms around him. 'Alf – if you want to, you know, I'm willing.'

'Are you sure?' He sounded uncertain himself. It had been a long six months without making love, after all.

'I'm sure,' she said. 'First, I got something to show you, that I should've before – then you'll know why I felt like I did.' She pushed back the bedclothes, lifted her nightdress. 'This awful scar. . . .'

Alf placed his large, warm hand over the place. 'Now, I understand,' he said simply. 'It just makes me love you all the more.'

The house next door was almost in darkness, too. Laura was sharing Granny Garter's room, and double bed, aware that Harry was just the other side of the bedroom wall.

'You ain't I hope,' Granny said after taking her medicinal brandy and settling down on her side of the bed, 'got yerself in the fam'ly way?'

'Oh, Granny, no! Harry's not that bold. . . .'

'Bit backward at comin' forward if you ask me,' Granny said frankly. 'I'm good at advice in that respect, so don't be afraid to ask.' Some time later she prodded Laura in the back. 'You still awake?'

'Mmm. . . .'

'I been thinkin'. You'd be foolish to elope – Harry would have to go off to sea and you'd be left, no home – no nothin'. You're not ready for that, nor is he. I reckon you should get in touch with your ma, and tell her you're goin' back on stage. You got a gift, and you oughter use it. Like she does, only we won't talk about that. . . . Get together with Polly. I reckon Arthur would prefer her to be one of the Garter Sisters again – he's jealous of her bein' in the spotlight on her own.'

'Where would I live – I can't go home.'

'Lula would welcome you back like a shot, as a payin' lodger.'
She turned over. 'Now that's settled – can I get some sleep?'

There was still a light on in Fred and Peg's room. It had been a long, happy day but both of them had been thinking, but hadn't said, that it was a shame Bess had not been there to share it. Though, of course, Peg reminded herself, I took her place as mother of the brides, and I couldn't have been prouder, if they'd really been my daughters.

Fred looked as if he was already asleep, with his hand cupping his cheek on his pillow. Peg sighed, glancing at the empty cardboard box which had been Puglet's bed: they hadn't liked to dispose of it. She put the light out, then whispered 'Goodnight old feller,' not expecting a response.

Fred stirred. 'I ain't asleep. I know you got somethin' on yer mind. Tell me, eh?'

'I'm afraid of the future, Fred. . . .'

'That's not like you.'

'You promised me you'd go down the doctor's—'

'I did, and I will. But we can both guess what he'll say.'

'Ain't *you* afraid, then?'

'No – not so long as I got you. Stop frettin', we'll get by.'

'D'you believe that?'

'I do,' he said firmly. 'Where's me goodnight kiss, Peg?'

Peg sighed again, with relief this time, before she obliged.

Thirty

June 1897

The date had come at last: it was Queen Victoria's Diamond Jubilee. The midsummer weather was notable for dramatic hail-storms, growling thunder and lightning flashes, but nothing could deter her loyal subjects from near and far from lining the route of the Jubilee Procession and waiting as it travelled through London to St Paul's Cathedral and returned to Buckingham Palace.

The Royal carriage was escorted by all the European Princes and troops from every part of the Commonwealth. There were scarlet uniforms and many plumed helmets; mounted senior military officers followed the band on beautiful horses and contributed to an unforgettable sight. The Colonial dignitaries in the coaches received a share of the cheers, and one of their wives waved her parasol at the crowd.

Photographers were out in force, with the latest cameras. Robert Paul was the most well-known of these, and like the rest of the film crews, he had paid handsomely for the privilege. Every aspect of the circular route of the procession was recorded on film. There would soon be long queues at the cinemas to view the event all over again.

The Queen was greeted by the Lord Mayor of London at the Law Courts and also at Mansion House. She coped admirably with all the fanfare despite her age, and the fact that she had already breakfasted at nine o'clock before her physician pronounced her fit and well enough to carry out her duties that day.

It was a public holiday, so Hester and Van asked permission to take Samuel out for the day, to watch the Queen go by and later to take him to have tea with them at Greenwich.

Samuel, standing in his chair to gain a better view was most impressed by the horses. 'Can I have a ride on one?' he asked.

'Not one of those, they belong to the Queen,' Van told him, 'But we'll take you somewhere another day perhaps where you can have a donkey ride.'

There was rejoicing all over the country, the papers reported. A new golf course had been opened in St Andrews in Scotland, with 12 holes only, intended for ladies and beginners – it seemed the perfect day for such minor celebrations, too.

The hailstones pattering noisily on the roof of the cab as they drove to Greenwich, excited Samuel – everything was a source of wonder.

'We just got back in time,' Hester said, as she put the kettle on, and piled the tea-time treats on a plate. She looked at Van, as he sat with Samuel at the kitchen table. 'Van – *you* tell him – I can't!'

'How would you like to come and live here with us?' Van asked Samuel.

'With you and Nurse Hester?'

'Yes. We would like to adopt you, if that's possible.'

'What does that mean?'

'It means, we'd like you to be our son. You'd be part of our family. Nurse Hester misses you since you both left the hospital, you know. You might even have a brother or sister later on – would you like that?'

The small boy nodded, thinking about it. 'You know how to rub my legs and arms when they hurt. You make me better, Nurse Hester. I want to live with you and Mr Van. Shall I still call you that?'

'You may call us whatever you want,' Van said smiling.

Hester left the tea cups and held out her arms to Samuel. She was too choked for a few minutes to say anything, but she thought,

I hope he will call us Ma and Pa, like I did my parents. . . .

'When can I come?' Samuel's voice was muffled as Hester hugged him to her.

'It will take a little while, but we can look forward to it,' Van said.

The kind staff at the Coram considered that the child and his prospective parents were well-suited already. Hester, with her nursing skills was the right person to care for him in a motherly role and Van was a father figure Samuel could look up to, and emulate. They had noted the twinkle in Van's eyes, too; the fact that he walked with a stick meant that he would understand Samuel's growing handicap. The boy's enquiring mind would be encouraged by this engineer and teacher.

It was September when they brought Samuel home for good. He was having a period of respite from the rheumatism and could climb the short flight of stairs which led to the two bedrooms unaided. One of these had been furnished specially for him. He unpacked his few possessions from his bag and opened and closed drawers. There was a box on his bed, tied with ribbon. 'Look inside,' Hester told him.

'Jumbo!' he cried excitedly, when he delved inside the box. The grey cloth elephant even had a howdah on its back. It wasn't really a plaything, but that didn't matter – Samuel would treasure it throughout his childhood, even after the moths got at it.

'Tomorrow,' Hester said, pleased at his reaction to his gift, 'We are going over to Poplar, because Granny Peg and Grandpa Fred are having a party to welcome you to the family.'

'Why can't they come here?'

'Well, it's difficult for Grandpa Fred because he only has one leg.'

'Was he a wounded soldier?'

'No, he was too young for the Crimean War, and he'll be too old if there's another war – but he's a very brave man, anyway.'

'What does he do?'

'He used to work at the docks, but now he helps Granny Peg at the Coffee House.'

'He plays the Penny Whistle,' Van added.

'Will he teach me?' Samuel asked.

'I shouldn't be surprised, he needs a boy to replace my brother Harry, since he went off to sea.'

'You went off to sea, too, didn't you, Pa?'

'I did indeed, for many years. . . . Did you know that I was born at sea on a dark and stormy night?'

'No – tell me!'

Hester tiptoed away. He hasn't called me Ma yet, but I hope he will, she thought. She could tell how much it meant to Van when he called him Pa for the first time.

Peg and Fred were thrilled to have their first grandson, even if, as Peg said privately to Fred, 'He ain't a home-grown one, but I hope they intend to do somethin' about that. I always knew Hester would make a lovely mother.'

'What about Poll?'

'She's too fly for that,' Peg said candidly.

They intended to break the news gently of Fred's condition, but Peg thought that Hester would probably see the difference in him physically, though surely she would be reassured by his attitude to what would now be an even more restricted life. His cheerful acceptance, the doctor said, would help him carry on and make the most of things. There was no cure, but he must eat a restricted diet.

Granny Garter's tactless reaction actually made Fred laugh. 'You always was too fond of sugar, Fred!'

'You mean I was too sweet for words, eh?' he returned.

After Polly and Arthur arrived, and Granny Garter had woken from her afternoon nap, they ate their sandwiches, sausage rolls, gingerbread and finished with jelly and junket. Then they walked to the park to admire all the flower beds, the newly mown grass, and to throw a ball to amuse Samuel.

Back at the house, Samuel had a request for Fred. 'Grandpa Fred, will you teach me to play the penny whistle?'

For the next hour before it was time to return to Greenwich, Samuel blew hard but managed a very few dulcet notes. 'Good for a first go,' Fred encouraged him. 'You'll make a Poplar Penny Whistler one day.'

'I should've brought my whistle,' Polly said, 'Then there would've been three of us again.'

She had seemed rather preoccupied, likewise her new husband. He raised his eyebrows at her expressively: she interpreted, Have you told them? She shook her head.

Polly could hardly believe it. Surely she couldn't be expecting a baby so soon after their marriage? She had her whole career ahead of her. It would mean no more cartwheels for several months if their suspicions were true. The only good thing at the moment, was that Arthur had just had his new appointment confirmed. She didn't notice her father's gaunt face, or the fact that he ate very little. Laura had been so excited to think they would be on stage together again, how could she let her down? The thought struck her: if I do have a baby, Hester could look after it for me.

'You take care of yourself, Pa,' Hester whispered, as she kissed him goodbye. As Peg had known she would, she had taken in the fact that Fred was not as well as he had been. 'Thank you for being so patient with Samuel.'

'You've chosen a good 'un there, Hester.'

Big Peg hugged them all in turn. 'We must all meet again soon!'

Granny Garter slipped a sixpence in Samuel's hand. 'A little something for you, lad. Don't spend it all at once.'

Back at Greenwich, Samuel had his bath, and a glass of milk, before he went off to bed. 'I like my family,' he said.

Van spread his books on the table. He had preparation to do for a lecture tomorrow. 'You go up, don't wait for me,' he told Hester later.

She lay in bed, contented after their happy day. She touched her stomach reflectively. Was it too early to tell Van yet that she hoped she might be pregnant? Was it really a good time for a baby when Samuel was still settling in with them?

She thought back over the years to when she was a child herself. They'd been poor, but there was plenty of love while her mother was alive. Life had been harder when Granny Garter came to live with them, but she could hardly believe the change in Granny over the past few years, although she was still acerbic. She recalled her early working days, with a little shudder as she thought of the grind of the laundry. Big Peg had brought them all closer together again after she joined their family – Hester blessed that day. She put to the back of her mind the fears that beset them when Fred had had his accident. That humble young working-class girl with her sore red hands who was faced with the prospect of endless years ahead of her in the laundry, had somehow realized her dream of becoming a nurse. She still marvelled at the fact that people had believed in her and encouraged her to succeed.

I didn't know, she said to herself, that I would meet Van and fall in love with him. I thought then that I would never marry, but rise in my profession, dedicated to my patients. The fact that I have Samuel to care for and can help him if he becomes ill, means I can still be fulfilled in a small way as a nurse.

Now, here I am, and I'm still bettering myself. I'm married to a man who has been brought up to be middle-class, a clever man, well educated and professional. I still have some social graces to master . . . But he loves me as much as I love him.

We have adopted a son, who is from a poorer family than mine. I must not let him become ashamed of his beginnings, but make him proud to say he was born in Poplar, as I am. I will always be a Poplar girl at heart.

'Are you asleep?' Van asked, as he made ready for bed.

Hester opened her eyes. 'Not now...'

'I'm sorry if I disturbed you. I won't read any more tonight. I'll turn the light out.'

'I was dreaming, I thought I heard the fog horn on the river.'

'No fog around tonight,' he told her. He drew her close. 'Is anything worrying you?'

She turned her face to his and kissed him. 'I do worry that Pa may be unwell, but they didn't say so . . . Van, I'm not sure yet, but—'

He put a finger over her lips. 'Don't say it, in case we are disappointed in a week or two.'

'You'd be pleased then?' she persisted.

'You know the answer to that,' he said tenderly.